THE ISLAND OF SHEEP

THE
ISLAND OF SHEEP

John Buchan

WORDSWORTH CLASSICS

This edition published 1998 by
Wordsworth Editions Limited
Cumberland House, Crib Street, Ware,
Hertfordshire SG12 9ET

ISBN 1 85326 276 5

Printed and bound in Great britain by
Mackays of Chatham plc, Chatham, Kent
Typeset in the UK by R & B Creative Services Ltd

INTRODUCTION

AMONG HIS MANY outstanding achievements, John Buchan produced a total of one hundred books during his relatively short lifetime. Thirty of these are novels of adventure that reflect the rich and varied experience of Buchan's own life. The Island of Sheep is the last book in a series of five thrillers about Richard Hannay, a former mining engineer from South Africa, now a British General with an exceptional talent for spy-catching. The first of the series, The Thirty-Nine Steps, was written in 1915 and brought Buchan international acclaim.

The Island of Sheep, like Buchan's first novel, Prester John, which he claims to have written for boys, is a thriller that will appeal to the young as much as it will to anyone with a love of adventure. Set in three main locations, Gloucestershire, Scotland and the Scandinavian 'Island of Sheep', with occasional scenes taking place in London, the action of the novel centres around the now middle-aged Sir Richard Hannay who leads an idyllic life with a considerable amount of leisure on his Gloucestershire estate. Hannay occasionally fears that life is too comfortable and that he is in danger of becoming staid. A chance meeting with an old friend, Lombard, a one-time companion in high adventure who has changed almost beyond recognition exacerbates the feeling, but curiously, it is Lombard who leads Hannay into thrilling and dangerous action. Some thirty years earlier, both men had sworn to uphold the cause of a man named Haraldsen, and now it is the dead Haraldsen's son who needs help. The plan to rid Haraldsen forever of his tormentors is masterminded by another redoubtable friend, Sandy, Lord Clanroyden, but it is Hannay's son, Peter John, and Haraldsen's daughter Anna who are the real heroes of the piece.

The story of The Island of Sheep reveals an intense romanticism, yet it has none of the mechanical excesses of many a modern thriller. Buchan's unusually wide range of interests is evident throughout the novel which shows an outstanding grasp of business and financial affairs, of history, geography, science, mythology and particularly of the natural world. Buchan's acute sense of landscape firmly establishes any setting he describes, and his love of birds permeates the story creating a further dimension. Buchan grew up on the coast of Fifeshire in Scotland and spent childhood holidays on his grandparents' sheep-farm. His intimate knowledge of the ways of farming is displayed in the section of The Island of Sheep which is set in Scotland, and his first-hand experience of coastal life comes into its own once the action moves to the island itself

Sound characterization lends conviction to his tale, and the clarity of Buchan's narrative makes for compelling reading. The protagonists in The Island of Sheep are great, good and essentially privileged, yet Buchan depicts shepherds, seamen, gamekeepers and other ordinary folk with equal respect and affection. Many of his other novels, particularly those set in Glasgow, feature heroes from a lowlier background.

The uncommonly strange events in the novel are recounted in a poised, lucid style that typifies Buchan. His romanticism and love of wild adventure is tempered by plain common-sense and a natural inclination towards moderate, concise expression that heightens rather than detracts from the tremendous pace and tension created in his stories, and makes his world entirely believable. A fundamental faith in the intrinsic magnanimity of his fellow men informs all his work and makes his adventure stories especially inspiring. The Island of Sheep is a stirring tale that casts a refreshing light on human nature, and strikes a welcome note of enthusiasm for life which is widely appealing.

John Buchan was born in Perth in 1876, the son of a Free Church of Scotland minister. He was educated locally before going to Hutcheson Grammar School in Glasgow, Glasgow University and Brasenose College, Oxford. He went to South Africa as one of 'Milner's young men' to assist in reconstruction after the Boer War. He was called to the Bar where he practised with considerable success, was elected to parliament in 1927, and he was created Baron Tweedsmuir in 1935 on his appointmnt as Governor General of Canada, where he died in 1940. He wrote poetry and biography as well as novels, but is best remembered for his adventure stories, the five Hannay novels, the three Gorbals Diehards books whose unlikely hero is the middle-aged and romantic grocer Dickson McCunn, and the two Sir Edward Leithen stories John McNab and Sick Heart River.

Further Reading:
Life of John Buchan, Janet Adam Smith, 1965
Memory Hold the Door, John Buchan, 1940

Contents

TO

J.N.S.B.

WHO KNOWS THE NORLANDS AND

THE WAYS OF THE WILD GEESE

PART I

Fosse

CHAPTER I

Lost Gods

I HAVE NEVER BELIEVED, as some people do, in omens and forewarnings, for the dramatic things in my life have generally come upon me as suddenly as a tropical thunderstorm. But I have observed that in a queer way I have been sometimes prepared for them by my mind drifting into an unexpected mood. I would remember something I had not thought of for years, or start without reason an unusual line of thought. That was what happened to me on an October evening when I got into the train at Victoria.

That afternoon I had done what for me was a rare thing, and attended a debate in the House of Commons. Lamancha was to make a full-dress speech, and Lamancha on such an occasion is worth hearing. But it was not my friend's eloquence that filled my mind or his deadly handling of interruptions, but a reply which the Colonial Secretary gave to a question before the debate began. A name can sometimes be like a scent or a tune, a key to long-buried memories. When old Melbury spoke the word 'Lombard,' my thoughts were set racing down dim alleys of the past. He quoted a memorandum written years ago and incorporated in the report of a certain Commission; 'A very able memorandum,' he called it, 'by a certain Mr. Lombard,' which contained the point he wished to make. Able! I should think it was. And the writer! To be described as 'a certain Mr. Lombard' showed how completely the man I once knew had dropped out of the world's ken.

I did not do justice to Lamancha's speech, for I thought of Lombard all through it. I thought of him in my taxi going to the station, and, when I had found my compartment, his face came between me and the pages of my evening paper. I had not thought much about him for years, but now Melbury's chance quotation had started a set of pictures which flitted like a film series before my eyes. I saw Lombard as I had last seen him, dressed a little differently from to-day, a little fuller in the face than we lean kine who have survived the War, with eyes not blurred from motoring, and voice not high-pitched like ours to override the din of our environment. I saw his smile, the odd quick lift of his chin – and I realized that I was growing old and had left some wonderful things behind me.

The compartment filled up with City men going home to their comfortable southern suburbs. They all had evening papers, and some had morning papers to finish. Most of them appeared to make this journey regularly, for they knew each other, and exchanged market gossip or commented on public affairs. A friendly confidential party; and I sat in my corner looking out of the window at another landscape than what some poet has called 'smoky dwarf houses,' and seeing a young man's face which was very different from theirs.

Lombard had come out to East Africa as secretary to a Government Commission, a Commission which he very soon manipulated as he pleased. I met him there when I was sent up on a prospecting job. He was very young then, not more than twenty-five, and he was in his first years at the Bar. He had been at one of the lesser public schools and at Cambridge, had been a good scholar, and was as full as he could hold of books. I remembered our first meeting in a cold camp on the Uasin Gishu plateau, when he quoted and translated a Greek line about the bitter little wind before dawn. But he never paraded his learning, for his desire was to be in complete harmony with his surroundings, and to look very much the pioneer. Those were the old days in East Africa, before the 'Happy Valley' and the remittance man and settlers who wanted self-government, and people's hopes were high. He was full of the heroes of the past, like Roddy Owen and Vandeleur and the Portals, and, except that he was a poor horseman, he had something in common with them. With his light figure and bleached fair hair and brown skin he looked the very model of the adventurous Englishman. I thought that there might be a touch of the Jew in his ancestry – something high-coloured and foreign at any rate, for he was more expansive and quickly fired than the rest of us. But on the whole he was as English as a Hampshire water-meadow. . . .

The compartment was blue with pipe-smoke. My companions were talking about rock-gardens. The man in the corner opposite me was apparently an authority on the subject, and he had much to say about different firms of nursery gardeners. He was blond, plump, and baldish, and had a pleasant voice whose tones woke a recollection which I could not fix. I thought that I had probably seen him at some company meeting. . . .

My mind went back to Lombard. I remembered how we had sat on a rock one evening looking over the trough of Equatoria, and, as the sun crimsoned the distant olive-green forests, he had told me his ambitions. In those days the after-glow of Cecil Rhodes's spell still lay on Africa, and men could dream dreams. Lombard's were majestic. 'I have got my inspiration,' he told me. His old hankerings after legal or literary or political success at home had gone. He had found a new and masterful purpose.

It was a very young man's talk. I was about his own age, but I had knocked about a bit and saw its crudity. Yet it most deeply impressed me. There were fire and poetry in it, and there was also a pleasant shrewdness. He had had his 'call' and was hastening to answer it. Henceforth his life was to be dedicated to one end, the building up of a British Equatoria, with the highlands of the East and South as the white man's base. It was to be both white man's and black man's country, a new kingdom of Prester John. It was to link up South Africa with Egypt and the Sudan, and thereby complete Rhodes's plan. It was to be a magnet to attract our youth and a settlement ground for our surplus population. It was to carry with it a spiritual renaissance for England. 'When I think,' he cried, 'of the stuffy life at home! We must bring air into it, and instead of a blind alley give 'em open country. . . .'

The talk in the compartment was now of golf. Matches were being fixed up for the following Sunday. My *vis-à-vis* had evidently some repute as a golfer, and was describing how he had managed to lower his handicap. Golf 'shop' is to me the most dismal thing on earth, and I shut my ears to it. 'So I took my mashie, you know, my *little* mashie' – the words seemed to have all the stuffiness of which Lombard had complained. Here in perfection was the smug suburban life from which he had revolted. My thoughts went back to that hilltop three thousand miles and thirty years away. . . .

All of us at that time had talked a little grandiloquently, but with Lombard it was less a rhapsody than a passionate confession of faith. He was not quite certain about the next step in his own career. He had been offered a post on the staff of the Governor of X—, which might be a good jumping-off ground. There was the business side, too. He had the chance of going into the firm of Y—, which was about to spend large sums on African development. Money was important, he said, and cited Rhodes and Beit. He had not made up his mind, but ways and means did not greatly trouble him. His goal was so clear that he would find a road to it.

I do not think that I have ever had a stronger impression of a consuming purpose. Here was one who would never be content to settle among the fatted calves of the world. He might fail, but he would fail superbly.

'Some day,' I said, 'there will be a new British Dominion, and it will be called Lombardy. You have the right sort of name for Empire-making.'

I spoke quite seriously, and he took it seriously.

'Yes, I have thought of that,' he said, 'but it would have to be Lombardia.'

That was not the last time I saw him, for a year later he came down to Rhodesia, again on Government business, and we went through a rather odd experience together. But it was that hour in the African twilight that stuck in my memory. Here was a man dedicated to a crusade, ready to bend every power of mind and body to a high ambition, and to sacrifice all the softer things of life. I had felt myself in the presence of a young knight-errant, gravely entering upon his vows of service. . . .

I looked round the compartment at the flabby eupeptic faces which offered so stark a contrast to the one I remembered. The talk was still of golf, and the plump man was enlarging on a new steel-shafted driver. Well, it required all kinds to make a world. . . .

I had not seen Lombard for more than a quarter of a century. I had not even heard his name till that afternoon when Melbury mentioned him in the House. But at first I had often thought of him and waited for his *avatar*. I felt about him as Browning felt about Waring in the poem, for I believed that sooner or later – and rather soon than late – he would in some way or other make for himself a resounding name. I pictured him striding towards his goal, scorning half-achievements and easy repute, waiting patiently on the big chance and the great moment. Death alone, I was convinced, would stop him. And then the War came. . . .

The compartment had nearly emptied. Only my *vis-à-vis* remained. He had put up his feet on the seat and was skimming a motoring journal. . . .

Yes, I decided, the War had done it. Lombard would of course have fought – he was the kind of man who must – and in some obscure action in some part of the world-wide battlefield death had closed his dreams. Another case of unfulfilled renown. The thought made me melancholy. The fatted calves had always the best of it. Brains and high ambitions had perished, and the world was for the comfortable folk like the man opposite me.

We passed a station, and the next was obviously my companion's destination, for he got up, stretched his legs, and took down a parcel from the rack. He was carrying back the fish for dinner. He folded up his papers and lit a cigarette. Then for the first time he had a proper look at me, and in his face I saw slowly the dawning of recognition. He hesitated, and then he spoke my name.

'Hannay?' he said. 'Isn't it Dick Hannay?'

The voice did the trick with me, for I remembered those precise tones which he had never managed to slur and broaden after our outland fashion. My eyes cleared, and a response clicked in my brain. I saw, behind the well-covered cheeks and the full chin and the high varnish of good living, a leaner and younger face.

'Lombard!' I cried. 'I haven't seen or heard of you for twenty years. Do you know that the Colonial Secretary referred to you in the House this afternoon? I have been thinking of you ever since.'

He grinned and he held out his hand.

'What did he say? Nothing uncomplimentary, I hope. We've been having a bit of a controversy with his department over Irak. I've often heard of *you*, and read about you in the papers, and I've been hoping to run across you some day. You made some splash in the War. You're a K.C.B., aren't you? They offered me a knighthood too, but my firm thought I'd better stand out. Bad luck we didn't spot each other sooner, for I should have liked a yarn with you.'

'So should I,' was my answer. 'We have plenty to talk about.'

He replied to the question in my eye.

'Those were funny old times we had together. Lord, they seem a long way off now. What have I been doing since? Well, I went in for oil. I wish I had taken it up sooner, for I wasted several years chasing my tail. My firm made a pot of money in the War, and we haven't done so badly since.'

He was friendly and obviously glad to see me, but after so long a gap in our acquaintance he found it difficult to come to close quarters. So did I. I could only stare at his bland comfortable face and try in vain to recapture in it something that had gone for ever.

He felt the constraint. As we slackened speed, he dusted his hat, adjusted an aquascutum on his arm, and looked out of the window. I seemed to detect some effort in his geniality.

'I live down here,' he said. 'We mustn't lose sight of each other now we have foregathered. What about lunching together one day – my club's the Junior Carlton? Or better still, come down to us for a week-end. I can give you quite a decent game of golf.'

The train drew up at a trim little platform covered with smooth yellow gravel, and a red station house, like a Wesleyan chapel, which in June would be smothered with Dorothy Perkins roses. There was a long line of fading geraniums, and several plots of chrysanthemums. Beyond the fence I could see a glistening tarmac road and the trees and lawns of biggish villas. I noticed a shining Daimler drawn up at the station entrance, and on the platform was a woman like a full-blown peony, to whom Lombard waved his hand.

'My wife,' he said, as he got out. 'I'd like you to meet her. . . . It's been great seeing you again. I've got a nice little place down here. . . . Promise you'll come to us for some week-end. Beryl will write to you.'

I continued my journey – I was going down to the Solent to see about laying up my boat, for I had lately taken to a mild sort of yachting – in an odd frame of mind. I experienced what was rare with me – a considerable dissatisfaction with life. Lombard had been absorbed into the great, solid, complacent middle class which he had once despised, and was apparently happy in it. The man whom I had thought of as a young eagle was content to be a barndoor fowl. Well, if he was satisfied, it was no business of mine, but I had a dreary sense of the fragility of hopes and dreams.

It was about myself that I felt most dismally. Lombard's youth had gone, but so had my own. Lombard was settled like Moab on his lees, but so was I. We all make pictures of ourselves that we try to live up to, and mine had always been of somebody hard and taut who could preserve to the last day of life a decent vigour of spirit. Well, I kept my body in fair training by exercise, but I realized that my soul was in danger of fatty degeneration. I was too comfortable. I had all the blessings a man can have, but I wasn't earning them. I tried to tell myself that I deserved a little peace and quiet, but I got no good from that reflection, for it meant that I had accepted old age. What were my hobbies and my easy days but the consolations of senility? I looked at my face in the mirror in the carriage back, and it disgusted me, for it reminded me of my recent companions who had pattered about golf. Then I became angry with myself. 'You are a fool,' I said. 'You are becoming soft and elderly, which is the law of life, and you haven't the grit to grow old cheerfully.' That put a stopper on my complaints, but it left me dejected and only half convinced.

CHAPTER II

Hanham Flats

ALL THAT AUTUMN and early winter I had an uneasy feeling at the back of my mind. I had my pleasant country-gentleman's existence, but some of the zest had gone out of it. Instead of feeling, as I usually did, that it was the only life for a white man, I had an ugly suspicion that satisfaction with it meant that I had grown decrepit. And at the same time I had a queer expectation that an event was about to happen which would jog me out of my rut into something much less comfortable, and that I had better bask while the sun shone, for it wouldn't shine long. Oddly enough, that comforted me. I wasn't looking for any more difficult jobs in this world, but the mere possibility of one coming along allowed me to enjoy my slippered days with a quieter conscience.

In the week before Christmas came the second of the chain of happenings which were the prelude to this story. My son came into it, and here I must beg leave to introduce Peter John, now in his fourteenth year.

The kind of son I had hoped for when he was born was the typical English boy, good at games, fairly intelligent, reasonably honest and clean, the kind of public-school product you read about in books. I say had 'hoped for,' for it was the conventional notion most fathers entertain, though I doubt if I should have had much patience with the reality. Anyhow, Peter John was nothing like that. He didn't care a rush for the public-school spirit. He was rather a delicate child, but after he had passed his seventh birthday his health improved, and at his preparatory school he was a sturdy young ruffian who had no ailments except the conventional mumps and measles. He was tall for his age and rather handsome in his own way. Mary's glorious hair in him took the form of a sandy thatch inclining to red, but he had her blue eyes and her long, slim hands and feet. He had my mouth and my shape of head, but he had a slightly sullen air which he could have got from neither of us. I have seen him when he was perfectly happy looking the picture of gloom. He was very quiet in his manner; had a pleasant, low voice; talked little, and then with prodigiously long words. That came of his favourite reading, which was the Prophet Isaiah, Izaak Walton, and an eighteenth-century book on falconry translated from the French. One of his school reports said he spoke to his masters as Dr. Johnson might have addressed a street-arab.

He was never meant for any kind of schoolboy, for talk about 'playing the game' and the 'team spirit' and 'the honour of the old House' simply made him sick. He was pretty bad at his books, though he learned to slog along at them, but he was a hopeless duffer at games, which indeed he absolutely refused to learn. He detested his preparatory school, and twice ran away from it. He took the lowest form at his public school, where, however, he was happier, since he was left more to himself. He was the kind of boy who is the despair of masters, for he kept them at arm's length, and, though very gentle and well-mannered, could not help showing that he didn't think much of them. He didn't think much of the other boys either, but most were wise enough not to resent this, for he was for his weight one of the handiest people with his fists I have ever seen.

Peter John's lack of scholastic success used to worry Mary sometimes, but I felt that he was going his own way and picking up a pretty good education. He was truthful and plucky and kindly, and that was what I chiefly cared about. Also his mind never stopped working on his own subjects. He scarcely knew a bat from a ball, but he could cast a perfect dry-fly. He was as likely to be seen with a doll as with a tennis-racquet, but before he was twelve he was a good enough shot with his 16-bore to hold his own at any covert shoot. He had a funny aversion to horses, and wouldn't get into a saddle, but he was a genius with other animals. He could last out a long day in a deer forest when he had just entered his teens. Also he had made himself a fine field naturalist, and even Archie Roylance respected his knowledge of birds. He took up boxing very early and entirely of his own accord, because he didn't like the notion of being hit in the face, and thought that he had better conquer that funk. It proved to be a game in which he was a natural master, for he had a long reach and was wonderfully light on his feet. I would add that in his solemn way he was the friendliest of souls. The whole countryside within twenty miles of Fosse had a good word for him. One habit of his was to call everybody 'Mr.' and it was a queer thing to hear him 'mistering' some ragamuffin that I had helped on the Bench to send to jail a few months before. Peter John was getting his education from wild nature and every brand of country folk, and I considered that it was about as good a kind as any.

But it made him rather a misfit as a schoolboy, since he had none of the ordinary ambitions. He wouldn't have thanked you for putting him into the Eleven or the Boat, and the innocent snobbery of boys left him untouched. He simply wasn't running for the same stakes. I think he was respected by other boys, and on the whole rather liked by the masters, for he was always being forgiven for his breaches of discipline. Certainly he had an amazing knack of getting away with things. He twice stayed out all night, and wasn't expelled for it, since no one thought of disbelieving his explanation that in one case he had been timing a badger, and in the other waiting for an expected flight of grey-lags. He must have poached and never been caught, for he once sent his mother a brace of woodcock with his compliments, after she had complained in a letter that the birds were scarce with us. Also he kept hawks from his second week as a lower boy and nobody seemed to mind. At the date of which I write he was in his fourth half at school, and had at various times possessed goshawks, sparrow-hawks, merlins, and innumerable kestrels. The whole aviary in bandboxes used to accompany him backwards and forwards in the car. He had generally a hawk of sorts tucked away in his change coat, and once a party of American tourists got the surprise of their lives when they stopped a gentle-looking child to ask some question about the chapel, and suddenly saw a bird come out of the heavens and dive under his jacket.

Mary announced at breakfast that Peter John was cutting down costs and reducing his establishment. Archie Roylance, who was staying with us, looked up sympathetically from his porridge bowl.

'What? Sending his horses to Tattersall's and shutting up the old home? Poor old chap!'

'He has lost his she-goshawk, Jezebel,' Mary said, 'and can't afford another. Also white horse-leather for jesses costs too much. He has nothing left now except a couple of kestrels. If you want to live with death, Archie, keep hawks. They perish at the slightest provocation. Hang themselves, or have apoplexy, or a clot or something, or they get lost and catch their jesses in a tree and die of starvation. I'm always being heartbroken by Peter John coming in with a sad face in the morning to tell me that another bird is dead. Last summer he had four kestrels, called Violet, Slingsby, Guy, and Lionel. The most beloved little birds. They sat all day on their perches on the lawn, and scolded like fishwives if one of Dick's cockers came near them, for they couldn't abide black dogs. Not one is left. Jezebel killed one, two died of heart-disease, and one broke its neck in the stable-yard.

Peter John got two eyasses to take their place from the Winstanleys' keeper, but they'll go the same road. And now Jezebel is a corpse. I never liked her, for she was as big as an eagle and had a most malevolent eye, but she was the joy of his soul, and it was wonderful to see her come back to the lure out of the clouds. Now he says he can't afford to buy any more and is putting down his establishment. He spent most of his allowance on hawks, and was always corresponding with distressed Austrian noblemen about them.'

Just then Peter John came in. He was apt to be late for breakfast, for, though he rose early, he had usually a lot to do in the morning. He was wearing old beagling breeches, and a leather-patched jacket which a tramp would have declined.

'I say, I'm sorry about your bad luck,' Archie told him. 'But you mustn't chuck falconry. Did you ever have a peregrine?'

'You mustn't talk like that,' Mary said. 'Say tassel-gentle or falcon-gentle, according to the sex. Peter John likes the old names, which he gets out of Gervase Markhan.'

'Because,' Archie continued, 'if you'd like it I can get you one.'

Peter John's eye brightened.

'Eyass or passage-hawk?' he asked.

'Eyass,' said Archie, who understood the language. 'Wattie Laidlaw got it out of a nest last spring. It's a female – a falcon, I suppose you'd call it – and an uncommon fine bird. She has been well manned too, and Wattie has killed several brace of grouse with her. But she can't go on with him, for he has too much to do, and he wrote last week that he wanted to find a home for her. I thought of young David Warcliff, but he has gone to France to cram for the Diplomatic. So what about it, my lad? She's yours for the taking.'

The upshot was that Peter John had some happy days making new hoods and leashes and jesses, and that a week later the peregrine arrived in a box from Crask. She was in a vile temper, and had damaged two of her tail feathers, so that he had to spend a day with the imping needle. If you keep hawks you have to be a pretty efficient nursemaid, and feed them and wash them and mend for them. She hadn't a name, so Peter John christened her Morag, as a tribute to her Highland ancestry. He spent most of his time in solitary communion with her till she got to know him, and in the first days of the New Year he had her in good train.

Always in January, if the weather is right, I go down to the Norfolk coast for a few days' goose-shooting. This year I had meant to take Peter John with me, for I thought that it would be a sport after his own heart. But it was plain that he couldn't leave Morag, and, as I wanted company, I agreed to her coming. So on the night of January 7 Peter John, his bird, and myself found ourselves in the Rose and Crown at Hanham, looking out over darkening mudflats which were being scourged by a south-west gale.

Peter John found quarters for Morag in an outhouse, and after supper went to bed, for he had to be up at four next morning. I looked into the bar for a word with the old fowlers, particularly my own man, Samson Grose, whom I had appointed to meet me there. There were only two in the place besides Samson, Joe Whipple and the elder Green, both famous names on the Hanham Flats, for the rest were at the evening flight and would look in later on their way home for the fowler's jorum of hot rum-and-milk. All three were elderly – two had fought in the Boer War – and they had the sallow skins and yellowish eyeballs of those who spend their lives between the Barrier Sands and the sea. I never met a tougher, and I never saw a less healthy-looking, breed than the Hanham men. They are a class by themselves, neither quite of the land nor quite of the water.

Samson had good news. The Baltic must be freezing, for wild fowl were coming in plentifully, though too thin to be worth shooting. Chiefly widgeon and teal, but he had seen a little bunch of pintail. I asked about geese. Plenty of brent, he said, which were no good, for they couldn't be eaten, and a few barnacle and bean. The white-fronts and the pink-foot were there, though they had been mortal hard to get near, but this gale was the right thing to keep them low. The evening flight was the better just now, Samson thought, for there was no moon, and geese, whose eyesight is no keener than yours or mine, left the shore fields early to get back to the sea, and one hadn't to wait so long. He fixed 4.15 as the time he was to meet us at the inn-door next morning; for dawn would not be till close on eight, and that gave us plenty of time to get well out into the mud and dig our 'graves.'

The three fowlers left for home, and I went into the bar-parlour to have a talk with the hostess, Mrs. Pottinger. When I first visited Hanham she and Job her husband were a handsome middle-aged pair, but Job had had his back broken in Hanham Great Wood when he was drawing timber, and his widow had suddenly become an old woman. It was a lonely business at the Rose and Crown, on the edge of the salt marshes and a couple of miles from any village, but that she minded not at all. Grieving for Job, and a kind of recurring fever which is common in those parts in the autumn, a sort of mild malaria, had taken the vigour out of her, and put a pathos like a dog's into her fine dark eyes. She ran the little inn for the fowlers, who had been Joe's friends, and did a small transport business with a couple of barges in the creek and an ancient carrier's cart along the shore. She took me in as a guest because Job had liked me, but, though the house had three or four snug little bedrooms, she did not hold it out as a place for visitors, and would have shut the door in the face of an inquisitive stranger.

I found her having a late cup of tea and looking better than I remembered her last time. A fire burned pleasantly, and window and roof-beams shook in the gale. She was full of inquiries about Peter John, who in his old-fashioned way had at once paid his respects to her and begged her tolerance for Morag. She shook her head when she heard that he was going out next morning. 'Pore little lad,' she said. 'Young bones want long lays abed.' Then she broke to me what I should never have suspected, that there was another guest in the Rose and Crown.

'Nice, quiet, young gentleman,' she said, 'and not so young neither, for he'll never see thirty-five again. Name of Smith – Mr. James Smith. He has been ill and wanted a place where folks wouldn't worrit him, and he heard of this house through my cousin Nance, her that's married on a groom at Lord Hanham's racin' stables. He wrote to me that pleadingly that I hadn't the heart to refuse, and now he's been a fortnight in the red room and become, as you might say, a part of the 'ousehold. Keeps hisself to hisself, but very pleasant when spoke to.'

I asked if Mr. Smith was a sportsman.

'No. He ain't no gunner. He lies late and goes early to bed, and in between walks up and down about the shore from Trim Head to Whaffle Creek. But this night he has gone out with the gunners – for the first time. He persuaded Jeb Smart to take him, for, like your little gentleman son, he has a fancy for them wild birds.'

Mrs. Pottinger roused herself with difficulty out of her chair, for in spite of her grief she had put on weight since her husband's death.

'I think I hear them,' she said. 'Job always said I had the ears of a wild goose. I must see if Sue has kept up the fire in the bar, and got the milk 'ot. The pore things will be perished, for it's a wind to blow the tail off a cow, as folks say.'

Sure enough it was the returning fowlers. Two men, whose short frieze jackets made them seem as broad as they were long, were stamping their feet on the brick floor. A third was peeling off an airman's leather coat with a fleece lining, and revealing long legs in trench-boots and a long body in home-spun. I thought him one of the biggest fellows I had ever seen.

I knew the two Smarts, Jeb and Zeb – their shortened Christian names were a perpetual confusion – and they introduced me to the third, for Mrs. Pottinger, after satisfying herself that all was well, had retreated to her parlour. The fowlers drank their rum-and-milk and between gulps gave me their news. They had not done much – only a 'Charlie,' which is a goose that has been pricked by a shot and has dropped out of the flight. But they thought well of the chances in the morning, for the gale would last for twenty-four hours, there were plenty of white-fronts and pink-foot now out on the sea, and in that hurricane they would fly in low. Jeb and Zeb had never much conversation, and in three minutes they grunted good-night and took the road.

I was left with the third of the party. As I have said, he was a very big man, clean-shaven except for a small fair moustache, and with a shock of sandy hair which had certainly not been cut by a good barber. He was wearing an old suit of home-spun tweeds, and he had a pull-over of a coarse black-and-white pattern, the kind of thing you see in a Grimsby trawler. I would have set him down as a farmer of sorts, but for the fact that his skin was oddly pallid, and that his hands were not those of a man who had ever done manual toil. He had bowed to me in a way which was not quite English. I said something about the weather, and he replied in good English with just a suspicion of a foreign accent.

Clearly he had not expected to find another guest in the Rose and Crown, for his first glance at me had been one of extreme surprise. More than surprise. I could have sworn that it was alarm, almost panic, till something about me reassured him. But his eyes kept searching my face, as if they were looking for something which he dreaded to find there. Then, when I spoke, he appeared to be more at his ease. I told him that I had come to Hanham for some years, and that I had brought my boy with me, and hoped to show him a little sport.

'Your boy?' he asked. 'He is young?'

When I told him nearly fourteen, he seemed to be relieved.

'The boy – he is fond of shooting?'

I said that Peter John had never been after geese before, but that he was mad about birds.

'I too,' he said. 'I do not shoot, but I love to watch the birds. There are many here which I have not seen before, and some which I have seen rarely are here in multitudes.'

As I went to bed I speculated about Mr. Smith. That he was a foreigner I judged both from his slight accent and from his rather

elaborate English. I thought that he might be a German or a Dutchman or a Swede, perhaps a field-naturalist who was visiting Hanham
just as Archie Roylance used to visit Texel. I liked his face, which
was kindly and shy, and I decided that, since he seemed to be a
lonely fellow, Peter John and I would offer to take him out with us.
But there were two things about him that puzzled me. One was that
I had a dim consciousness of having seen him before, or at least some
one very like him. The set of his jaw and the way his nose sprang
sharply from below his forehead were familiar. The other was that
spasm of fright in his eyes when he had first seen me. He could not
be a criminal in hiding – he looked far too honest and wholesome for
that – but he was in fear, in fear of some one or something coming
suddenly upon him even in this outlandish corner of England. I fell
asleep wondering what might lurk in the past of this simple, substantial being.

At four o'clock we were called, and after a cup of tea joined
Samson on the jetty, and by the light of an exiguous electric torch
started to find our way over the dry sand, and out into the salt
marshes. The gale had dropped a little, but the wind blew cruelly on
our right cheek, and the whole dark world was an ice-box. Peter
John and I wore rubber knee-boots, beastly things to walk in, and,
not having Samson's experience, we plunged several times up to the
waist in the little creeks. Both of us had 8-bore guns firing cartridges
three and a half inches long, while Samson had a 12-bore with a
barrel as long as a Boer *roer*. By and by we were free of the crab grass
and out on the oozy mud-flats. There Samson halted us, and with
the coal-shovels from our goose-bags we started to dig our 'graves,'
piling up a rampart of mud on the sea side from which the birds
were coming. After that there fell a silence like death, while each of
us crouched in our holes about a hundred yards apart, peering up
with chattering teeth into the thick darkness, and waiting for that
slow lightening which would mean the dawn.

A little after six there came a sound above us like the roar of a
second gale, the first having subsided to a fairly steady south-west
wind. I knew from experience what it was, and I had warned Peter
John about it. It was thousands and thousands of waders, stints and
knots and redshanks and the like, flying in batches, each batch
making the noise of a great wave on a beach. Then for a little there
was stillness again, and the darkness thinned ever so little, so that I
believed that I must be seeing at least fifty yards. But I wasn't, for
when the duck began I could only hear the beat of their wings,
though I knew that they were flying low.

There was another spell of eerie quiet, and then it seemed that the world was changing. The clouds were drifting apart, and I suddenly saw a brilliant star-sown patch of sky. Then the whole horizon turned from velvet-black to grey, grey rimmed in the east with a strip of intense yellow light. I looked behind me and could see the outlines of the low coast, with blurs which I knew were woods, and with one church-steeple pricking fantastically into the pale brume.

It was the time for the geese, and in an instant they were on us. They came in wedge after wedge, shadowy as ghosts against the faintly flushing clouds, but cut sharp against the violet lagoon of clear sky. They were not babbling, as they do in an evening flight from the fields to the sea, but chuckling and talking low to themselves. From the sound I knew they were pink-foot, for the white-fronts make a throatier noise. It was a sight that always takes my breath away, this multitude of wild living things surging out of the darkness and the deep, as steady in their discipline as a Guards battalion. I never wanted to shoot and I never shot first; it was only the thunder of Samson's 12-bore that woke me to my job.

An old gander, which was the leading bird in one wedge, suddenly trumpeted. Him Samson got; he fell with a thud five yards from my head, and the echo of the shot woke the marshes for miles. It was all our bag. The birds flew pretty high, and Peter John had the best chance, but no sign of life came from his trench. As soon as the geese had passed, and a double wedge of whistling widgeon had followed very high up, I walked over to investigate. I found my son sitting on his mud rampart with a rapt face. 'I couldn't shoot,' he stammered; 'they were too beautiful. To-morrow I'll bring Morag. I don't mind hawking a goose, for that's a fair fight, but I won't kill them with a gun.' I respected his feelings, but I thought him optimistic, for, till he had learned to judge their pace, I was pretty sure that he would never get near them.

We had a gargantuan breakfast, and then tumbled into bed for four hours. After luncheon we went out on the sand dunes with the falcon, where Peter John to his joy saw a ruff. He wouldn't fly Morag, because he said it was a shame to match a well-fed bird of prey against the thin and weary waders which had flown from the Baltic. On our road back we met Smith, who had been for a long walk, and I introduced Peter John. The two took to each other at once, in the way a shy man often makes friends with a boy. Smith obviously knew a good deal about birds, but I wondered what had been his observation ground, for he was keenly interested in ducks like teal and widgeon, which are common objects of the seashore, while he spoke of rarities like the purple sandpiper as if they were old acquaintances. Otherwise he was not communicative, and he had the same sad, watchful look that I had noticed the night before. But he brightened up when I suggested that he should come with us next morning.

That evening's flight was a wash-out. The wind capriciously died away, and out of the marshes a fog crept which the gunners call a 'thick.' We tried another part of the mud-flats, hoping that the weather would clear. Clear it did for about half an hour, when there was a wonderful scarlet and opal sunset. But the mist crept down again with the darkening, and all we could see was the occasional white glimmer of a duck's wing. The geese came from the shore about half-past five, not chuckling as in the morning, but making a prodigious clamour, and not in wedges, but in one continuous flight. We heard them right enough, but we could see nothing above us except a thing like a grey woollen comforter. At six o'clock we gave it up, and went back to supper, after which I read *King Solomon's Mines* aloud to Peter John before a blazing fire, and added comments on it from my own experience.

I thought that the weather was inclining to frost and had not much hope for next morning. But the gale had not finished, and I was awakened to the rattle of windows and the blatter of sleet on the roof. We found Smith waiting for us with Samson, looking as if he had been up for hours or had not slept, for his eyes were not gummy like Peter John's and mine. We had a peculiarly unpleasant walk over the crab grass, bent double to avoid the blizzard, and when we got to the mud our hands were so icy that they could hardly grip the coal-shovels. Smith, who had no gun, helped Peter John to dig his 'grave,' the latter being encumbered by Morag, who needed some attention. Never was an angrier bird, to judge by her vindictive squeaks and the glimpses I had in the fitful torchlight of her bright, furious eyes.

We had a miserable vigil, during which the sleet died away and the wind slightly abated. My hole was close to a creek, and I remember that, just as dawn was breaking, the shiny, water-proof head of a seal popped up beside me. After that came the usual ritual – the thunderous flocks of waders, the skeins of duck, and then in the first light the wedges of geese, this time mainly white-fronts. They were a little later than usual, for it must have been half-past seven before they came, and well after eight before they had passed.

The guns did nothing. Samson never fired, and though I had two shots at the tail birds of a wedge, I was well behind them. The birds were far out, and there was something mightily wrong with the visibility. . . . I was just getting up to shake the mud out of my boots when I squatted down again, for I was the spectator of a sudden marvellous sight. Smith, who shared the hole with me, also dropped on his knees.

Peter John had flown Morag, and the falcon had picked a gander out of a wedge and driven him beyond the echelon. The sky had lightened, and I saw the whole drama very clearly. Morag soared above her quarry, to prepare for her deadly stoop, but the goose had been at the game before and knew what to do. It dropped like a stone till it was only a couple of yards above the mud, and at that elevation made at its best pace for the shore. Fifty feet or so above it the falcon kept a parallel flight. She had easily the pace of the goose, but she did not dare to strike, for, if she had, she would have killed her prey, but, with the impetus of her stoop, would have also broken her own neck.

I have watched sensational horse-races and prize-fights in my time, but I have never seen anything more exciting than the finish of that contest. The birds shot past only about ten yards to my right, and I could easily have got the white-front, but I would as soon have shot my mother. This was a show in which I had no part, the kind of struggle of two wonderful winged things that had gone on since the creation of the world. I fairly howled in my enthusiasm for the old goose. Smith, too, was on his feet on the top of the rampart yelling like a dervish, and Peter John was squelching through the mud after the combatants. . . .

The whole business can scarcely have lasted a full minute, for the speed was terrific; but I seemed to be living through crowded hours. The white-front turned slightly to the left, rose a little to clear a hillock in the crab grass, and then the two became mere specks in the distance. But the light was good enough to show us the finish. The lower speck reached a pinewood and disappeared, and the upper speck was lost against the gloom of the trees. The goose had won sanctuary. I found myself babbling, 'Well done – oh, well done!' and I knew that Peter John, now frantically waving the lure, would be of the same mind.

Suddenly my attention was switched on to the man Smith. He was sitting in the mud, and he was weeping – yes, weeping. At first I thought it was only excitement, and wasn't much surprised, and then I saw that it was something more. I gave him a hand to help him up, and he clutched my arm.

'It is safe,' he stammered. 'Tell me, it is safe? '

'Safe as the Bank,' I said. 'No falcon can do anything against a bird in a wood.'

He gripped me harder.

'It is safe because it was humble,' he cried. 'It flew near the ground. It was humble and lowly, as I am. It is a message from Heaven.'

Then he seemed to be ashamed of himself, for he apologized for being a fool. But he scarcely spoke a word on the way back, and when I got out of bed in time for luncheon, Mrs. Pottinger brought me the news that he had left the Rose and Crown. . . . That moment on the mudflats had given me a line on Smith. He was a hunted man, in desperate terror of some pursuer and lying very low. The success of the old white-front had given him hope, for its tactics were his own. I wondered if I should ever meet him again.

CHAPTER III

The Tablet of Jade

THE NEXT CHAPTER in this tale came at the end of March when the Clanroydens stayed with us at Fosse for a long week-end. Sandy, after his return from South America and his marriage, had settled down at Laverlaw as a Scots laird, and for the better part of a year you couldn't dig Barbara and him out of that heavenly fastness. Then came a crisis in the Near East on which he felt called upon to hold forth in the House of Lords, and gradually he was drawn more and more into public affairs. Also Barbara took a long time to recover from the birth of her daughter, and had to be much in London within reach of doctors. The consequence was that Mary and I saw a good deal of the Clanroydens. Mary was one of the daughter's godmothers, and Lady Clanroyden stayed at Fosse with us most of the time that Sandy was in China as chairman of an international Commission. He had only returned from the Far East at the end of February.

It was the most perfect kind of early spring weather. In February we had a fortnight's snow, so the ground was well moistened and the spring full, and in the first week of March we had drying blasts from the north-east. Then came mild south-west winds, and a sudden outburst of life. The blackthorn was in flower, the rooks were busy in the beeches, the elms were reddening, and the lawns at Fosse were framed in gold drifts of daffodils. On the Friday after tea Sandy and I went for a walk up on to the Sharway Downs, where you look east into the shallow Oxfordshire vales and north over ridge upon ridge of green, round-shouldered hills. As the twilight drew in there was a soft bloom like peach-blossom on the landscape, a thrush was pouring out his heart in a bush, and the wild cry of lapwings, mingled with the babble of young lambs, linked the untamable with our comfortable human uses.

Sandy, as he sniffed the scents coming up from the woods and the ploughlands, seemed to feel the magic of the place.

'Pretty good,' he said. 'England is the only really comfortable spot on earth – the only place where man can be utterly at home.'

'Too comfortable,' I said. 'I feel I'm getting old and soft and slack. I don't deserve this place, and I'm not earning it.'

He laughed. 'You feel like that? So do I, often. There are times at Laverlaw when it seems that that blessed glen is too perfect for fallen humanity, and that I'm not worthy of it. It was lucky that Adam was kicked out of Paradise, for he couldn't have enjoyed it if he had remained there. I've known summer mornings so beautiful that they depressed me to my boots. I suppose it is proper to feel like that, for it keeps you humble, and makes you count your mercies.'

'I don't know,' I said. 'It's not much good counting your mercies if you feel you have no right to them.'

'Oh, we've a right to them. Both of us have been through the hards. But there's no such thing as a final right. We have to go on earning them.'

'But we're not. I, at any rate. I'm sunk in cushions – lapped about in ease, like a man in a warm bath.'

'That's right enough, provided you're ready to accept the cold plunge when it comes. At least that's the way I look at it. Enjoy your comforts, but sit loose to them. You'll enjoy them all the more if you hold them on that kind of tenure, for you'll never take them for granted.'

We didn't talk much on the way home, for I was meditating on what Sandy had said and wondering if it would give me that philosophy for advancing age which I was seeking. The trouble was, that I couldn't be sure that I would ever be willing to give up my pleasant ways. Sandy would, for he would always have open ears, but I was getting pretty dull of hearing.

That night at dinner he was in his best form. Till last year he had never been farther east than India, though he knew the Near and Middle East like a book, and he was full of his new experiences. Sandy rarely talked politics, so he said nothing about the work of his Commission, but he revelled in all the whimsies and freaks of travel. Adventures are to the adventurous, and his acquaintance was so colossal that wherever he went he was certain to revive old contacts. He had something to tell me about common friends whom I had long lost sight of, and who had been washed up like driftwood on queer shores.

'Do you remember a man called Haraldsen?' he asked.

'Yes,' I said. 'I once knew a Haraldsen, a Dane. Marius Eliaser Haraldsen.'

He nodded. 'That's the chap.'

It was odd to hear that name spoken, for though I had not thought of it for years, just lately it had come back to my memory, since it was in a way connected with Lombard.

'I haven't seen him for a quarter of a century, and he was an old man then. What's he doing? Did you run across him?'

'No. He is dead. But I knew him at the end of the War – and after. I've got something to tell you about Haraldsen, and something to show you.'

After dinner we sat round the fire in the library, and Sandy went up to his bedroom and brought down a small flat object wrapped in chamois leather. 'First of all, Dick,' he said, 'what do you remember about Haraldsen?'

I remembered a good many things, especially a story into which Lombard came. But since I wanted to hear what Sandy had to tell, I only said that I had known him in Rhodesia as a rather lucky speculator in gold-mining propositions. He had been a long time in South Africa, and was believed to have made a pot of money in the earlier days of the Rand. But he was always looking for new fields, and might have dropped some of it in his Rhodesian ventures. When I had last seen him he had been exploring north of the Zambezi, and had a dozen prospectors working for him in the bend of the Kafue.

'Yes,' said Sandy. 'That was Haraldsen. Let me tell you something more about him. He was the professional gold-seeker *in excelsis*, with a wonderful nose for the stuff and the patience of Buddha. But he wasn't the ordinary treasure-hunter, for he had a purpose which he never lost sight of. He was a Dane, as you say, a native of Jutland, and he was bred a mining engineer. He was a pretty good mineralogist, too. But he was also, and principally, a poet. His youth was before the days of all this Nordic humbug, but he had got into his head the notion that the Northern culture was as great a contribution to civilization as the Greek and Roman, and that the Scandinavian peoples were destined to be the true leaders of Europe. He had their history at his fingers' ends, and he knew the Sagas better than any man I've ever met – I'm some judge of that, for I know them pretty well myself. He had a vision of a great Northern revival, when the spirit of Harald Fairhair would revive in Norway, and Gustavus Adolphus and Charles XII. would be reborn in Sweden, and Valdemar the Victorious in Denmark. Not that he wanted any conquests or federations – he wasn't interested in politics: his ideal was a revival of the Northern mind, a sort of Northern Renaissance of which he was to be the leader. You remember what a tough bird he was in any practical question, but how he could relax sometimes and become the simplest of souls when you pressed the right button.'

I certainly remembered one instance when Haraldsen had talked to me about a house he was building in a little island somewhere in the north, and had rhapsodized over it like a boy. Otherwise he was regarded as rather a hard citizen.

'Well, for his purpose he wanted money, and that would be difficult to come by if he stayed at home. So he started out like the gooseherd in Hans Andersen in search of fortune – a proper big fortune, for he had a lot to do with it. Somehow he drifted to Egypt, and he was one of the prospectors that Ismail sent out to look for an El Dorado in the Sudan. At that time he must have been in his early twenties. Then by way of Abyssinia and Madagascar he moved south, until he fetched up in Mozambique, where he started out to look for the Queen of Sheba's gold-mines.

'He wasted a lot of time in that barren game, and more than once nearly had his throat cut, and then he was lucky enough to turn up on the Rand when that show was beginning. He did well – exceedingly well in a way, but not enough to satisfy him. He had still to find his own private special Golconda. So he went north into Rhodesia, where you met him, and farther north into the Eastern Congo. And then he decided that he had had enough of Africa, and would try Asia.'

'So that's where he went,' I said. 'The old hero! When I knew him he was nearer sixty than fifty.'

'I know. He was as tough as one of his own Saga-men. Well, he had a good many adventures in Asia – principally in Siberia and in the country east and south of the Caspian. When I came across him in Persia early in 1918 he was rather the worse for wear. You remember what a big fellow he was, with his enormous long arms and his great shoulders? When I met him he wasn't much more than a framework, and his clothes hung on him like the rags on the props of a scarecrow. But he wasn't ill, only indecently lean, and he was quite undefeated. He was still hunting for his Ophir.'

'That must have been during the War,' I put in. 'How on earth was he allowed to wander about in those parts? '

'He wasn't. He simply went – there were more of those uncharted libertines in the war zones than people imagined. You see, he was an impressive old gentleman, and he had money, and he knew the ropes – all the many ropes. He travelled in some style, too, with servants and a good cook and an armed escort who were more afraid of him than of any possible enemies. He wasn't a business man for nothing. I had about a week of his company, and in the cool of the morning, when we ate white mulberries together in the garden, he told me all about himself. He spoke to me freely, for we were two civilized men alone in the wilds, and he took a fancy to me, for I knew all about his blessed Sagas. How did he impress you, Dick, when you knew him? '

'I liked him – we all did, but we were a little puzzled about what he was after. We thought that a Rand magnate of well over fifty would be better employed enjoying himself in Europe than in fossicking about in the bush. He was very capable and ran his outfit beautifully. You would have had to rise uncommonly early to get the better of old Haraldsen.'

'He must have changed before I met him,' said Sandy. 'In Africa you have to fight hard to prevent matter dominating mind, but in Asia the trouble is to keep mind in reasonable touch with matter. Haraldsen, when I knew him, was about as much mystic as gold-hunter. He told me about his past life, as if it were a thing very far away. I mentioned your name, I remember, and he recollected you, but didn't seem greatly interested in anything that happened in Africa. He had a son somewhere in Europe, but he said very little about him – also a house, but I never discovered where. What filled his thoughts was this treasure which he was going to find some day, and which had been waiting for him since the foundation of the world. I gathered that he was a rich man, and that he was not looking for mere wealth. He told me about his dreams for the future of the Northern races, but rather as if he were repeating a lesson. The fact was that to find his Ophir had become for him an end in itself, quite apart from the use he meant to make of it. You sometimes find that in old men who have led a strenuous life. They become monomaniacs.'

'Did he find it?' I asked.

'Not in Persia. The Middle East at that time wasn't propitious for treasure-hunting. You must understand that Haraldsen wasn't looking for gold in the void. He was proceeding on a plan, and he had his data as carefully marshalled as any Intelligence Department. He was following the reports of a whole host of predecessors, whose evidence he had collected and analysed – chiefly the trail of old caravan-routes along which he knew that gold had been carried. Well, he failed in Persia, and the next I heard of him was in Sinkiang – what they used to call Chinese Turkestan. I was in India then, keeping a watchful eye on Central Asia, and my old friend managed to give me a good deal of trouble. He got into Kashgar, and we had the deuce of a job getting him out. Sinkiang at that time was a kind of battleground between Moslem home-rulers and Soviet emissaries, with nobody to keep the peace except some weak Chinese officials and a

ragtime Chinese army. However, in the end it was arranged that he
should come to India, and I was looking forward to welcoming him
at Simla, when news came that the Tungans had won, and that the
garrison and the foreigners had been booted out and were fleeing
eastward to China. I decided that it was all up with Haraldsen. He
would never make the two thousand miles of desert that separated
Sinkiang from China. I wrote something pious in my diary about the
foolishness of treasure-hunting.'

'Poor old chap!' I murmured. 'It was the kind of end he was bound
to have.'

'It wasn't the end,' said Sandy. 'That was twelve years ago. Haraldsen is dead, but after he left Sinkiang he lived for ten years. He
must have been eighty when he died, so he had a goodish run for his
money. Moreover, he found his Ophir.'

'How do you know?' I asked excitedly.

'It's a queer story,' said Sandy, and he took the object in his hands
out of its chamois-leather wrappings. It was a tablet, about eight
inches by six, of the most beautiful emerald jade I have ever seen.
Sandy handed it to Mary, who handed it to me. I saw that it was covered on both sides with spidery marks, but if it was any known language it was one I couldn't read. Mary, who loved all jewels,
exclaimed at its beauty.

'I got that in Peking,' he said. 'There were times when we weren't
very busy, and I liked to go foraging about the city in the sharp,
bright autumn afternoons. There was one junk-shop up near the An
Ting gate where I made friends with the owner. He was an old
Mohammedan from Kansu whose language I could make a shot at
talking, and his place was an education in every corner and century
of Asia. In the front, which was open to the street, there was a glorious muddle of saddlery and rugs and palanquins and bows and
arrows and furs, and even a little livestock like red desert-hawks in
bamboo cages. As you went farther in the stock got smaller in size,
but more valuable, things like marvellously carved walking-sticks,
and damascened swords, and mandarin hats, and temple furniture,
and every sort of lacquer. Some outlandish things, too, like an ordinary English grandfather's clock marked 'London, 1782.' At the very
back was the inner shrine which the old man only took you into
when he knew all about you. It smelt of scented woods and spices
and the dust of ages, and it was hard to find your way about in it with
no light but the owner's little green lamp. Here were the small precious things, some on shelves, some in locked cabinets, and some in
cheap glazed cases of deal. There was everything, from raw Bhotan

turquoises to mandarin's buttons of flawed rubies, from tiny celadon cups to Ming bowls, from ivory Manchu combs to agate snuff-boxes. I was looking for something for Barbara when I found this.

'I always liked good jade, and even in that dusk I saw that this was a fine piece. The old fellow let me take it into the light in the front shop, and I had no doubts about it. It was an exquisite bit of the true imperial stone, with the famous kingfisher's-back colour. As you see, one side is covered with hieroglyphics which I can't read. The other side has also an inscription, which at first I took to be in the same jargon. I asked the shop-keeper what the writing meant, and he shook his head. It was some hieratic language, he thought, which the monks used on the Tibetan border.

'I took a tremendous fancy to the piece, and we chaffered over it for the better part of an afternoon. In the end I got it at quite a reasonable price – reasonable, that is, for jade, which would keep its value in China if the bottom dropped out of everything else. I think that the only reason why it was unsold was its size, which made it too clumsy for personal adornment, and because of the inscriptions on it which made it hard to fashion it into an ordinary jewel. The old fellow was doubtful about its *provenance*. From the quality of the stone he thought that it should have come from Siberia, from the Lake Baikal neighbourhood, but at the same time he was positive that the inscriptions belonged to the south-west corner of China. He couldn't read them, but he said he recognized the characters.

'That night in my hotel, when I examined the tablet by the light of a good lamp, I got the surprise of my life. The close lettering on one side, all whorls and twists, I could make nothing of. But on the other side the few lines inscribed were perfectly comprehensible. They consisted of a Latin sentence, a place-name, and a date. The Latin was *"Marius Haraldsen moriturus haec scripsit thesauro feliciter invento"* – "Marius Haraldsen, being on the point of death and having happily found his treasure, has written these words." The place-name was Gutok. The date was the fifteenth of October the year before last. What do you think of that for a yarn?'

I looked at the translucent green tablet in which the firelight woke wonderful glints of gold and ruby. I saw the maze of spidery writing on one side, and on the other the Latin words, not very neatly incised – probably with a penknife. It seemed a wonderful thing to get this news of my old friend out of the darkness four thousand miles from where I had known him. I handled it reverently, and passed it back to Sandy. 'What do you make of it?' I asked.

'I think it's simple,' he said. 'I raced back next morning to the old man to find out how he had got hold of it. But he could tell me nothing. It had come to him with other junk – he was always getting consignments – some caravan had picked it up – bought it from a pedlar or a thief. Then I went to the Embassy, and one of the secretaries helped me to hunt for Gutok. We ran it to earth at last – in a Russian gazetteer published just before the War. It was a little place down in the province of Shu-san, where a trade-route sent a fork south to Burma. An active man with proper backing could have reached it in the old days from Shanghai in a month.'

'Are you going there?' I asked.

'Not I. I have never cared about treasure. But I think we can be certain what happened. Haraldsen found his Ophir – God knows what it was – an old mine or an outcrop or something – anyhow, it must have been the real thing, for he knew too much to make mistakes. But he discovered also that he was dying. Now Gutok is not exactly a convenient centre of transport. He probably wrote letters, but he couldn't be certain that they would ever get to their destination. Two years ago all that corner of Asia was a rabble of banditry and guerrillas. So he adopted the sound scheme of writing poorish Latin on a fine bit of jade, in the hope that sooner or later it would come into the hands of some one who could construe it and give his friends news of his fate. He probably entrusted it to a servant, who was robbed and murdered, but he knew that the jade was too precious to disappear, and he was pretty certain that it would drift east and fetch up in some junk-shop in Peking or Shanghai. That was rather his way of doing things, for he was a fatalist, and left a good deal to Providence.'

'Yes, that was the old chap,' I said. 'Well, he has won out. You and I were his friends, and we know when and where he died and that he had found what he was looking for. He'd have liked us to know the last part, for he wasn't fond of being beaten. But his treasure wasn't much use to him and his Northern races. It's buried again for good.'

'I don't know,' said Sandy. 'I'm fairly certain that that spidery stuff on the other side is an account of how to reach it. It was done at the same time as the Latin, either by Haraldsen himself or more likely by one of his Chinese assistants. I can't read it, but I expect I could find somebody who can, and I'm prepared to bet that if we had it translated we should know just what Haraldsen discovered. You're an idle man, Dick. Why not go out and have a shot at digging it up? '

'I'm too old,' I said, 'and too slack.'

I took the tablet in my hands again and examined it. It gave me a queer feeling to look at this last testament of my old friend, and to picture the conditions under which it had been inscribed in some godless mountain valley at the back of beyond, and to consider the vicissitudes it must have gone through before it reached the Peking curio-shop. Heaven knew what blood and tears it had drawn on its road. I felt too – I don't know why – that there was something in this for me, something which concerned me far more closely than Sandy. As I looked at my pleasant library, with the fire reflected from the book-lined walls, it seemed to dislimn and expand into the wild spaces where I had first known Haraldsen, and I was faced again by the man with his grizzled, tawny beard and his slow, emphatic speech. I suddenly saw him as I remembered him, standing in the African moonlight, swearing me to a pact which I hadn't remembered for twenty years.

'If you are not sleepy, I'll tell you a story about Haraldsen,' I said.

'Go on,' said Sandy, as he lit his pipe. He and Mary are the best listeners I know, and till well after midnight they gave their attention to the tale which is set down in the next chapter.

CHAPTER IV

Haraldsen

IN THE EARLY YEARS of the century the land north of the Limpopo
River was now and then an exciting place to live in. We Rhodesians
went on with our ordinary avocations, prospecting, mining, trying
out new kinds of fruit and tobacco, pushing, many of us, into wilder
country with our ventures. But the excitement did not all lie in front
of us, for some of it came from behind. Up from the Rand and the
Cape straggled odd customers whom the police had to keep an eye
on, and England now and then sent us some high-coloured gentry.
The country was still in many people's minds a no-man's-land,
where the King's writ did not run, and in any case it was a jumping-
off ground for all the wilds of the North. In my goings to and fro I
used to strike queer little parties, often very ill-found, that had the
air of hunted folk, and were not very keen to give any information
about themselves. Heaven knows what became of them. Sometimes
we had the job of feeding some starving tramp, and helping him to
get back to civilization, but generally they disappeared into the
unknown and we heard no more of them. Some may have gone
native, and ended as poor whites in a dirty hut in a Kaffir kraal.
Some may have died of fever or perished miserably of thirst or
hunger, lost in the Rhodesian bush, which was not a thing to trifle
with. In the jungles of the middle Zambezi and the glens of the
Scarp and the swamps of the Mazoe and the Ruenya there must have
been many little heaps of bleached and forgotten bones.

I had come back from a trip to East Africa, and in Buluwayo to my
delight I met Lombard, with whom I had made friends in the Rift
valley. He had finished his work with his Commission, and was on
the road home, taking a look at South Africa on the way. He had
come by sea from Mombasa to Beira, and was putting up for a few
days at Government House. When he met me he was eager to go on
trek, for he had several weeks to spare and, since I was due for a trip
up-country, he offered to go with me. My firm wanted me to have a
look at some copper indications in Manicaland, north of the upper
Pungwe in Makapan's country. Lombard wanted to see the fantastic

land where the berg and the plateau break down into the Zambezi flats, and he hoped for a little shooting, for which he had had no leisure on his East African job. My trip promised to be a dull one, so I gladly welcomed his company, for to a plain fellow like me Lombard's talk was a constant opening out of new windows.

In the hotel at Salisbury we struck a strange outfit. It was a party of four, an elderly man, a youngish man, and two women. The older man looked a little over fifty, a heavily built fellow, with a square face and a cavalry moustache and a loud laugh. I should have taken him for a soldier but for the slouch of his shoulders, which suggested a sedentary life. He spoke like an educated Englishman – a Londoner, I guessed, for he had that indefinable clipping and blurring of his words which is the mark of the true metropolitan. The younger man was an American from his accent, and at the first glance I disliked him. He was the *faux bonhomme*, if I knew the breed, always grinning and pawing the man he spoke to, but with cold, cunning grey eyes that never smiled. We were not a dressy lot in Rhodesia, and the clothes of these two cried out like a tuberose in a cottage window. They wore the most smartly cut flannels, and soft linen collars, which were then a novelty, and they had wonderful buckskin shoes. The cut of their jib was not exactly loud, but it was exotic, though no doubt it would have been all right at Bournemouth. Even Lombard, who was always neat in his dress, looked shabby by contrast.

The women were birds of Paradise. They were both young, and rather pretty, and they were heavily rouged and powdered, so that I wondered what their faces would be like if the African sun got at them. They wore garden-party clothes, and in the evening put themselves into wonderful fluffy tea-gowns. They seemed to belong to a lower class than their male escort, for they had high vulgar voices and brazen Cockney accents. The party, apparently, had money to burn. They made a great outcry about the food, which was the ordinary tinned stuff and trek-ox, but they had champagne to all their meals, and champagne was not a cheap beverage in Salisbury.

I had no talk with any of them except the young fellow. He was very civil and very full of questions, after he had mixed me a cocktail which he claimed was his own patent. He and his friends, he said, were out to cast an eye over the Rhodesian proposition and sort of size-up what kind of guy the late C. J. Rhodes had been. Just a short look-see, for he judged they must soon hurry home. He talked a ripe American, but I guessed that it was not his native wood-notes, and sure enough I learned that he was a Dane by birth, name of Albinus, who had been some years in the States. He mentioned Montana, and I tried to get him to talk about copper, but he showed no interest. But he appeared curiously well-informed about parts of Rhodesia, for he asked me questions about the little-known north-eastern corner, which showed that he had made some study of its topography.

Lombard had a talk with the elder man, but got nothing out of him, except that he was an Englishman on a holiday. 'Common vulgar trippers,' said Lombard. 'Probably won some big sweepstake or had a lucky flutter in stocks, and are now out for a frolic. Funny thing, but I fancy the old chap tries to make himself out a bigger bounder than God meant him to be. When he is off his guard he speaks almost like a gentleman. The women! Oh, the eternal type – Gaiety girls – salaried *compagnons de voyage*. The whole crowd make an ugly splash of aniline dye on this sober landscape.'

We were to be off at dawn next morning. Before turning in I went into the bar for a drink, and there I met a policeman I knew – Jim Arcoll, who was a famous name anywhere north of the Vaal River. I didn't ask him what he was doing there, for that was the kind of question he never permitted, but I told him my own plans. He knew every corner of the country like his own name, and, when he learned where we were going, he nodded. 'You'll find old Haraldsen up there,' he said. 'He's fossicking somewhere near Mafudi's kraal. Give him my love if you see him, and tell him to keep me in touch with his movements. It's a rough world, and he might come by a mischief.'

Then he jerked his thumb to the ceiling.

'You've got a gay little push upstairs,' he said.

'I've only Lombard – the man you met in Buluwayo!' I replied.

'I didn't mean your lot. I mean the others. The two dudes with the pretty ladies. Do you know who the older man is? No less than the illustrious Aylmer Troth.'

People have long ago forgotten the Scimitar case, but a year before it had made a great stir in England. It was a big financial swindle, with an ugly episode in it which might have been suicide, or might have been murder. There was a famous trial at the Old Bailey, and five out of the twelve accused got heavy terms of penal servitude. One of the chief figures had been a well-known London solicitor called Troth, who was the mystery man of the whole business. He had got off after a brilliant defence by his counsel, but the judge had been pretty severe in his comments and a heavy mist of suspicion remained.

'Troth!' I said. 'What on earth is he doing here? I thought the chap upstairs looked too formidable for the ordinary globe-trotter.'

'He is certainly formidable. As for his purpose, ask me another. We've nothing against him. Left the court without a stain on his character and all that. All the same, he's a pretty mangy lad, and we have instructions to keep our eye on him till he gets on to the boat at Beira or Capetown. I don't fancy he's up to any special tricks this time. With his pretty love-birds he carries too heavy baggage for anything very desperate.'

Some days later, after a detour westward to pick up part of my outfit, we were on the hills between the Pungwe and the Ruenya. I thought that we had said good-bye to Troth and his garish crew, and had indeed forgotten all about them, when suddenly one noon, when we off-saddled at a water-hole, we struck them again. There were the four sitting round a fire having luncheon. The men had changed their rig, and wore breeches and leggings and khaki shirts, with open necks and sleeves rolled up, very different people from the exquisites of the hotel. Albinus looked a workmanlike fellow who had been at the game before, and even Troth made a presentable figure for the wilds. But the women were terrible. They too had got themselves up in breeches and putties and rough shirts, but they weren't the right shape for that garb, and they had a sad raddled look like toy terriers that had got mixed up in a dog-fight. The sun, as I had anticipated, was playing havoc with their complexions.

The four did not seem surprised to see us, as indeed why should they, for they were on the regular trail into Makapan's country, and a fair number of people passed that way. They were uncommonly forthcoming, and offered us drinks, of which they had plenty, and fancy foods, of which they had a remarkable assortment. They seemed to be in excellent spirits, and were very full of chat. Troth was enthusiastic about everything – the country and the climate, and the delight of living in the open, of which, he lamented, a busy man like himself had never before had a chance. Alas, they could only have a few days of this Paradise, and then they must make tracks for home. No, they were not hunting; they had shot nothing but a few guinea-fowl for the pot. He wished that he wasn't such a rotten bad naturalist, or that he had somebody with him to tell him about the beasts and birds. Altogether you couldn't have met a more innocent Bank Holiday tripper. The girls too spoke their piece very nicely, though I couldn't believe that they were really enjoying themselves. Albinus said little, but he was very assiduous in helping us to drinks.

I asked if we could do anything for them, but they said they were all right. They proposed to have a look at a place called Pinto's Kloof, which they had been told was a better view-point than the

Matoppos, and then they must turn back. It seemed odd that a man with Troth's antecedents should be enjoying himself in this simple way, and Albinus didn't look as if he had any natural taste for the idyllic, nor the high-coloured ladies. But I must say they kept up the part well, and Troth's last word to me was that he wished he was twenty years younger and could have a life like mine. He said it as if he meant it.

When we had ridden on, Lombard observed that he thought that they were anxious to make themselves out to be greater novices and greenhorns than they really were. 'I caught a glimpse of their iron-mongery,' he said, 'and there was more there than scatter-guns. I'll swear there were rifles – at least one Mauser and what looked like an express.'

I nodded.

'I noticed that too,' I said. 'And did you observe their boys? Two they may have hired in Salisbury, but there was a half-caste Portu-goose whom I fancy I've seen before, and who didn't want to be rec-ognized. He dodged behind a tree when he saw me. Arcoll is right to keep an eye on that lot. Not that I see what mischief they can do. This part of the world can't offer much to a shady London solicitor and an American crook.'

Three days later we were well into Makapan's country and I had started on my job, verifying the reports of our prospectors in a land of little broken kopjes right on the edge of the Scarp. I had with me a Cape half-caste called Hendrik, who was my general factotum, and who looked after the whole outfit. There was nothing he could not turn his hand to, hunting, transport-riding, horse-doctoring, or any job that turned up: he was a wonderful fellow with a mule team, too, and he was the best cook in Africa. We had four boys with us, Mashonas whom I had employed before. Lombard spent his time shooting, and, as it was a country where a man could not easily get lost if he had a compass, I let him go out alone. He didn't get much beyond a few klipspringer and bushbuck, but it was a good game area, and he lived in hopes of a kudu.

Well, one evening as we were sitting at dinner beside our fire, I looked up to see Peter Pienaar standing beside me. It was not the Peter that you knew in the War, but Peter ten years younger, with no grey in his beard, and as trim and light and hard as an Olympic athlete. But he had the same mild face, and the same gentle sleepy eyes that you remember, and the same uncanny quietness. Peter made no more noise in his appearances than the change from night to morning.

I had last heard of him in the Kalahari, which was a very good reason why I should expect to find him next on the other side of Africa. He ate all the food we could give him and drank two bottles of beer, which was his habit, for he used to stoke up like a camel, never being sure when he would eat or drink again. Then he filled a deep-bowled pipe with the old Transvaal arms on it, which a cousin had carved for him when a prisoner of war in Ceylon. I waited for him to explain himself, for I was fairly certain that this meeting was not accidental.

'I have hurried to find you, Dick,' he said, 'for I think there is going to be dirty work in Makapan's country.'

'There's sure to be dirty work when you're about, you old aas-vogel,' I said. 'What is it this time? '

'I do not know what it is, but I think I know who it is. It is friends of yours, Dick – very nasty friends.'

'Hullo!' I said. 'Was it Arcoll who sent you? Are you after the trip-pers that we found on the road last week?'

'*Ja*! Captain Jim sent me. He said, ' Peter, will you keep an eye on two gentlemen and two ladies who are taking a little holiday?' He did not tell me more, and he did not know more. Perhaps now he knows, for I have sent him a message. But I have found out very bad things which Captain Jim cannot stop, for they will happen quickly. That is why I have come to you.'

'But those four tourists can't do anything,' I said. 'One I know is a crook, and I think the other is, and they've got an ugly Portugoose with them that I swear I've seen before. But that's only three, and they are cumbered with two women.'

'The *vrows* have gone back to the town,' said Peter solemnly. 'They will wait quietly there till the others return. They will make the whole thing seem innocent – naughty, perhaps, but innocent. But the three you speak of are not the only ones. By this time they have been joined by others, and these others are very great scoundrels. You say, how do I know? I will tell you. I am at home in Makapan's country and Makapan's people do what I ask them. They have brought me news which is surer and speedier than Captain Jim can get. There is very bad mischief brewing. Listen, and I will tell you.'

The gist of Peter's story was that after they had got rid of the women Troth and Albinus had moved down from the scarp into the bush-veld. The third, the Portugoose, Peter knew all about. His name was Dorando, and Peter had come across his tracks in many queer places; he had done time for I.D.B. and for selling illicit liquor, and was wanted in Mozambique on a variety of charges from highway robbery to cold-blooded murder. An odd travelling companion for two innocent sight-seeing tourists! Down in the flats the three had been joined by two other daisies, one an Australian who had been mixed up in the Kruger Treasure business, and one a man from the Diamond Fields called Stringer. I opened my eyes when I heard about the last, for Jim Stringer was an ill-omened name at that time in South Africa. He was the typical 'bad man,' daring and resourceful and reputed a dead shot. I was under the impression that he had been safely tucked away for his share in a big Johannesburg burglary.

'He came out of *tronk* last month,' said Peter, 'and your friends must have met him as they came up-country and arranged things. What do you say, Dick? Here are three skellums that I know well, and your two friends who are not good people. They have with them four boys, Shangaans whom I do not know, but they are Makinde's people, and Makinde's kraal is a dirty nest. What are they after, think you? They are not staying in the flats. They have already moved up into the Berg, and they are moving fast, and they are moving north. They are not looking for gold, and they are not hunting, and they are not admiring the scenery. Where are they going? I can tell you that, for I found it out before they joined Jim Stringer. The two English do not drink, or if they drink they do not babble. But Dorando drinks and babbles. One of Makapan's people, who is my friend, was their guide, and he heard Dorando talk when he was drunk. They are going to Mafudi's kraal. Now who is at Mafudi's kraal, Dick? They do not want to see old Mafudi in his red blanket. There is somebody else there.'

'Haraldsen!' I exclaimed.

'*Ja*! The Baas.' Peter always called Haraldsen the Baas, for he had often worked for him, as guide and transport-rider, and Haraldsen had more than once got him out of scrapes. Peter was a loyal soul, and if his allegiance was vowed to anyone alive it was to the old Dane.

'But what on earth can they have to do with Haraldsen?' I demanded.

'I do not know,' he said; 'but they have got it in for the Baas. Consider, Dick. He is not a young man, and he is up there alone, with his little band of Basutos and the Dutchman Malan, who is clever but not a fighter, for he has but the one arm. The Baas is very rich, and he is believed to know many secrets. These skellums have some business with him and it will not be clean business. Perhaps it is an old quarrel. Perhaps he has put it across your friends Troth and Albinus in old days. Or perhaps it is just plain robbery, and they mean to make him squeal. He cannot have much money with him, but they may force him to find them money. I do not know, but I am certain of one thing, that they mean to lay hands on the Baas – and he will not come happily out of their hands – perhaps not alive.'

I was fairly flabbergasted by Peter's tale. At first I thought he was talking through his hat, for we were civilized folk in Rhodesia, and violence was more or less a thing of the past. But Peter never talked wildly, and the more I thought of it the less I liked it. Five desperadoes up in that lonely corner could do pretty much what they pleased with Haraldsen and his one-armed assistant. I remembered the old fellow's reputation for having hunted gold all his life and having struck it in a good many places. What more likely than that some hungry rogues should try to get him alone in the wilds and force out of him either money or knowledge?

'What do you mean to do?' I asked.

'I am going straight to Mafudi's,' said Peter. 'And I think you are coming with me, Dick.'

Of course I couldn't refuse, but I felt bound to go cautiously. Would it not be better to get Arcoll and the police? I didn't relish the notion of a private scrap with people who would certainly not stick at trifles. Besides, could we do any real good? Haraldsen and Malan might be ruled out as combatants, and we three would be up against five hefty scallywags.

Peter overruled all my objections in his quiet way. Arcoll was a hundred miles off. A native runner had been sent to him, but it was impossible for him to arrive at Mafudi's in time, for Troth and his little lot would be there by to-morrow morning. As for being outnumbered, we were five honest men against five rascals, and in all rascals he believed there was a yellow streak. 'I can shoot a little,' he said, 'and you can shoot a little, Dick.' He turned inquiringly to Lombard.

'I can loose off at any rate,' said Lombard. He was looking rather excited, for this adventure was a piece of luck he had not hoped for.

The upshot was that we had no rest that night. I sent off one of my boys with another message for Arcoll, giving him more details than Peter had given him, and suggesting a road in by the north-west which I feared he might not think of. I left Hendrik and the mules and the rest of the outfit to come on later – and I remember wondering what kind of situation they would find when they reached Mafudi's. The three of us took the road just after ten o'clock. Peter's boy accompanied us, a tough little Bechuana from Khama's country.

I had travelled the route several times before, and Peter knew it well, but in any case it was not hard to find, for it kept to the open ground near the edge of the scarp, bending inland only to avoid the deep-cut kloofs. There was a wonderful moon which made the whole landscape swim in warm light – an African moon, which is not the pale thing of the north, but as masterful as the sun itself. When it set we were on high ground, a plateau of long grass and thorns, with the great hollow of the lower veld making a gulf of darkness on our right. The road was easy enough to follow, and when dawn came with a rush of gold and crimson out of the east we were close to the three queer little peaks between which lay Mafudi's kraal.

We went straight to Haraldsen's camp, which was about half a mile from the kraal on one of the ridges. It was the ordinary prospector's camp of which at that time you could have found a score or two in Rhodesia, but more professional than most, for Haraldsen had the cash with which to do things properly. Gold is not my pidgin, but the heaps of quartz I passed looked healthy. He had struck an outcrop which he thought promising, and was busy tracing the run of the reef, having sunk two seventy-foot shafts about a quarter of a mile apart. But I wasn't concerned with old Haraldsen's operations, but with Haraldsen himself. We had been sighted by his boys, and he stood outside his tent awaiting us, a figure like a patriarch with the sun on his shaggy head.

While our breakfast coffee was being made I told him our story, for there was no time to lose, since Peter calculated that Troth and his lot, by the road they were coming, could not be more than five miles off. Haraldsen had a face so weathered and set in its lines that it didn't reveal much of his thoughts, and he had grey eyes as steady as a good dog's. But the mention of Troth woke him up and the name of Albinus didn't please him. He seemed to be more worried about them than about the other scallywags.

'Troth I know,' he said in his deep voice and his precise accent, for he always spoke English as if he had got it from old-fashioned books. 'He is a great scoundrel and my enemy. Once – long ago – he was my partner for a little. He does not like me, and he has a reason, for I most earnestly laboured to have him put in *tronk*. He comes now like a ghost out of the past, and he means evil.' Of Albinus, he would only say that his father had had a great devil in him, and that he did not think that the devil had been exorcized in the son.

He had not the smallest doubt that the gang were after him, but he didn't explain why. All he said was, 'They will try to make me do their will, and if I do not consent they will kill me. Unless, indeed, I first kill them.'

I tried as usual to put the common sense of it. 'If they find us with you,' I said, 'they won't dare to do anything. A quiet murder might be in their line, but they won't want to fight a battle.'

But Haraldsen shook his head. He knew Troth, he said, and he knew about Albinus. He must have laid these gentry out pretty flat some time or other for them to have such a murderous grudge against him, or else he knew the depth and desperation of their greed. But what impressed me most was Peter's view. He knew about Stringer and Dorando, and was clear that they would not go home without loot. They would not think of consequences, for they could leak away into the back-world of Africa.

I was never one for a fight except in the last resort, so I proposed that Haraldsen should take his best horse and make a bolt for it, leaving us to face the music, since there was nothing much to be got out of Peter and Lombard and myself. But Haraldsen wouldn't hear of this. 'If I flee,' he said, 'they will find me later and I shall live with a menace over my head. That I will not face. Better to meet them here and have done with it.'

That was all very well, but I wasn't keen on being mixed up in any Saga-battle. I asked him if his boys were any use. 'None,' he said. 'They are Mashonas and are timid as rabbits. Besides, I will not have them hurt.'

'What about Mafudi's men?' I asked.

It was Peter who answered. 'Mafudi is always drunk, and also very old. Once his people were warriors, but now they have no guns. They will not fight.'

'Well, then, it's the five of us – and one of us crippled – against the five of them.'

But it was worse than that, for it appeared that Malan had a bad go of fever and might be counted out. Also Haraldsen had run out of ammunition and had sent a boy off to get a fresh supply, and as his rifles were Mannlichers and ours Mausers we could do nothing to help him out. This seemed to me fairly to put the lid on it, but Peter did not lose his cheerfulness. 'We must make a plan,' he said – a great phrase of his; and he delicately scratched the tip of his left ear, which was always a sign that his mind was working hard.

'This is my plan,' he said at last. 'We must find a place where we can defend ourselves. Captain Arcoll will be here to-day – or perhaps to-night – at any rate not later than to-morrow. We cannot fight these skellums on fair terms in the open, but in a strong fort we may beat them off for perhaps twelve hours, perhaps more.'

'But where is your fort?' I asked. As I looked round the bright open place, the jumble of kopjes with the green of Mafudi's crops in the heart of it, I didn't see much hopes of a refuge we could hold. It was all open and bare, and we hadn't time to dig trenches or build a *scherm*.

'There is the Hill of the Blue Leopard,' said Peter, using a Mashona word. 'It is above the kraal – you can see the corner of it beyond that ridge. It is a very holy place where few go but the priests, and it has round it a five-foot hedge of thorns and a big fence of stakes. I do not know what is inside except a black stone which fell from heaven. It is there that the young men must watch during the Circumcision. If we get in there, Dick, I think we could laugh at your friends for a little – long enough to give Captain Arcoll time to get here. There is another thing. If the skellums were strong enough to break in, I think that Mafudi's men might be very angry. It is true that they have no guns, but very angry men can do much with knobkerries and axes.'

'But they'll never let us enter,' I protested.

'Perhaps they will. I will try. I have always been good friends with Mafudi's folk.' And without another word he strode off in the direction of the kraal.

I was doubtful about his success, for I knew how jealous the natives were of their sacred places, especially the Mashonas, who have always been in the hands of their priests. Still I knew that Peter had an amazing graft among the tribes, for he was not the kind of man who damned them all as niggers. People used to say that he was the only white man who had ever been present at the great Purification Dance of the Amatolas. It was a nervous business waiting for his return, for he took a long time about it. I made Haraldsen collect his valuables, and we prepared a sort of litter for Malan, who was at that stage of fever when a man is pretty well unconscious of his surroundings. Always I kept my eye on the corner of the kloof where any moment Troth and his gang might be expected to appear.

But they did not come, and at last Peter did. He had succeeded in persuading the elders of the tribe to let us inside the sacred enclosure. He did not tell me what arguments he had used, for that was never his way; he presented the world with results and left it to guess his methods. We bundled up our traps in a mighty hurry, for there was no time to lose, hoisted Malan into his litter, and told Haraldsen's boys to take the horses up into the berg and to lie low till we sent for them. In the kraal, in the open space in the centre of the kyas, we were met by most of Mafudi's people, all as silent as the tomb, which is not common among Kaffirs. We had to have water poured on our heads – what the books call a lustration – and to have little dabs of green paint stuck on our foreheads. Peter's Bechuana boy was not allowed to be of our party, only the white men. Then we were solemnly conducted up a narrow bush road to the Hill of the Blue Leopard, and as we started there was a great 'Ouch,' a sound like a sigh, from all the natives. There was a kind of cattle-gate in the wall of the *scherm*, which a priest ceremonially opened, and the four of us and Malan in his litter passed into the holy place.

At first sight it looked as if we had found a sanctuary. The hill was perhaps a hundred feet high, and most of it was covered with thick bush, except a bald cone at the top where the sacred stone lay. The bush was mostly waak-em-beetje thorn and quite impenetrable, but it was seamed and criss-crossed by dozens of little paths, worn smooth like a pebble by ages of ceremonial. One of the items in the Circumcision rite was a kind of demented hide-and-seek in this maze. Around the foot of the hill, as I have said, was a dense quick-set *scherm* which it would have taken a regiment to hack through. The only danger-point was the gate, and I thought that in case of trouble two of us might manage to hold it, for I didn't envy the job of the men who tried to rush it in the face of concealed rifles. Anyhow, we could hold it long enough, I thought, to give Arcoll time to turn up. Indeed, I had hopes that Troth and his gang would miss us altogether. They would find Haraldsen's camp deserted and conclude that he had moved on.

In every bit of my forecast I was wrong. In the first place our ene-mies came round the edge of the kloof in time to see the movement of Mafudi's people toward the little hill, and if they didn't guess then what had happened, they knew all right when they got to Harald-sen's camp. For his boys had been too slow over the job of scattering into the woods. One of them they caught, and, since they meant business and were not fastidious in their methods, they soon made the poor devil blab what he knew or guessed. The consequence was that half an hour after we were inside the *scherm* the others were making hell in Mafudi's kraal. I had found a lair well up the hill where I could spy out the land, and I saw that Troth's party was bigger than I had supposed. I made out Troth and Albinus, their natty outfit a little the worse for wear, and the trim figure of Dorando, and Jim Stringer's long legs. They had left their natives behind, but they had four other white men with them, and I didn't like the cut of their jib. They were eight to our four, odds of two to one. I called Peter up beside me, and his eyes, sharp as a berghaan's, examined the reinforcements. He recognized the Australian and one other, a Lydenburg man whose name he mentioned and then spat. 'I think we must fight, Dick,' he said quietly. 'The greed of these men is so great that it will make them brave. And I know that Dorando and Stringer are bad, but not cowards.'

I thought the same, so I started out to make my dispositions, for I had learned some soldiering in the late war. Haraldsen I kept out of sight, for his life was the most valuable of the lot, and besides I meant to pretend that we knew nothing about him. Peter, who was far the best shot among us, I placed behind a rock where he had a good view of the approaches. I told him not to shoot unless they tried to rush the gate, and then to cripple if possible and not kill, for I didn't want bloodshed and a formal inquiry and screeds in the papers – that would do no good to either Haraldsen or me. Lombard and I took our stations near the gate, which was a solid thing of log and wattle jointed between two tree trunks. We had a rifle and a revolver apiece; but I would have preferred shot-guns. I could see that Lombard was twittering with excitement, but he kept a set face, though he was very white.

The affair was slow in beginning. It was after midday before Dorando and Stringer appeared on the track that led up from the kraal. They had a handkerchief tied to a rifle muzzle by way of a white flag. I halted them when they were six yards from the gate, and asked what they wanted.

Butter wouldn't have melted in their mouths. They had come to see Mr. Haraldsen, who was a friend of theirs – to see him on business. They understood that he was on the hill. Would he step out and come down to luncheon with them? They were kind enough to include me in the invitation.

I said that I knew nothing about Mr Haraldsen, but that I knew a good deal about them. I proposed another plan: let them leave their guns where they stood, and come inside the *scherm* and take a bite with us. They thanked me, and said they would be delighted, and moved to the gate, but they did not drop their rifles, and I saw the bulge of revolvers in their pockets. 'Stop,' I shouted. 'Down guns or stay where you are,' and Lombard and I showed our pistols.

'Is that a way to talk to gentlemen?' said Dorando with a very ugly look.

'It's the way to talk to you, my lads,' I said. 'I've known you too long. Strip yourselves and come inside. If not, I give you one minute to get out of here.'

Dorando was livid, but Stringer only smiled sleepily. He was the more dangerous of the two, for he was mighty quick on the draw and didn't miss. He had a long thin face, and few teeth, which made his mouth as prim as a lawyer's. I kept my eye on him, having whispered to Lombard to mark Dorando. But they didn't try to rush us, only said a word to each other and turned and went back. That was the end of the first bout.

All afternoon nothing happened. The heat was blistering, and as there was no water on the hill and we had nothing liquid but a flask of brandy, we suffered badly from thirst. Malan babbled in his fever, and Haraldsen, who was in the shade beside him, went to sleep. Old Haraldsen had been in so many tight places in his life that he was hard to rattle. Little green lizards came out and basked in the sun on the tracks, widow-birds flopped among the trees, and a great ugly aasvogel dropped out of the blue sky and had a look at us. The whole land lay baking and still, and down in the kraal there was not a sound. There was nobody in the space between the huts, not a child or a chicken stirred, and we might have been looking down at a graveyard.

Suddenly from one of the kyas there came a cry as of some one in deadly pain. In the hot silence it had a horrible eeriness, for it sounded like a child's scream, though I knew that a Kaffir in pain or terror often gives tongue like an infant. I saw Lombard's face whiten.

'Oughtn't we to do something?' he croaked, for his mouth was dry with thirst.

'We can't,' I told him. 'I don't know what these swine are up to, but it will soon be our turn. Our only hope is to sit tight.'

When the twilight began to fall Peter descended from his perch. Being higher up the hill he had had a better view and he brought news.

'The stad is quiet,' he told us. 'All Mafudi's people are indoors, for they have been told that they will be shot if they show their faces. Of the others, two are on guard and the rest have not been sleeping. They have been pulling down a kya to get the old straw from the roof, and they have been down at the byres where the hay is kept. As soon as it is dark they will be very busy.'

'Good God!' I cried, for I saw what this meant. 'They mean to burn us out.'

'Sure,' he said. 'They are clever men. The moon will not rise till nine o'clock. Soon it will be black night, and we cannot shoot in the dark. There are eight of them, and of us only four. At this time of year there is no sap in the thorns, so they will burn like dry tinder. The gate will no longer matter. They can fire this *scherm* at six places, and we cannot watch them all. We are in a bad fix, Dick.'

There was no doubt about that. At in-fighting those scallywags –
leaving out Troth and Albinus, whom I knew nothing about – were
far more than our masters. If Peter was right, our sanctuary would
very soon be a trap. I summoned Haraldsen, and the four of us had a
solemn council. We couldn't hold the place against fire, and we
couldn't escape, for the gaps made by the flames would all be
watched, and likewise the gate.

'Have you any plan?' I asked Peter.

He shook his head, for even he was at the end of his resources.

'We can only trust in God,' he said simply, and his mild quizzical
face was solemn. 'Perhaps Jim Arcoll may come in time.'

Haraldsen said nothing. He had no weapon, so I offered him my
rifle. But he preferred to take an axe which Peter had insisted on
bringing from the camp, and he swung it round his head, looking
like some old Viking. I apologized to Lombard for having got him
into such a hole, but he told me not to worry. That cry from the
kraal had stripped him of all nervousness or fear. He was thinking
only of what mischief he could do to the eight devils at the foot of
the hill.

The short mulberry gloaming faded out of the sky, and night
came down on the world like a thick black shawl. I had sent Lombard and Peter up to the summit where they could get early news of
what was happening, for I knew that an attempt would be made to
fire the *scherm* in several places at once. I stayed at the gate, and Haraldsen for some reason of his own insisted on staying beside me. We
moved the sick Malan out into the open, for I feared that the firing
of the *scherm* might kindle all the bush on the hill.

I can't say that I enjoyed the hour we had to wait. I saw no chance
for us, short of a miracle, and the best we could hope for was a good
scrap and a quick death. You may ask why we didn't parley with our
enemies to gain time. The answer is that we were convinced that
they meant black murder if we gave them half a chance; at least they
meant to do in Haraldsen, and we couldn't allow that. Haraldsen
himself had wanted to be let out and to go down and face them
alone, but Peter and I told him not to be a fool.

The crisis came, as such things do, when I wasn't expecting it.
Suddenly I saw a red glow in the night, apparently on the other side
of the hill. The glow spread, which must mean that other fires had
been started. There was a rifle shot, which I assumed to be Peter's,
and then Lombard stumbled down with the news that the *scherm* was
burning in four places. The next thing I knew was that there was a
big burst of flame about five yards from me, and at the same moment

faces appeared in the gate. I fired at one, there was an answering crackle of shots, and I felt a raw pain in my left shoulder. Then I saw the gate in a sheet of flame, for the wattles had been fired.

After that there was a wild confusion. I found an ugly face close to me, fired at it, and saw it go blind. That was the man from Lydenburg, for we found the body later. I saw other figures in the gap, and then I saw an extraordinary sight. Haraldsen, looking like a giant in the hellish glow, had leaped forward and was swinging his axe and shouting like a madman. The spectacle must have confounded the attackers, for they made wild shooting. He had a bullet through one pocket and another through his hair, but he got none in his body. I saw him jump the blazing remnant of the gate and bring his axe down on somebody's head. And then he was through them and careering out into the dark.

I was pretty dazed and wild, and I decided that it was all up now, when suddenly the whole business took a new turn. Above the crackle and the roar of the flames I heard a sound which I had not heard since the Matabele Rising, the deep throaty howl of Kaffirs on the war-path. It rose to heaven like a great wind, and I clutched at my wits and realized what had happened. Mafudi's men were up. They had been like driven cattle all day, but this outrage on their sacred place had awakened their manhood. Once they had been a famous fighting clan and the old fury had revived. They were swarming like bees round the *scherm*, and making short work of our assailants. The Kaffir sees better in the dark than a white man, and a knobkerrie or an axe is a better weapon in a blind scrap than a gun. Also there were scores of them, the better part of a hundred lusty savages, mad with fury at the violation of their shrine.

There was nothing I could do except join Peter and Lombard on the top. But there was no sign of them there, for they had each made for one of the burning gaps to do what they could to hold the fort. As a matter of fact the fires at no place had gone far enough to make an opening, so none of our assailants had got inside the *scherm*. Pandemonium was in full blast around it, where some of Mafudi's men were rounding up Troth's lot and the rest were beating out the flames. This latter wasn't an easy job and the moon was up before it was over. I simply sat on the bald crest beside the sacred stone and waited. This was no work for me. Peter and Lombard were somewhere on the hill, but it was impossible to find them in that dark maze. The noise of native shouting soon died away, so I realized that they had finished their business. The fires were all mastered except one that kept breaking out afresh. Then over the rim of the horizon

rose the moon, and the world was bright again. I was just starting
out to look for the others when I heard the jingle of bridles and the
clatter of hoofs and knew that Arcoll's police had arrived at last.

Arcoll made a fine bag of miscreants – five, to be accurate, who
were firm in the grip of Mafudi's people. Three were dead – the man
from Lydenburg whom I shot, one of the new fellows whose skull
Haraldsen split with his axe, and, as the fates would have it, Troth
himself. Peter had got Troth at the very start, when he showed up
for a second in the gleam of the first fire. There he lay with his neat
London outfit punctured by Peter's bullet, a home-bred hound
among jackals, but the worst jackal of the pack.

'That's a pleasant yarn,' said Sandy. 'Old Haraldsen told me a
good many of his adventures, but not that one. It had the right sort
of ending.'

'That wasn't quite the end,' I said. 'Haraldsen had burst through
the ring into the arms of Mafudi's men, who knew him well and recognized him and kept him out of danger. But as soon as Arcoll
arrived and took charge the old man got busy. He had been berserk
at the gate, and now he seemed to be 'fey.' He said there was something still to do, and he insisted on Peter and Lombard and me
accompanying him to the top of the Hill of the Blue Leopard. There
he made us a speech, looking more like an old Norseman than ever.
He said that we were his blood-brothers, who had been ready to
stand by him to the end. But the end hadn't come, though Troth was
dead and the others would soon be in quod. There was a legacy of ill
will that would follow him to his last day, and the dead Troth would
leave it as a bequest to his successors. So he wanted the three of us to
swear that if he called for us we would come to his aid wherever in
the world we might be. More, we must be ready to come to his son's
help, for he considered that this vendetta might not end with his
own life, and we were to hand on the duty to our own sons. As none
of us was married that didn't greatly worry us.

'It was like something out of one of his Sagas. There we stood
above the silvered bush on rocks which were like snowdrifts in the
strong moonlight. We took his right hand in turn in ours and put it
to our foreheads, and then we raised our right arms and repeated a
mad formula about dew and fire and running water. . . . Lord, how it
all comes back – that white world, and the smell of charred bush, and
the pain in my shoulder, and Lombard, who had had about as much
as he could stand, whimpering like a scared dog!'

'Well, he's dead now,' said Sandy, 'and your oath is finished, for it's not likely that his son will trouble you. Heigh-ho! The old wild days have gone. Peter long ago entered Valhalla. What about the third – Lombard, I think you called him? '

'Curiously enough,' I said, 'I met him last autumn. He's not thinking about any Saga oath nowadays. He is bald and plump and something in big business.'

CHAPTER V

Haraldsen's Son

THE CLANROYDENS WENT OFF to Laverlaw for a fortnight, Sandy to
fish his Border burns, and Barbara to attend to her garden, and I was
settling down to my farming, when I got a letter from Lombard. I
had heard nothing of him since our meeting in the train the previous
autumn. He had not invited me for a week-end as he had suggested –
at which I rejoiced, for I would have had to invent some excuse for
refusing; nor had he repeated his proposal to lunch together in
London.

His letter began with apologies for this neglect; he had been very
busy all winter and had had to make two trips abroad. But now he
wanted to see me – wanted to see me urgently. Was there any
chance of my being in town in the coming week, and if so, could we
meet? He would keep any appointment, but he suggested luncheon
and then going back to his office to talk. I couldn't imagine what he
had to say to me, and I had an unpleasant suspicion that he wanted
me for one of his financial ventures, but, as I had to go to London on
other business, I had no grounds for declining. So I wired asking him
to lunch at my own club, a quiet place with a smoking-room on the
top floor which we could have to ourselves.

Lombard was looking worried, and he had also a heavy cold. His
ruddy face had gone white, his eyes watered, and his voice was like a
cracked tin-can. He had been drenched golfing, he told me, and the
east wind had done the rest. But his bodily ailment was the least of
his troubles, and I had the impression that this plump, four-square
personage had been badly shaken. At luncheon I made him drink hot
whisky-and-water, but he only picked at his food, and had very little
conversation. There was something on his mind, and I was glad
when I got him to the upper smoking-room, settled him in an armchair, and told him to get on with it.

His first question startled me.

'Do you remember a chap called Haraldsen?' he asked. 'Thirty
years ago in Rhodesia? The time I went on trek with you when I was
on my way home? '

'I do,' I said. 'Oddly enough I was talking about him last week.'

'Well, I've seen him.'

'Then you've seen a ghost,' I replied; 'for he is dead.'

He opened his rheumy eyes.

'I don't mean the old man – I mean his son. But how do you know that Haraldsen is dead? The young one doesn't know it.'

'Never mind,' I said. 'It's too long a story to tell you now, but it's a fact. What about the young one? I knew there was a son, but I never heard anything about him. What sort of age? '

'Over thirty. Perhaps nearer forty. He wrote to me and asked for an interview – found my name in the telephone-book – didn't say what he wanted. I thought he might have something to do with a Swedish wood-pulp proposition, for I've been doing a little in that line lately, so I agreed to see him, though I was very busy. I had completely forgotten the name, and it never suggested Rhodesia.'

He stopped, and then broke out quite fiercely. 'Why on earth should it? It's all more than thirty years ago, and I've long ago buried the callow boy who went vapouring about Africa. Hang it all, I've made a position for myself. Next year I hope to be a Director of the Bank of England. I've my reputation to consider. You see that, don't you?'

I didn't know what he was driving at, but it was plain that Lombard was no longer the sleek suburbanite. Something had jostled him out of his rut.

'But there was nothing in the old Haraldsen business to hurt your credit,' I said. 'So far as I remember, you behaved well. There's no skeleton in that cupboard.'

'Wait till you hear,' he replied dismally. 'This chap came to my office, and he told me a dashed silly story. Oh, a regular blood-and-thunder yarn of how he was in an awful mess, with a lot of crooks out gunning for him. I didn't follow him very clearly, for he was in a pitiable state of nerves, and now and then lost command of the English language altogether. But the gist of it was that he was in deadly danger, and that his enemies would get him unless he found the right kind of friends. I don't know how much was true, but I could see that he believed it all. There must be some truth in it, for he didn't look a fool, and I'll swear that he's honest.'

He stopped, and I waited, for I guessed what was coming.

'He asked me to help him,' Lombard continued, 'though God knows what he thought I could do. I'm not a Cabinet Minister or a Chief of Police. Did you ever hear anything more preposterous? '

'Never,' I said heartily – and waited.

'He had got it into his head that he had some claim on me. Said I once helped his father in a tight place, and that his father had sworn me to stand by him if called upon – or by his son. Apparently the old man had put it all down in writing, and this Haraldsen had the document.'

'Well, it's not the kind of thing you could sue on,' I said cheerfully.

'I know that. . . . But, I say, Hannay, do you remember the occasion? '

'Perfectly. We stood on the top of a kopje in the moonlight, and the old boy swore us by one of his Viking oaths. Oh, I remember it all right.'

'So do I,' said Lombard miserably. 'Well, what the devil is to be done about it? '

'Nothing,' I said stoutly. I had sized up Lombard, and I realized that to expect this sedentary middle-aged fellow to take a hand in a wild business was beyond all reason. My old liking for him had returned, and I didn't want him to have an uneasy conscience. But what puzzled me was why young Haraldsen had gone to him. 'There were three of us in it,' I said. 'You and I and Peter Pienaar. Peter is in a better world, but I'm still to the fore. Why didn't he tackle me? I had much more to do with his father than you had.'

'Perhaps he didn't think of you as a major-general with a title. He probably heard my name in the City. Anyhow, there we are, and an infernal worrying business it is.'

'My dear chap, you needn't worry,' I said. 'We have all been foolish in our young days, and we can't be expected to go on living up to our folly. If I had made a pact with a man when I was twenty-one to climb Everest, and he turned up to-day and wanted to hold me to it, I should tell him to go to blazes. But I should like to hear more of young Haraldsen's yarn.'

'I didn't get it quite straight,' he replied, 'for the fellow was too excited. Besides, I didn't try to, for I could think of nothing except that ridiculous performance in Rhodesia. But I jotted down one or two names he mentioned, the names of the people he was afraid of.' From his pocket he took a sheet of notepaper. 'Troth,' he read, 'Lancelot Troth. And a name which may be Albius or Albion – I didn't ask him to spell it. Oh, and Barralty – you know, the company-promoter that came down in the Lepcha goldfield business.'

This made me open my eyes. 'God bless my soul, but Troth is dead. You know that yourself, for you saw old Peter Pienaar account for him. Your second name is probably Albinus – you must remember him too. If he's still alive I can't think what the Devil is waiting for. Barralty I know nothing about. I tell you what, Lombard, this all sounds to me like sheer hallucination. Young Haraldsen has come on Troth and Albinus in his father's papers, and has let himself be hag-ridden by ghosts from the past. Most likely the man is crazy.'

He shook his head. 'He didn't impress me that way. Scared if you like, but quite sane. Anyhow, what do you advise me to do about it? He made an appeal to me – he was almost weeping – and I had to promise to give him an answer. My answer is due to-morrow.'

'I think you had better turn the thing over to me,' I said. 'I've had some news lately about old Haraldsen, and I'd like to meet his son. Have you got his address? '

'I know how to get on to him. He's desperately secretive, but he gave me a telephone number which I could ring up and leave a message for a Mr. Bosworth.'

'Well, send the message. I must go home to-morrow, but to-night I'm free. Tell him to dine with me here to-night at eight. Give him my name, and mention that I was deeper in the old business than you were. If the thing's genuine, he is bound to have some record of me. If it's bogus, he'll never turn up.'

'What will you do with him?' he asked.

'I'll cross-examine him and riddle out the business. I know enough about old Haraldsen to be able to cross-examine with some effect. I suspect that the whole thing is a lunatic's fancy, for there's a good deal of lunacy in the Northern races. In that case, you and I will be able to go to bed in peace.'

'But if it's serious?' he asked, and his face showed that he had not much doubt about that.

'Oh, if there's anything in it, I suppose I must take a hand. After all, I was a pretty close friend of his father, which you never were. You needn't worry about the Moonlight Sonata stuff, for I put noth-ing on that. That was only old Haraldsen's taste for melodrama. Consider yourself as clean out of the affair, like Peter Pienaar. You've been a responsible citizen for the better part of thirty years, with a big business to manage and a settled life and all the rest of it. No sane man would expect you to butt into a show of this kind. Besides, you'd be no sort of good at it. I've settled down, too, but I've led a different kind of life from you, and crime is a little bit more in my line. I've made several excursions into the under-world, and I know some of the ropes.'

There was an odd change in his face, which had hitherto regis-tered only anxiety. I could have sworn that he was getting cross.

'If you were in my position, would you take that advice?' he asked in a flat voice.

'Most certainly I should,' I replied.

'You're a good fellow, Hannay,' he said, 'and you mean well. But you're a damned liar. If you were in my position, you'd do nothing of the kind, and you'd have the blood of anybody who advised you to. I can see what you take me for – I could see it in your eyes when we foregathered in the train. You believe I'm a fatted calf that has made a success in the City, and thinks only of his bank balance and his snug house, and his Saturday's golf. You believe that I'm the sort of herring-gutted creature that would take any insult lying down, or at the best run round to my solicitors. Well, you're wrong. I've had a soft life compared to you, but it hasn't been all fur-lined. I've had to take plenty of risks, and some of them mighty big ones. I had no wish to see you again after we met last autumn, for I saw that you despised me, and I didn't see how I could ever get you to change your mind. You're right in some ways. I'm a bit flabby and out of training in body and mind. But by God you're wrong about the main thing. I've never gone back on my word or funked a duty. And I'm not going to begin now. If there's anything in Haraldsen's story, my promise stands, and I'm in the business up to my neck, the same as you. If you don't agree to that, then you'll jolly well stand out, and I'll take it on myself.'

I felt the blood surging to my cheeks. Lombard had got up from his chair, and I had done the same, and we stood staring at each other across the hearth-rug. I saw in his face what I had missed altogether on the last occasion we met, a stubborn resolution and a shining honesty. In spite of his baldness and fleshiness and bleared eyes and snuffling, he looked twenty years younger. I recognized in him the boy I had known in Equatoria, and I felt as if I had suddenly recovered an old friend.

'Never mind what I thought,' I said. 'If I thought as you say I did I made a howling mistake and I grovel in apologies. We've picked up our friendship where we left it at Mafudi's kraal, and we'll see this thing through together.'

All the anger had gone out of his face.

'Mafudi,' he repeated. 'Yes, that's the name. I couldn't get to sleep last night for trying to remember it.'

I had two things to think about that evening. One was the revelation I had had of the true Lombard. That gave me extraordinary pleasure, for it seemed to remove the suspicion I had had all winter that I was myself old and stale and that all my youth had gone. If the fire still burned in this padded City magnate, it could not have died altogether in me. The second thing was Haraldsen, and I confess I felt solemn when I reflected that the week before Sandy Clanroyden had brought news of him out of the remotest East, news acquired by the wildest of chances. I had an eerie sense that this was all a sort of preparation engineered by Providence.

Lombard telephoned to me that 'Mr. Bosworth' would come to my club at eight o'clock. There was nobody in the smoking-room as I waited for my guest, and I remember trying to imagine what kind of fellow I should meet, and to reconstruct a younger version of old Haraldsen.

I got one of the shocks of my life when he appeared. For it was the man Smith, whom Peter John and I had met in the Rose and Crown at Hanham.

His surprise when he saw me was quite equal to mine.

'You!' he cried. 'Oh, thank God, I have found you. I never dreamed. . . .'

'You heard my name at Hanham,' I said.

'Ah, but I was looking for a South African engineer called Dick Hannay. In you I saw only an English general and a grandee. I took to you then – I do not know when I have so taken to a man, for I saw that you were wise and kind. But I did not imagine that you were my Dick Hannay.'

'Well, I am,' I said. 'I've seen Lombard, so two of your father's friends are with you. The third, the pick of the bunch, is dead.'

'You will stand beside me?' he stammered.

'Certainly,' I said. 'You may count us both in. Lombard told me that this afternoon.'

It was wonderful to see the effect these words had on him. As I have said, he was a very big fellow, but he slouched as if he were afraid of his size, and he had a shy, confused manner, like a large thing trying to hide behind something too small to cover it. He had cut an odd enough figure at Hanham, but in London he was clean out of the picture. When he entered the room my impression had been of a being altogether maladjusted to his environment, out of focus, so to speak, built on a wrong scale. But with his recovery of confidence he became almost normal, and I saw that the bucolic impression I had got of him was false. In his old-fashioned dinner-jacket he was more like a scholar than the farmer I had taken him for. His brow was broad and high, and his eyes had the unmistakable look of having peered a good deal over white paper.

At dinner he told me his story. He had not seen his father for eight years, or heard from him for three years, but it was clear that the old man was the dominant influence in his life. He had been brought up from childhood on a plan. While the elder Haraldsen was ranging the world the younger stayed in Europe, preparing himself for the task for which the former was laying up a fortune. He was to be the leader of the Northern peoples to a new destiny, and from a small boy he was put into the strictest training. First he was to be a master of all Northern learning, and imbibe its spirit. Then he was to know every corner of the North and every type of Northman. After that he was to have a first-class business education and learn how to handle big affairs. The old man's ambition for his son seemed to have been a kind of blend of Sir Walter Scott and Bismarck and Cecil Rhodes.

Of course, it didn't work – that kind of scheme never does. The young Valdemar (his Christian name was Valdemar) went stolidly through an immense curriculum, for he was clay in his father's hands, but the result was not the Admirable Crichton of the old man's dreams. He went to college in Denmark and Germany; he did two years in a Copenhagen bank; he travelled from Greenland in the west to the White Sea in the east, and even got as far as Spitzbergen, and there were not many places in Scandinavia and its islands on which he had not turned his unseeing eyes. But he did it all as a round of duty, for he had not a spark of his father's ardour. A scholar indeed he became, and a keen naturalist, but nothing more. He wanted a quiet life, and the future of the Northern races was no more to him than a half-forgotten fairy tale.

So at twenty-six there was Valdemar Haraldsen, sound in wind and limb, stuffed with much curious learning, but with no more ambition than a mole. I gathered that the old man had been disappointed, but had made the best of it. His son was young, so there was still hope, for there must be some fruit from so arduous a sowing. It seemed that his mother had come out of the Norland Isles, the daughter of a long line of what they called King's Yeomen there. She had inherited an island, and there the elder Haraldsen, on one of his longer sojourns in Europe, had built a house. He seemed to have made a minor hobby of it, for he had spent a good deal of money and filled it with Northern furniture and antiques. He agreed to Valdemar settling down there, after the boy had married with his consent, for no doubt he thought that the *genius loci* would have something to say to him. But the marriage had soon a tragic ending, for the young wife died with her first child.

I asked about the child.

'She lives and is well,' he said. 'She is now in her thirteenth year. She is at a school in England.'

He had stayed on in his lonely isle, and I gathered had become a good deal of a recluse, rarely coming south, and filling his time with his hobbies, which were principally natural history and an inquiry into the interaction of the old Norse and Celtic peoples.

'But I was happy,' he said in his gentle voice. 'I was indeed always anxious about my father, who did not come to me and would not permit me to go to him. But I had my girl Anna with me till she was of age for school, and I had my house and my books and my little kingdom. And I had good health and a quiet mind.'

'You're well off?' I asked.

A pained look came into his eyes, as if his mind had been engaged with pleasant things and now saw something hideous.

'I believe I am very rich,' he said slowly. 'I do not know how rich, for money has never interested me. There are bankers in Copenhagen who look after these things for me, and they tell me I need not stint myself.'

I thought what bad luck it was on old Haraldsen to go on piling up a fortune for a son who never wanted to hear how much it was.

'Well,' I said, 'I think I've got the lay-out. You've been squatting peacefully up in your island while your father has been gold-digging in the ends of the earth. What has happened now? What is the trouble?'

'The trouble,' he said slowly, and his eyes were full of pain again, 'is that I have lost my quiet mind.'

Then he told me, with long stops when he seemed to be hunting for words, the following story.

Two years before he had had a letter from a London firm of solicitors who said that they wrote on behalf of a client who had a claim on his father, and asked for his father's address. He replied that he did not know where his father was, and thought no more about it. Then came a second letter, asking whether the old man was alive or dead, and Haraldsen duly replied that he couldn't be sure, but hoped for the best. After that he was informed that an action at law would be begun, and that, if his father did not appear, an attempt would be made to have his death presumed, so that recourse might be had against his estate. I didn't quite get the hang of the argument, for Valdemar was not very clear himself. The correspondence was all perfectly civil in tone, but the last letter gave him a nasty shock, for the solicitors disclosed that their client was a Mr. Lancelot Troth.

Now Valdemar had a great quantity of his father's papers, which he had been at pains to read and arrange, and among them were records of his old days in Africa, and especially of his early work on the Rand. The name of Troth appeared in some of them. Troth had been the old man's partner at one time and had tried to swindle him. There had been a terrific row, and Troth had cleared out, but Haraldsen had been certain that he would come back again and make mischief. He took the trouble to write out a detailed statement of the case, and Valdemar said that it left the impression on him that while Troth was no doubt a rogue, he might have had some kind of a grievance, and that his father's conscience was not quite easy about the business.

Among the papers, too, was a full account of the affair at the Hill of the Blue Leopard, and of how he had sworn three men, Lombard, Peter Pienaar, and myself, to stand by him or his son, if there was any further trouble on that score. The funny thing was that he did not mention that Troth had been killed. He seemed to have the Saga notion that a vendetta went on from generation to generation, and that Troth's son, if he had one, might make things unpleasant for his own son. He mentioned Albinus too, who had apparently been a subordinate figure in the first row on the Rand, but a leader at Mafudi's.

So when Valdemar saw the name of Troth in the solicitors' letter he began to feel uncomfortable. I gathered that his father had been very solemn about the affair, and had gone out of his way to warn his son. Valdemar did his best to put the thing out of his head, but not with much success. And then he got a letter signed Lancelot Troth which had effectively scared him. The lawyers' correspondence had been, so to speak, only ranging shots, and now the guns started in earnest.

The writer said that his father had been grievously wronged by the old Haraldsen, and that he demanded restitution. If the old man was dead, or lost to the world, the son must pay, for he had ascertained that he was very rich. There need be no unpleasantness, if the writer were fairly treated, for he was convinced that his claim must be patent to any reasonable man. He suggested that a meeting should be arranged in Copenhagen or London, to which Valdemar could bring one adviser, while he, Troth, would bring his partner, Mr. Erick Albinus, who was a party to his claim. There was no talk now of any legal action. It was a straight personal demand to stand and deliver.

Valdemar was mightily put out, and, not being a man of the

world, would in all likelihood have done something silly – seen Troth, agreed to his terms, and so put himself in his power for the rest of his life. But luckily he met an Englishman who came up that summer to fish in the Norlands, and in the course of conversation asked him some vague questions, in which he managed to mention Troth's name. The Englishman was a well-known barrister whose practice was largely at the Old Bailey, and he could tell him a good deal about Troth, though he had never heard of Albinus. Troth had succeeded to his father's business as a solicitor, and bore a pretty shady repute. The fisherman described him as one who didn't stick at trifles, but had so far been clever enough to keep on the sunny side of the law. He was believed to be at the moment in the environs of Queer Street, for he was mixed up with Barralty in the Lepcha Reef flotation, and that was beginning to look ugly. 'I hate the fellow,' said the Englishman, 'but I wouldn't go out of my way to cross him. He has an eye like a gunman's, and a jowl like a prize-fighter.'

That talk opened Valdemar's eyes to the dangers of his position. He had sense enough to see that it was a case of large-sized black-mail, and that any sum he paid would only be a lever for further extortions till he was bled white. He went off his sleep, and worried himself into a fever, for he couldn't decide what his next step should be.

While he was still cogitating he got a second letter from Troth. Mr. Haraldsen need not trouble to come south, for the writer was about to pay a visit to the Norlands in his friend Mr. Barralty's yacht. He proposed a meeting in Hjalmarshavn some three weeks ahead.

This screwed Valdemar up to the point of action. Alone on his island he was at the mercy of any gang of miscreants that chose to visit him. His ignorance of the world made him imagine terrible things. He hungered for human society, for a crowd in which he could hide himself. So he buried his papers and some of the things he most valued, shut up his house, left the island to the care of his steward, and along with his daughter fled from the Norlands. He left an address in Copenhagen for forwarding letters, but he did not mean to go there, for he was known in Denmark and would be recognized. He determined to go to London, where he would be utterly obscure.

Troth and his friend duly arrived in the Norlands. They visited the Island of Sheep – this was the name of Valdemar's place – and, when they found it empty, pretty well ransacked the house, just like so many pirates from the sea. But they did no mischief, for they were playing a bigger game. Valdemar heard of this from his steward, his letter going first to his bank in Copenhagen, then to a friend in Sweden, and finally to his English address. He placed his child in an English school, and took to wandering about the country, calling himself Smith and other names, and never staying long in one place. He heard of the crash of the Lepcha Reef and Barralty's difficulties, and realized that this would make the gang keener than ever on his scent. He had letters from Troth – three I think – and the last fairly put the wind up. 'You have refused to meet me frankly,' said Troth, 'and you have run away, but don't imagine you can escape me. I will follow you till I track you down, though I have to give up my life to the job, and the price you will have to pay will double with each month I have to wait.' It was brigandage now, naked brigandage.

I am not sure that I believed all this tale, but there was one thing I couldn't doubt – Valdemar believed it, and was sweating with terror. That big man, who should have marched stoutly through life, had eyes like a hunted deer's.

'What an infernal nuisance for you!' I said. 'You can't go home, because of the threats of those scallywags! Well, anyhow, you're safe enough here, and can have an easy mind till we think out some plan.'

'I am not safe here,' he said solemnly. 'At first I thought that no one knew me in England. But I was wrong. They have had descriptions of me – photographs – from the Norlands and from Copenhagen. They have found people who can identify me. . . . One day in the street I saw a barber from Denmark who has often shaved me, and he recognized me, and tried to follow me. He is a poor man and would not have come here on his own account. He has been brought to London. The net is drawing in on me, and I know from many small things that they are very close on my trail. I change my dwelling often, but I feel that I cannot long escape them. So I am very desperate, and that is why I have sought out my father's friends.'

He sat huddled in his chair, his chin sunk on his breast, the image of impotence and despair. I realized that Lombard and I were going to have a difficult job with him. I had an uneasy suspicion, as I looked at him, that his story might be all moonshine, the hallucination of a lonely neurotic, and I wished I had never heard of him. Keeping a promise was one thing, but nursing a lunatic was quite another.

'It is not only for myself I fear,' he said in a leaden voice. 'There is my little daughter. I dare not visit her in case they follow me. They might kidnap her, and then I should assuredly go mad.'

To that I had nothing to say, for the mention of kidnapping always made me windy. I had had too much of it in the affair with Medina, which I have already written about.[1]

'There is my father, too,' he went on. 'He may at any moment go to the Norlands or come to England, and I cannot warn him.'

'You needn't worry about that,' I said gently. 'Your father died two years ago – at a place called Gutok, in Chinese Tibet.' And I repeated briefly what Sandy Clanroyden had told me.

You never saw such a change in a man. The news seemed to pull him together and put light into his eyes. To him, apparently, it was not a matter of grief, but of comfort.

'*Thesauro feliciter invento,*' he repeated. 'Then he succeeded – he has died happy. I cannot sorrow for him, for he has greatly ended a great life.'

He put his chin on his hand and brooded, and in that moment I was possessed by one of those queer irrational convictions which I have always made a habit of accepting, for I have never found them wrong. This Valdemar Haraldsen was as sane as myself, and he was in deadly peril. I believed implicitly every word of his tale, and my duty to help him was plain as a pikestaff. My first business must be to tuck him away comfortably somewhere out of the road.

I asked him where he was living and if he was sure he had not been followed here. He said that he had only moved into his new quarters two days before, and was pretty certain that he was safe for the moment. 'But not for long,' he added dismally.

'Well, you must clear out,' I said. 'Tomorrow you pack your kit. You are coming to stay with me for a little. I will go down by an earlier train, for we shouldn't be seen together. Put on your oldest clothes and travel third-class – I'll send my keeper to meet you, and he'll bring you up in the old Ford. Your name is still Bosworth.'

I fixed up a train, offered him a whisky-and-soda, which he declined, and saw him shamble off in the direction of his Bayswater lodgings. He looked like a store-farmer who had borrowed an ancient suit of his father's dress-clothes, and that was the rôle I wanted him to play. Then I rang up Macgillivray in his Mount Street rooms, found that he was at home, and went round to see him.

[1] In *The Three Hostages.*

CHAPTER VI

Sundry Doings at Fosse

I FOUND MACGILLIVRAY READING Greek with his feet on the mantel-piece and the fire out. He was a bit of a scholar and kept up his classics. Of all my friends he was the one who had aged least. His lean, dark head and smooth, boyish face were just as I remembered them twenty years ago. I hadn't seen him for months, and he gave me a great welcome, rang for beer to which he knew I was partial, and settled me in his best armchair.

'Why this honour?' he asked. 'Is it friendship or business? A sudden craving for my company, or a mess you want to be helped out of? '

'Both,' I said. 'But business first.'

'A job for the Yard?'

'No-o. Not just yet, anyhow. I want some information. I've just got on the track of a rather ugly affair.'

He whistled. 'You have a high standard of ugliness. What is it? '

'Blackmail,' I said.

'Yourself? He must be a bold blackmailer to tackle you.'

'No, a friend. A pretty helpless sort of friend, who will go mad if he isn't backed up.'

'Well, let's have the story.'

'Not yet,' I said. 'It's a private affair which I would rather keep to myself for a little till I see how things shape. I only want an answer to a few questions.'

He laughed. 'That was always your way, Dick. You ' keep your ain fish-guts for your ain sea-mews,' as they say in Scotland. You never let in the Yard till the fruitiest episodes are over.'

'I've done a good deal for you in my time,' I said.

'True. And you may always count upon us to do our damnedest.'

Then he suddenly became serious.

'I'm going to talk to you like a grandfather, Dick. You're not ageing properly.'

'I'm ageing a dashed sight too fast,' I said.

'No, you're not. We're all getting old, of course, but you're not acquiring the virtues of age. There's still an ineradicable daftness about you. You've been lying pretty low lately, and I had hoped you had settled down for good. Consider. You're a married man with a growing son. You have made for yourself what I should call a happy life. I don't want to see you wreck it merely because you are feeling restless. So if it's only a craze for adventure that is taking you into this business, my advice to you as a friend is to keep out of it.'

He picked up the book he had been reading.

'Here's a text for you,' he said. 'It is Herodotus. This is the advice he makes Amasis give to his friend Polycrates. I'll translate. ' I know that the Gods are jealous, for I cannot remember that I ever heard of any man who, having been constantly successful, did not at last utterly perish.' That's worth thinking about. You've been amazingly lucky, but you mustn't press your luck too far. Remember, the Gods are jealous.'

'I'm not going into this affair for fun,' I replied. 'It's a solid obligation of honour.'

'Oh, in that case I have no more to say. Ask your questions.'

'Do you know anything about a fellow called Albinus, Erick Albinus? A man about my own age – a Dane by birth who has lived in America and, I should think, in many parts of the world? Dabbles in finance of a shady kind.' I gave the best description I could of how Albinus had looked thirty years ago, and what his appearance to-day might be presumed to be.

Macgillivray shook his head. 'I can't place him. I'll have our records looked up, but to the best of my knowledge I don't know anybody like him. I certainly don't remember his name.'

'Well, then, what about a man called Lancelot Troth? '

'Now we're getting on familiar ground,' he said. 'I know a good deal about Troth. The solicitor, I suppose you mean? He belongs to a firm which has been going on for several generations and has never been quite respectable. The father was a bit of a rogue who died years ago somewhere in Africa. That was before my time, but in the last ten years we have had to keep an eye on the activities of the son. He operates on the borderland of rather dubious finance, but so far he has never quite crossed the frontier, though sometimes he has had to be shepherded back. Company promotion is his chief line, and he is uncommonly clever at taking advantage of every crack in our confused company law. I thought we had him the other day over the Lepcha business, but we were advised that a prosecution would fail. He has several side lines – does a good deal of work for Indian rajahs which may now and then be pretty shady – made a pot of money over grey-hound-racing in its early days – a mighty gambler, too, they tell me, and fairly successful. Rich! So-so. Flush one day and hard up the next – he leads the apolaustic life, and that's an expensive thing nowadays.'

I asked about his appearance and Macgillivray described him. A man in his early forties, strongly made, with the square, clean-shaven face of his profession. Like a cross between a Chancery barrister and a Newmarket trainer.

'He doesn't make a bad impression at first sight,' he added. 'He looks you in the face and he has rather pleasant eyes. On the occasions when I've met him I've rather liked him. A tough, no doubt, but with some of the merits of the breed. I can imagine him standing stiffly by his friends, and I have heard of him doing generous things. He's a bit of a sportsman too – keeps a six-ton cutter, and can be seen on a Friday evening departing in old clothes from his City office with his kit in a pillow-case. If your trouble is blackmail, Dick, and Troth is in it, it won't be the ordinary kind. The man might be a bandit, but he wouldn't be a sneak-thief.'

Then I spoke the name of Barralty, and when he heard it Macgillivray's attention visibly quickened. He whistled, and his face took on that absent-minded look which always means that his brain or his memory is busy.

'Barralty,' he repeated. 'Do you know, Dick, you've an uncommon knack of getting alongside interesting folk? Whenever you've consulted me it has always been in connection with gentry about whom I was pretty curious myself. Barralty – Joseph Bannatyne Barralty! It would take a cleverer man than me to expound that intricate gentleman. Did you ever see him?'

I said No – I had only heard of him for the first time that day.

'How shall I describe him? In some lights he looks like a half-pay colonel who inhabits the environs of Cheltenham. Tallish, lean, big-nose, high cheek-bones – dresses generally in well-cut flannels or tweeds – age anything round fifty. He has a moustache which has gone grey at the tips, and it gives him a queer look of innocence. That's one aspect – the English country gentleman. In another light he is simply Don Quixote – the same unfinished face, the same mild sad eyes and general air of being lost that one associates with the Don. That sounds rather attractive, doesn't it? – half adventurer, half squire? But there's a third light – for I have seen him look as ugly as sin. The pale eyes became mean and shallow and hard, the rudimentary features were something less than human, and the brindled moustache with its white points looked like the tusks of an obscene boar. . . . I dare say you've gathered that I don't much like Mr. Barralty.

'But I don't understand him,' he went on. 'First of all, let me say that we have nothing against him. He came down in the Lepcha business, but there was never any suggestion against his character. He behaved perfectly well, and will probably end by paying every creditor in full, for he is bound to come on top again. He has had his ups and downs, and, like everybody in the City, has had to mix with doubtful characters, but his own reputation is unblemished. He doesn't appear to care for money so much as for the game. Yet nobody likes him, and I doubt if many trust him, though every one admits his ability. Now if you find a man unpopular for no apparent reason, it is generally safe to assume some pretty rotten patch in him. I assume the patch all right in Barralty's case, but I'm hanged if I can put my finger on it, or find anything to justify my assumption except that now and then I've seen him look like the Devil.'

I asked about his profession.

'He's a stockbroker – a one-man firm which he founded himself. His interests? Not financial exclusively – indeed, he professes to despise the whole money-spinning business. Says he is in it only to get cash for the things he cares about. What are these? Well, yachting used to be one. In the days of his power he had the *Thelma* – six hundred tons odd – that might be the original link with Troth. Then he's a first-class, six-cylindered, copper-bottomed highbrow. A gentlemanly Communist. An intellectual who doesn't forget to shave. The patron of every new fad in painting and sculping and writing. Mighty condescending about all that ordinary chaps like you and me like, but liable to enthuse about monstrosities, provided that they're brand-new and for preference foreign. I should think it was a genuine taste, for he has that kind of rootless, marginal mind. He backs his fancy too. For years he has kept the – going (Macgillivray mentioned a peevishly superior weekly journal), and he imports at his own expense all kinds of exponents of the *dernier cri*. His line is that he despises capitalism, as he despises all orthodoxies, but that as long as the beastly thing lasts, he will try to make his bit out of it, and spend the proceeds in hastening its end. Quite reasonable. I blame nothing about him except his taste.'

'Isn't he popular with his progressive lot?' I asked.

Macgillivray shook his head. 'I should doubt it. They flatter him when necessary, and sponge on him, but I'm pretty certain they don't like him.'

I asked if all this intelligentsia business might not be a dodge to help Barralty's city interests. It made him a new type of financier, and simple folk might be inclined to trust a man who declared that his only object in getting money was to prevent anybody, including himself, piling it up in the future.

Macgillivray thought that there might be something in that.

'He's a cautious fellow. His name is always being appended to protests in the newspapers, but he keeps off anything too extreme. His line is not the fanatic, but the superior critic of human follies. He does nothing to scare the investor. . . . Well, I'll keep an eye on him, and see if I can find out more about his relations with Troth. And the other fellow – what's his name – Erick Albinus? You've given me an odd triangle.'

As I was leaving, Macgillivray said one last thing, which didn't make much impression at the time, but which I was to remember later.

'I should back you against the lot, Dick. They're not natural criminals, and their nerve might crack. The danger would be if they got into the hands of somebody quite different – some really desperate fellow – like yourself.'

I went down to Fosse next morning by the early train, and Haraldsen duly arrived at midday. He put up with my keeper Jack Godstow, who had a roomy cottage in which I reserved a couple of rooms for bachelor guns when Fosse was overcrowded during a big shoot. I hunted him up after tea, and we went for a walk on the Downs.

My impression of the day before was confirmed. Haraldsen was as sane as I was. Whatever his trouble was, it was real enough, and not a mental delusion. But he was in an appalling condition of nerves. He was inclined to talk to himself under his breath – you could see his lips moving, and he had a queer trick of grunting. When we sat down he kept twitching his hands and fussing with his legs, and he would suddenly go off into an abstraction. He admitted that he had been sleeping badly. I was distressed by his state, for he was a fifty per cent. sicker man than he had been at Hanham in January. I discovered that he had two terrors: one that something very bad might at any moment happen to himself or his daughter – especially his daughter. The other was that this miserable thing might simply drag on without anything happening, and that he would be shut off for ever from his beloved home in the north.

I did my best to minister to his tattered nerves. I told him that he was perfectly safe with me, and that I wouldn't let matters drag on – Lombard and I would take steps to clear them up. I encouraged him to talk about his Island of Sheep, for it did him good to have something pleasant to think about, and he described to me with tremendous feeling the delight of its greenery and peace, the summer days when it was never dark, the fresh, changing seas, the tardy, delicate springs, the roaring, windy autumns, the long, snug, firelit winters.

I impressed upon him that for the present he must lie low. He would have the run of the house and the library, and Mary and I would see a lot of him, but to the countryside he must be an invalid friend of a friend of mine, who had come to Fosse for quiet and mustn't be disturbed. Jack Godstow would take him out fishing and show him the lie of the land. I gathered that he had some belongings scattered up and down London which he would like to have beside him, and I said that I would arrange for Lombard to collect them quietly and send them on. But I chiefly told him to be quite assured that this persecution was going to be brought to an end, for I saw that it was only that hope which would soothe him.

I spoke confidently, but I hadn't a notion how it was to be done. Haraldsen's safety depended on his being hidden away – I was quite clear about that – so we couldn't draw the fire of his enemies so as to locate them. About these enemies I was wholly in the dark. An Americanized Dane, a shady sporting solicitor, a highbrow financier who looked like Don Quixote and had just crashed; it didn't sound a formidable combination. I had only met one of them, Albinus, and about him I only knew the episode at Mafudi's kraal; Macgillivray rather liked Troth, and Barralty sounded unpleasant but ineffective. Yet the three were engaged in something which had put the fear of death on a very decent citizen, and that had to be riddled out and stopped. There was nothing to do but to wait on developments. That night I wrote a long letter to Lombard, telling him the result of my talk with Macgillivray, asking him to keep his ears open for any news which would connect the three names, and warning him that I might summon him at any moment. As we went to bed I told Mary that I had not much to do for the next few weeks, and that I meant to devote them to getting Haraldsen back to an even keel.

But next day I had news which upset all my plans. Peter John at school was stricken with appendicitis, and was to be operated on that day. Mary and I raced off at once and took rooms near the nursing-home. The operation went off well, and after two days, which were purgatory to me and hell to Mary, he was pronounced to be out of danger. He made an excellent quick recovery, being as healthy as a trout, but it was a fortnight before he was allowed up, and three weeks before he left the home. Then, since the weather was hot, we took him to a seaside place on the East coast for a couple of weeks, so it was not till the beginning of June that we returned to Fosse.

Meanwhile I had heard nothing about Haraldsen. Lombard and Macgillivray had both been silent, and Jack Godstow had only reported weekly that the gentleman was doing nicely and was looking forward to the May-fly season. When I got back to Fosse I expected to find him rested and calmed and beginning to put on flesh, for all these weeks he had been deep in country peace and must have felt secure.

I found exactly the opposite. Haraldsen looked worse than when I had left him, leaner, paler, and his eyes had more of a hunted look than ever. He had little to say to me except to repeat his thanks for my kindness. No, he had not been disturbed; nothing had happened to alarm him; he was quite well and had got back a bit of his appetite, he thought; he wasn't sleeping so badly. But all the time his eyes were shifting about as if he expected any moment to see something mighty unpleasant, and he started at every noise. He was the very model of a nervous wreck.

I had a long talk about him with Jack Godstow. I won't attempt Jack's dialect, for no words could reproduce the odd Cotswold lilt and drawl, and the racy idiom of every sentence. The gist of his report was that Mr. Haraldsen was a difficult one to manage, since he never knew his own mind. He would make a plan to fish the evening rise, and then change it and start out at midnight when there was nothing doing. He didn't like the daylight no more than an owl, and he didn't like other folks neither, and would get scared if he saw a strange face. He was always asking about new folk in the neighbourhood, but Lord bless you, said Jack, new folk didn't come this way, except for an odd hiker or two, and the extra hands for the hay harvest, and the motor gentry on the Fosse Way. The gentleman needn't worry himself, and he had told him so, but it was no good speaking. I explained to Jack that my friend was a sick man, and that part of his sickness was a dread of strange faces. Jack understood that and grinned. 'Like that new 'awk of Master Peter John's,' he said.

The mention of Peter John gave me an idea. The boy was not going back to school that half, and was settling down to a blissful summer at Fosse before he went north to Sandy Clanroyden at Laverlaw. He had six little kestrels sitting all day on the lawn, and Morag on her perch in the Crow Wood, and a young badger called Broccoli that rootled about in the stable straw and gave him heart disease at night by getting down into the entrails of the greenhouses. He was still under a mild doctor's régime, but was picking up strength very fast. Haraldsen had taken to him at Hanham, and I thought that his company might be wholesome for him. So I asked him to take on the job of being a good deal with my guest, for everything about Peter John suggested calm nerves and solid reason. There was something else in my mind.

'Mr. Haraldsen is an invalid,' I said, 'and must keep quiet. He has been through rather a beastly experience, which I'll tell you about some day. It's just possible that the experience isn't over yet, and that some person or persons might turn up here who wouldn't be well disposed to him. I want you to keep your eyes very wide open and let me know at once if you see or hear anything suspicious. By suspicious I mean something outside the usual – I don't care how small it is. We can't afford to take any chances with Mr. Haraldsen.'

Peter John nodded and his face brightened. He asked no questions, but I knew that he had got something to think about.

Nothing happened for a week. The boy did Haraldsen good; Mary and I both noticed it, and Jack Godstow admitted as much. He took him to fish in the early mornings both in our little trout stream and in the Decoy ponds. He took him on the Downs in the afternoon to fly Morag. He took him into the woods after dinner to watch fox cubs at play, and try to intercept Broccoli's cousin on his way from his sett. Haraldsen began to get some colour into his face, and he confessed that he slept better. I don't know what the two talked about, but they must have found common subjects, for I could hear them conversing vigorously – Peter John's slow, grave voice, and Haraldsen's quicker, more staccato speech. If we were making no progress with Haraldsen's business we were at any rate mending his health.

Then one evening Peter John came to me with news.

They had been out hawking with Morag on the Sharway Downs, and on their way home had met a young man on horseback. At first Peter John had thought him one of the grooms from the Clipperstone Racing Stables exercising a horse, but as they passed he saw that the rider was not dressed like a groom. He wore white linen breeches, a smartly cut flannel coat, and an O.E. tie. He had taken a good look at the falconers, and the impression left by him on Peter John was of a florid young man with a small dark moustache and slightly projecting upper teeth. To their surprise they met him again, this time apparently in rather a hurry, for he was going at a quick trot, and again he scrutinized them sharply. Now, said my son, that meant that he had made a circuit by the track that led to Sharway Lodge Farm, and cut through the big Sharway Wood – not an easy road, and possible only for one who knew the country. Who was this young man? Did I know anybody like him, for he had never seen him before? Why was he so interested in the pair of them?

I said that he was no doubt a stranger who was intrigued by the sight of the falcon, and wanted to have another look at it.

'But he didn't look at Morag,' was the answer. 'It was Mr. Haraldsen that interested him – both times. You might have thought that he knew him and wanted to stop and speak.'

'Did Mr. Haraldsen recognize him?' I asked, and was told No. He didn't know him from Adam, and Peter John, not to alarm him, had pretended he was one of the racing-stable people.

Two days later I had to be at Gloucester for the Agricultural Show. When I was dressing for dinner in the evening Mary was full of the visitors she had had that afternoon at tea.

'The Marthews, no less!' she said. 'I can't think what brought them here, for Caythorp is thirty miles off and I scarcely know them. Claire Marthew was a god-daughter of one of my Wymondham aunts – I used to meet her here in the old days when she was Claire Serocold and a very silly affected girl. She hasn't improved much – her face lacquered like a doll's, and her eyes like a Pekinese, and her voice so foolish it made one hot to hear it. She's by way of being uncommonly smart, and she babbled of grandees. But she was amiable enough, though I can't explain this sudden craving for my society. She brought her whole party with her – in several cars – you never saw such a caravan. Mostly women who had to be shown the house and the garden – I wish I were a better show-woman, Dick, for I become paralysed with boredom when I have to expound our possessions. There was one extraordinarily pretty girl, a Miss Ludlow – a film actress, I believe, who was content to smile and look beautiful. There were a couple of young men, too, who didn't say much. I told Peter John to look after them, and I think he took them to see the hunters at grass, and Morag, and Broccoli. By the way, I haven't seen him since. I wonder what he's up to?'

Peter John was very late for dinner. In theory he should have been in bed by nine, but it was no good making rules for one whose habits, in summer at any rate, were largely nocturnal. At ten o'clock, when I was writing letters in the library, he appeared at my side.

'Did my mother tell you about the people who came to tea?' he asked. 'There was a flock of them, and one was the man that Mr. Haraldsen and I met on Tuesday – the chap on horseback who wanted to have another look at us.'

'What was his name?' I asked.

'They all called him Frankie. My mother thinks it was something like Warrender – but not Warrender. I took him to see the horses, and he asked a lot of questions.'

'Wasn't there another man?' I asked.

'Yes, but he didn't count. He was a sort of artist or antiquarian, and couldn't be got away from the tithe-barn. It was this Frankie chap that mattered. He made me take him all over the place, and he asked me all sorts of questions about who lived here, and what their jobs were, and who our friends were, and if many people came to stay with us. It would have been cheek in anybody else, but he did it quite nicely, as if he liked the place enormously and wanted to know all about it. But you told me to look out for anything suspicious, and I thought him a bit suspicious.

'And that isn't the end,' he went on. 'Frankie didn't go off with the rest. He started with them in a little sports car of his own, but he turned off at the lodge gate and tucked away his car in the track that leads to the old quarry. I was following him and saw him skirt the water-meadow and have a look at the back of Trimble's cottage. Then he moved on to Jack's, and lay up in the hazel clump behind it, where he could get a good view. I nipped in by the side door, and luckily caught Mr. Haraldsen, who was just starting out, and told him to stick indoors. Frankie was so long in the clump that I got tired of waiting and decided to flush him, so I made a circuit and barged in beside him, pretending I had lost Broccoli. He took it quite calmly, and said he was a keen botanist and had stayed behind to look for some plant that he had heard lived here. But he didn't want to stay any longer, so I saw him to his car, and he socked me two half-crowns, and then I went back to give the 'All Clear' to Mr. Haraldsen.'

I told Peter John that he had done very well, and had better get off to bed. His story had disquieted me, for this Frankie man had clearly been interested in Haraldsen, and it looked as if he had spotted his lair. That wasn't difficult, for, if there was anybody at Fosse who was not staying in the house, Jack's cottage was the only one big enough for a guest. I cross-examined Mary about Frankie, but she could tell me little. He had seemed a very ordinary young man, with pleasant manners and a vacant face – she remembered his prominent teeth. But she had got his name – not Warrender, but Varrinder. 'He's probably the son of the snuffy old Irish peer – Clongelt? – Clongelly? – who was said to be a money-lender in Cork Street.'

It was, I think, three days later that Sandy Clanroyden came to visit us. He wired that he wanted exercise, and proposed that I should meet him at a distant railway station, send his kit back in the car, and walk with him the fifteen miles to Fosse. We had a gorgeous walk through the blue June weather, drank good ale at the little pubs, and dropped down from the uplands nearly opposite our lodge gates, where a wild field of stunted thorns formed the *glacis* of the hills. We had a clear view of a patch of highway, where two men were getting into a little sports car.

Sandy sank to the ground as if he had been shot. 'Down, Dick,' he commanded, and, after a long stare, fixed in his eye the little single glass which he used for watching birds. All I saw was two young men, who seemed to be in rather a hurry. One was hatless, and the other had his hat pulled far down on his head. At that distance I couldn't be sure, but I had the impression that both were a little the worse for wear, for their flannel suits didn't seem to hang quite right on them.

When they had gone, Sandy pocketed his glass and grunted. He didn't say one word till we reached the house and were being greeted by Mary. Instead of replying to her inquiries about Barbara, he asked, like a cross-examining counsel, if she had had any visitors at Fosse that afternoon.

'Oh yes,' she said. 'The Varrinder youth, who came with the Marthews, turned up again. I told you about him, Dick. He's a great botanist, and there is something very rare here, which he wanted to show to his friend. He said that on his last visit he had found the dwarf orchis.'

Sandy whistled. 'Not very clever,' he said. '*Ustulata* is impossible on this soil. Who was his friend? '

'A Frenchman, a Monsieur Blanc. Mr. Varrinder called him Pierre.'

'Describe him.'

Mary wrinkled her brows. 'A man about thirty-five or forty, I should say. Very slim and elegant and beautifully dressed. A queerly shaped head that rose to a peak, rather like a faun's – clean-shaven, and with the kind of colour that people get from living in hot climates. His chin was paler than the rest of his face, so I expect he once had a beard. They wouldn't stay to tea – only wanted permission to explore the home woods.'

'Did Peter John see them?' I asked.

'I don't know. He has been out for the whole day, but he's back now, for I heard his bath running.'

As I was showing Sandy his room he said solemnly, 'We must have a long talk after dinner, Dick.'

'We must,' I said. 'I have a good deal I want to tell you.'

'And I have something rather startling to tell you,' he replied.

That night I brought Peter John into our conference, for I judged that he had better know everything. I began by going fully into the Haraldsen business, of which, of course, Sandy knew nothing. I told him of my talk with Lombard, and my talks with Haraldsen himself, and my conviction that the man was not dreaming, but was really in danger. I repeated what Macgillivray had told me about Troth and Barralty. I explained that I had thought it best to bring him down to Fosse, which seemed to me a safe hiding-place. Then I recounted what had happened since he came here, his growing restlessness and misery, which Peter John seemed to be in the way of curing, and finally the episode of young Varrinder. I said that I hadn't liked the business of that youth, for he appeared to have a morbid interest in Haraldsen, and I told of his lying up behind Jack's cottage, and I added that I liked less his coming here to-day with his tale of a bogus orchis. 'Do you know anything about him?' I asked.

'Not much,' said Sandy. 'I've heard of him. He's reputed to be something of a waster, gambles high at Dillon's, and so forth. But I can tell you a good deal about his friend Monsieur – Pierre – Blanc.' Sandy repeated the name slowly as if each syllable had its flavour.

'Listen, Dick,' he said, 'and you, Peter John, though you'll have to get your father to explain a lot afterwards. I've told you pretty fully the story of what happened in Olifa two years ago.[1] You remember that the Gran Seco was a sort of port of missing ships, where all kinds of geniuses and desperadoes who had crashed their lives were inspanned in Castor's service. They were like the servants of the Old Man of the Mountain in the Crusades, and drugged themselves into competence and comfort. Well, you know what happened. The gang – they called themselves the Conquistadores – was cleaned out. Some were killed in our final scrap, and the rest were bound to die slowly when they were deprived of their dope. There was one of them, almost the boldest, called Jacques D'Ingraville, who had been in his day a famous French ace. He was as big a blackguard as the others, but more wholesome, for, though he doped, his work in the air kept his body from becoming quite so sodden. I was never very sure what became of him in the end. We had no certain news of his death in the fight at Veiro, but there was a strong probability that he had stopped a bullet there, and anyhow, I knew that his number was

[1]The tale of Lord Clanroyden's doings in Olifa will be found in *The Courts of the Morning.*

up, since the supply of *astura* was cut off. I pictured him creeping to some hole in South America or Europe to die.

'Well, I was wrong,' he continued. 'Alone of those verminous Conquistadores – almost certainly alone – D'Ingraville lives. And I should say that he had recovered. He looked quite a fit man when I saw him this evening.'

Nobody spoke for a little. To me the whole affair suddenly began to wear a blacker complexion. It wasn't so much the appearance of D'Ingraville, for I had always suspected that Troth and Barralty and Albinus were not the whole of the gang. It was the fact that they had managed to trace Haraldsen here in spite of all our care. I reckoned that they must be far cleverer and more powerful than I had believed, and that my job of standing by Haraldsen was going to be a large-sized affair. I suddenly felt very feeble, and rather timid and old. But the sight of Sandy's face cheered me, for instead of being worried it was eager and merry.

'Who are in with you, Dick?' he asked. 'Only Lombard? Well, I think I must make a third. Partly because I've been funnily mixed up with Haraldsen, for Fate made me his father's legatee. The jade tablet was put in my hands for a purpose. Partly because of Monsieur le Capitaine Jacques D'Ingraville, *alias* Pierre Blanc. He's too dangerous a lad to be left at large. I haven't finished my Olifa job till I have settled with him. The time, I think, has come for me to take a hand.'

He got up and found himself a drink. I looked at him as he stood half in the dusk, with the light of a single lamp on his face – not much younger than me, but as taut as a strung bow and as active as a hunting leopard. I thought that Haraldsen's enemies had unloosed a force of pretty high velocity. Peter John must have thought the same. He had listened to our talk with his eyes popping out of his head, and that sullen set of his face which he always wore when he was strongly moved. But as he looked at Sandy his solemnity broke into a smile.

'I go up to town to-morrow,' said Sandy, 'and I must get busy. I want a good deal more information, and I have better means of getting it than Macgillivray. I wish I knew just how much time we have. The gang are on Haraldsen's track – that's clear – but the question is, have they located him? The Varrinder lad can't be sure, or he wouldn't have come back twice. . . . Of course they may have done the business to-day. I wonder how far they got this evening?'

Peter John spoke. 'They didn't get very far. They couldn't. You see, they both fell into the Mill pool.'

Sandy took his pipe from his mouth and beamed on the boy. 'They fell into the Mill pool? Explain yourself, my son.'

'I spotted them when they arrived,' said Peter John, 'and I knew they would be a little time in the house anyhow, so I nipped off and warned Mr. Haraldsen to keep cover. When they came out I trailed them. They went through the garden to the High Wood, but I was pretty certain that they meant to go to the hazel clump behind Jack's cottage. To get there they had to cross the Mill lead by the plank bridge just above the pool. The stone at the end of the bridge isn't safe unless the planks are pushed well up the bank. So I loosened it a bit more, and pulled down the planks so that they rested on it.'

'Well?' Sandy and I demanded in one breath.

'They both fell into the pool, and it's pretty deep. I helped to pull them out and asked them to come up to the house to change. They wouldn't, for they were very cross. But Mr. Varrinder socked me another five bob.'

CHAPTER VII

Lord Clanroyden Intervenes

SANDY DEPARTED NEXT MORNING, and, as usual, was not communicative about his plans. I wanted him to see Haraldsen, but he said that there was no need, and that the sooner he was in London the better. He asked for Lombard's address and a line of introduction to him, and his only instruction was to keep Haraldsen safe for the next week. He suggested that to look after him might be made a whole-time job for Peter John.

Peter John took on the task joyfully, for here was something after his own heart. He worshipped Sandy, and to be employed by him thrilled him to the marrow. Besides, he had struck up with Haraldsen one of those friendships that a shy, self-contained boy very often makes with a shy man. Haraldsen came twice to dinner during the week after Sandy left, and there was no mistake about the change for the better in his condition. He spoke of his daughter at school without the flicker of fear in his eyes which had distressed me. He was full of questions about our small woodland birds, which were mostly new to him, and to which Peter John was introducing him. He was even willing to talk about his Island of Sheep without a face of blank desolation.

Then on the morning of Midsummer Day I got a shock on opening my *Times*. For on the leader page was a long letter from Sandy, and it was headed, 'The late M. E. Haraldsen.'

It told the story of the jade tablet and of how he had picked it up in a Peking junk-shop. He quoted the Latin in which Haraldsen had said good-bye to the world, but he didn't mention the place where the words had been written. The letter concluded as follows:

'Marius Haraldsen was known to many as one of the most successful prospectors and operators in the early days of the South African gold-fields. But his friends were aware that he was more than an ordinary gold-seeker. He had great dreams for his own Northern peoples, and his life was dedicated, as in the case of Cecil Rhodes, to building up a fortune for their benefit. He must have made great sums of money, but he always cherished the dream that before his death he would find a true Ophir which would enable him to realize fully his grandiose plans. I met him on this quest in the Middle East and others have met him elsewhere. He was no casual prospector, but, with ample means and the most scientific methods, was engaged in following up the trail of earlier adventurers.

'Now it would seem that before his death he had made good on the biggest scale. The jade tablet in my possession tells us that he had found his treasure. The inscription on the obverse no doubt contains the details, for Marius Haraldsen was above all things a practical man, and did not leave a task half finished. The writing is difficult, but when it is translated, as I hope it will shortly be, the world will know something of what may well prove an epoch-making discovery.

'Meantime, I thought that this interim report might give satisfaction to the surviving friends of a great man and an intrepid adventurer.'

The thing was signed 'Clanroyden,' and dated from Laverlaw, and the *Times* had as its fourth leader a pleasant little essay on the survival power of material objects and the ingenious ways of Providence.

I pondered long over that letter. The first thing that struck me was that it was not written in Sandy's usual fastidious style. It was frank journalism, and must be meant to appeal to a particular audience.

My second reflection was that I knew what that audience was. It was the gang who were persecuting Haraldsen's son. Sandy, in so many words, told them that the old man had brought off his great *coup*, and that the Haraldsen fortune was potentially far bigger than any of them had dreamed. Here was a new strong scent for the pack.

My last thought was that Sandy had now put himself into the centre of the hunt. Any one reading that letter must assume that he knew all about the Haraldsen family and its affairs. He wrote himself down as the possessor of what might be worth millions – he professed confidence about the meaning of the writing on the tablet and the certainty of its being translated. . . . His purpose was clear. It was to draw off the hounds.

I wired to him at once at his London club asking when I could see him, but I got no answer. Instead I had a telegram in the afternoon from Lombard requesting me to come at once to his country house. The telegram concluded: 'Lock up carefully behind you,' and that could only have one meaning. I brought up Haraldsen to stay at the Manor, with instructions to Mary and Peter John not to let him out of their sight, and by five o'clock I had started in the car for Surrey.

I reached Lombard's house about half-past seven. It was on the skirts of an old-fashioned village which had become almost a London suburb by the building of a ring of big villas round it. The house wasn't bad of its kind, a pseudo-Georgian edifice of red brick with stone facings, and its six acres or so of ground had been shaped into a most elaborate garden. There was a sample of everything – miniature park, lily pond, water-garden, pergolas, arbours, yards of crazy paving; and he must have kept a largish staff of gardeners, for the place was blazing with flowers and manicured to the last perfection. Fosse was a shabby, old farm-house compared to it. It was the same indoors. Everything was shining white enamel, and polished wood, and glowing brass and copper. Some of the pictures looked to me good, but they were over-varnished and too pretentiously framed. There was overmuch glitter about the place, the masses of cut flowers were too opulent, the red lacquer was too fresh, there was no sober background to give the eye relief.

In the drawing-room I found the Lombards, and I recognized the inspiration which had created this glossiness. His wife, whom I had caught a glimpse of at the station in the preceding autumn, proved to be the most sumptuous of Lombard's possessions. She was dressed, I remember, in white and purple, and she had a wonderful cluster of orchids at her breast. As a girl she must have been lovely, and she was still a handsome woman of the heavy Madonna type – a slightly over-coloured Madonna. Being accustomed to slim people like Mary and Barbara Clanroyden and Janet Raden, I thought her a little too 'fair of flesh,' in the polite phrase of the ballads. I learned afterwards that she had been a tempestuous beauty, and well-dowered as well, for it was his marriage that first launched Lombard on his career.

'We are not to wait,' she told me. 'The fourth of our little party may be late. And we are not to use names, please, at table. Barton (that was the butler) is a confidential person, but it is not desirable that anybody else should know who is dining here. So you are to be Dick, please, and the fourth will be Sandy. These are Lord Clanroyden's own instructions.'

Dinner was announced, and I hadn't been seated five minutes at the table before I had Mrs. Lombard placed. She was a warm-hearted woman, without much brains, but with certain very definite tastes, and she dominated her environment. She was deeply in love with Lombard and he with her, and, since they had no children, each had grown into the other's ways. He had been swallowed up in the featherbed of her vast comfortableness, but she in turn had caught a spark from him, for she had a queer passion for romance, which I don't think she could have been born with. She amazed me by the range and variety of her not very intelligent reading, she had odd sensitive strains in her, and she sat in her suburban paradise expectant of marvels. Lombard had probably not told her very much about the present business, but he had told her enough to thrill her. I found her eyes looking at me sometimes just like an excited child, and I could see that she anticipated the coming of Sandy almost with awe. A few people no doubt knew my name, but half the world knew Sandy's.

He did not appear till the June twilight filled the big french windows, through which he slipped as if he had been a guest staying in the house. Barton and a footman were in the room at the time, and Mrs. Lombard behaved as if he were an old friend. 'So glad to see you at last, Sandy,' she said. 'I hope you had a pleasant journey.'

'Pleasant but longish,' he said. 'The air is the best route on a summer night. What a jolly place! I never smelt such roses.'

'Have you come from Laverlaw?' I asked when we were alone.

'No, only from London. But I didn't think it wise to come direct. I've been half round the southern counties, and I did the last stage on a bicycle – from Heston. You must give me a lift back there in your car, Dick.'

Sandy made an excellent meal and set himself to draw out Mrs. Lombard. I could see that he was asking himself the same question that I had asked, what part she played in her husband's life; and I think that he reached the same conclusion. She was not going to make any difficulties. Soon he had her talking about all her interests, the pleasantness of the neighbourhood, her brief season in London, her holiday plans – it was to be the Pyrenees, but her husband might not get away till later in the summer. He looked on her with favour, for her kindness and comeliness were manifest, and the embarrassment left her eyes as she spoke to him, not as a notable, but as a sympathetic human being. She had a delicious voice, and her prattle was the most soothing thing conceivable. It explained Lombard's smug contentment with his life, but it convinced me that in that life the lady was not an active force. She would neither spur nor impede him.

In the library after dinner I got my notion of Lombard further straightened out, for the room was a museum of the whole run of his interests. Sandy, who could never refrain from looking round any collection of books, bore me out. The walls on three sides were lined to the ceiling with books, which looked in the dim light like rich tapestry hangings. Lombard had kept his old school and college texts, and there was a big section on travel, and an immense amount of biography. He had also the latest works on finance, so he kept himself abreast of his profession. But the chief impression left on me was that it was the library of a man who did not want the memory of any part of his life to slip from him – a good augury for our present job.

'I've burned my boats, as you saw from the *Times* this morning,' said Sandy. 'I dare say you guessed the reason. The pace was becoming too hot – for Haraldsen.'

'How about yourself?' said Lombard.

'I have better wind and a better turn of speed,' was the answer. He filled his pipe, and sat himself crosswise in an armchair with his legs dangling over an arm.

'What do you make of Haraldsen, Dick?' he asked. 'Apart from his father and all that, is he worth taking trouble about? '

'Yes,' I said firmly. 'I have come to like him enormously. He is a high-strung being and has gone through a very fair imitation of hell, but there's no crack in his brain, and I'm positive there is none in his character.'

'Apart from the old man, and your promise, and one's general dislike of letting the Devil have the upper hand, you think he's worth saving? '

'Most certainly I do.'

'Good,' said Sandy. 'I asked, because this affair looks like being infernally troublesome, and it is as well to be sure about the principal personage. . . . Well, I haven't let the grass grow under my feet since I saw you last. I've seen Macgillivray, who didn't know much, but gave me some hints that were more useful than he imagined. Lombard here has been doing good work on the Barralty trail – by the way, the reason why I've been so melodramatic about coming here to-night is that Lombard must be kept free from suspicion as long as possible, or half his usefulness goes. I'm deeply suspect by this time; so are you, Dick; but Lombard has still a clean sheet. And I can assure you that the people we are up against are very active citizens. Chiefly, I've been busy with some of my old channels – very nearly silted up, some of them were, and one way and another I've con-ُnced myself that Haraldsen is the quarry of a very dangerous and ̇rate gang. The most dangerous kind, for they range from stolid respectability down to the dirtiest type of criminal. They have every weapon in their armoury, and they are organized like an American football team.'

'Hold on,' I said, much impressed, for Sandy didn't use words like 'dangerous' or 'desperate' very readily. 'I don't quite see their purpose. I can understand a vulgar attempt to blackmail a simple Norlander. But isn't this organization you speak of a bit too elaborate, like using a steam-hammer to crack a nut? '

'No,' was the reply, 'for the possible reward is immense. Quite apart from what my jade tablet may have to contribute, old Haraldsen's fortune was very large. Those blackguards could milk his son to the tune of hundreds of thousands of pounds, if not millions. Lombard has been good enough to verify that.'

'It took some doing,' said Lombard; 'but I had a pull with the Scandinavian banks. Haraldsen holds the bulk of the preference stock in' – he mentioned some famous companies – 'and he has ludicrous balances on current account.'

Sandy nodded. 'There's no doubt then about the bigness of the prize. And it should have been easy fruit. They had only to get hold of Haraldsen, a shy, unworldly recluse, to strip him bit by bit of his possessions – all by proper legal process. The man's a baby in these things. I can see him in Troth's hands assigning great blocks of his gilt-edged stuff – for consideration, of course, such as a holding in some of Barralty's shaky concerns. Then there would be a little peace for him, and then another cut at the joint. All very simple and pleasant, if ugly snags like us three hadn't got in the way. We won't be popular in certain quarters.'

'Have you a line on the gang?' I asked.

'So-so,' he said. 'I know a good deal about Troth, not all to his disadvantage. He has his enemies and plenty of critics, but he has also his friends. A sharp practitioner, of course, but there's more in his persecution of Haraldsen than mere greed. I haven't got the facts quite straight yet, but at the back there is some kind of family vendetta, which he inherited from his father. The elder Troth and the elder Haraldsen were once partners on the Rand, and I gather that they were together in a big venture which turned out well. Troth did something dirty, and Haraldsen kicked him out, as apparently he was justified in doing under their contract. But Troth thought that he had been badly treated and was entitled to his share in the profits of the big *coup*, and he was determined to make Haraldsen disgorge. That was the reason of the scrap on the Rhodesian hills you told me about. Troth believed that he was trying to get what belonged to him, and his son is on the same tack. Also, I suppose, Albinus.'

'Have you got in touch with Albinus?' I asked.

'Yes, and it wasn't hard. He's quite a prominent figure in his own line. He has lived for the last two years in a fashionable West-End hotel, and done himself pretty well. He seems to be comfortably off, for, though he does a little in the City, he spends most of his time amusing himself – races a bit and patronizes the drama, and entertains lavishly. Quite a popular citizen. I had him pointed out to me at Epsom – a fellow a little more than your own age, Dick, who has kept his figure as well as you have, but far better dressed than you could ever hope to be. His hair has gone grey, and he has the air of a retired cavalry colonel. I didn't care for his looks, for I don't like a face that is perpetually smiling while the eyes never change, but people don't seem to mind him. He's a member of –.' And he mentioned a highly respectable club. 'They say his finances are dicky.'

Lombard nodded. 'I heard for a fact that his bank has pulled him up about his overdraft. He has been too thick with Barralty.'

'Ah! Barralty!' Sandy's face took on that look of intense absorption which meant that his interest was really awakened. 'There's the puzzler. I can place Troth and Albinus – they're types – but Barralty is his own species and genus. I've been collecting data about him and it's mighty interesting. It's going to take us a long time to get the measure of that lad. But I've managed to see him – from a distance, and I confess I was fascinated.'

Sandy laughed.

'I got a young friend to take me to a party – golly, such a party! I was a French artist in a black sweater, and I hadn't washed for a day or two. A *surréaliste*, who had little English but all the latest Paris studio argot. I sat in a corner and worshipped, while Barralty held the floor. It was the usual round-up of rootless intellectuals, and the talk was the kind of thing you expect – terribly knowing and disillusioned and conscientiously indecent. I remember my grandfather had a phrase for the smattering of cocksure knowledge which was common in his day – the ' culture of the Mechanics' Institute.' I don't know what the modern equivalent would be – perhaps the 'culture of the B.B.C.' Our popular sciolism is different – it is a smattering not so much of facts as of points of view. But the youths and maidens at this party hadn't even that degree of certainty. They took nothing for granted except their own surpassing intelligence, and their minds were simply nebulae of atoms. Well, Barralty was a king among those callow anarchists. You could see that he was of a different breed from them, for he had a mind, however much he debased it. You could see too that he despised the whole racket.'

'What is he like?' I asked, for I had never had him properly described to me.

'Quite ordinary, except for his eyes. His pupils don't appear to be quite in the centre of the eyeballs, but rather high up, so he has always the air of looking over your head. And those pupils are intensely bright. An impressive face, but the more repellent the more you look at it. I have only begun my study of Mr. Barralty, but I have reached one firm conclusion. The man is inordinately, crazily ambitious. He has to assert himself even if it is only to be a Pope among the half-baked. I should say that he had about as much morals as a polecat, but he has what often does fairly well as a substitute, worldly wisdom. He is a cautious fellow, and up to now he has kept his feet on a very slippery floor, at least as far as repute goes. He wants to keep that repute, but he must have money, great quantities of money, so that he can prove to the world that a fastidious and cynical intellectual can beat the philistines at their own game. It's one version of the Grand Manner that our ancestors used to talk about. Do you follow me? Do you see how tempting the Haraldsen affair must be to him? Here is something quite secret and far away from the ordinary swim, which promises immense loot and not a word said. I think we can be certain that he is the brain in the enterprise and will get the biggest share. And that he won't stick at trifles. I can imagine Troth having scruples, but not Barralty.'

Sandy's tone was so grave that for a moment there was silence. Then I felt bound to put in a word of caution.

'You realize,' I said, 'that we are taking all this story of a plot on Haraldsen's word? '

'I do,' he said. 'That's why we must go slowly and wait on developments.'

'And the other two,' I said. 'We have nothing to link the young Varrinder and your Conquistador friend with the business except that they seem to have come sniffing round Haraldsen.'

'True,' was the answer. 'On that point we have no evidence, only suspicions. Therefore we must go very cannily. But not too cannily, or we may be caught. Who was it said that behind every doubt there lurked an immoral certainty? We must take suspicions for facts till they are disproved, for I don't think that in this affair we can afford to give away any weight. I'm coming in, partly because I don't like the Devil to score, and partly because I'm pretty certain that D'Ingraville is in it, and I have a rendezvous with D'Ingraville as long as he is above the sod. Therefore I'm going to follow my instinct and treat the thing seriously from the start. Our immediate duty is to safeguard Haraldsen.'

'Your *Times* letter to-day will help,' I said.

'It is a step in the right direction. But only a step. We must make it impossible for those blackguards to get at his money. So Lombard and I have made certain arrangements. To-morrow morning he goes back with you to Fosse with a bagful of papers which Haraldsen will sign. I assume that he'll agree, for it's the only way. We're making a trust of his possessions, with several most responsible trustees, and he must give Lombard his power of attorney. He will have enough free income for his modest needs, but till the trust is revoked he won't be able to touch the capital. That means that there can be no coercion on him to part with his fortune without considerable delays and a good many people knowing about it.'

'That sounds common sense,' I said. 'But will the gang that is after him ever discover it? '

'I shall take steps to see that they are informed,' he replied. 'I want to get them off his trail and gunning for me. My *Times* letter will have put them on my track. By the way, I propose presently to announce in the same admirable newspaper that I intend to present old Haraldsen's jade tablet to the British Museum.'

'Whatever for?' I asked.

Sandy grinned in his impish way. 'More ground bait. They won't believe it. They'll think it's a dodge to put them off the scent. They'll think too that something has happened to rattle me, which is what I intend. I don't want them to consider me too formidable. They'll fumble for a little and make one or two false casts, but soon I shall have the pack in full cry.'

It seemed to me that Sandy was going a little beyond the mark in his quixotry, and I told him so. His face was so lit up and eager that I thought it was simply another ebullition of the boy in him that could not die, and I reminded him he was a married man. That at once made him grave.

'I know, Dick,' he said. 'I've thought of that. But Barbara would be the first to agree. It isn't only saving Haraldsen, poor devil, though that is a work of necessity and mercy. It's putting a spoke in D'Ingraville's wheel, for if that sportsman is left on the loose there will be hell to pay for others than Haraldsen. You needn't worry about me, for as I've told you, they're bound to fumble at the start. They won't know what to make of me, and, if I may say it modestly, they may be a little worried. Presently, they'll pull themselves together, but not just yet. I must put in a week or two in London. I'll stay at the club, which I don't fancy they'll attempt to burgle. Violence won't be their line, at least not at the start. You see, I must get a line on D'Ingraville to make sure.'

I asked him how he proposed to get that, and he said 'Varrinder. I have found out a good deal about that lad, and I think I may make something of him. He's still only a novice in crime, and his nerve isn't steady. I fancy he may be turned into what the French police call an *indicateur*, half-apache and half-informer. We shall see. And meantime, Dick, I have a whole-time job for you. You are responsible for Haraldsen.'

He spoke the last sentence in the tone of a general giving orders to his staff. There was nothing boyish now about his face.

'Haraldsen,' he said, 'is the key of the whole business. I can't think how on earth he has escaped them so long. Probably his blundering simplicity. If he had been cleverer most likely they would have caught him. Well, we can't afford to let them catch him. God knows what might happen if they got a weak-nerved fellow into their clutches! Apart from what he might be made to suffer there's a good chance that they might win, for a trust can be revoked, and I can imagine a shattered Haraldsen giving them all the legal authority they want. He's our Achilles-heel, and we must guard him like a child. And there's the daughter, too, the little girl at school – I'm not easy about her if her father is left anywhere in the neighbourhood. It's a queer business to have as our weak point a neurotic Viking. All the same, I've a notion that in the last resort Haraldsen might surprise us – might go clean berserk and turn and rend them. I don't know him, but I remember the old man.'

'You mean that Fosse isn't safe?' I asked.

'Just that. It is almost certain that they have their eyes on it already, and even if they haven't they soon will have. It doesn't do to underrate the intelligence of that crowd. The place is not much more than seventy miles from London on a knuckle of upland accessible from every side – with a trunk road close to your gates, and hikers and tourists thick around it all summer. You're as defenceless as an old sow basking in the sun. Your own people are trusty, but your frontiers are too wide to watch. You must get yourself into a sanctuary, and there's one place only that fills the bill.'

I asked its name, but I had already guessed the answer.

'Laverlaw,' he said. 'I want you to shift your camp there at once – you and Mary and Peter John and Haraldsen. You'll only be antedating your yearly visit by a few weeks. There's nothing to keep you in the south, is there? '

'Nothing,' I said. 'But are you sure it's wise? They're still doubtful about Fosse, but now that you're in the business, they will be certain about Laverlaw.'

'I mean them to be,' he replied. 'The fight must come, and I want to choose my own ground for it. Fosse is hopeless – Laverlaw pretty well perfect. Not a soul can show his face in that long glen of mine without my people knowing it. Not a stray sheep can appear on my hills without my shepherds spotting it. Not the smallest unfamiliar thing can happen but it is at once reported. Haraldsen will be safe at Laverlaw till we see how things move. You remember in the Medina business that I advised you to get straight off to Machray? Well, Laverlaw is as good as any Highland deer forest – better, for there are more of my own folk there. So, Dick, you've got to move to Laverlaw at once – as inconspicuously as possible, but at once. I've warned Babs, and she's expecting you.'

I saw the reason in Sandy's plan, but I wasn't quite happy. For I remembered what he seemed to have forgotten, that when I went to Machray to keep out of Medina's way I had had an uncommonly close shave for my life.

PART II

Laverlaw

CHAPTER VIII

Sanctuary

LAVERLAW, MARY USED TO SAY, was her notion of the end of the world. It is eight miles from a railway station and the little village of Hangingshaw, and the road to it follows a shallow valley between benty uplands till the hills grow higher, and only the size of the stream shows that you have not reached the glen head. Then it passes between two steep hillsides, where there is room but for it and the burn, rounds a corner, and enters an amphitheatre a mile or two square, bounded by steep heather hills, with the Lammer Law heaving up its great shoulders at the far end. The amphitheatre is the park of the castle, mountain turf, diversified with patches of the old Ettrick Forest and a couple of reedy lakes. The house stands at the junction of four avenues of ancient beeches – the keep thirteenth century, most of it late sixteenth century, and nothing more modern than the Restoration wing built by Bruce of Kinross. There are lawns and pleasaunces and a wonderful walled garden, and then you are among heather again, for the moorlands lap it round as the sea laps a reef.

All the land for miles is Sandy's, and has been in his family for centuries, and though there is another property – Clenry Den, in Fife, from which, by an absurd eighteenth-century transformation, they take their title of Clanroyden – Laverlaw has always been their home. From Hangingshaw southward there are no dwellings but hill-farms and shepherds' cottages. Beyond the containing walls of the valley lie heathy uplands hiding an infinity of glens and burns, nameless except to herds and keepers and the large-scale Ordnance map. The highway stops short at the castle, and beyond it a drove road tracks the ultimate waters of the Laver, and makes its way, by a pass called the Raxed Thrapple, to the English Border. The place is so perfect that the first sight of it catches the breath, for it is like a dream of all that is habitable and gracious; but it is also as tonic as mid-ocean and as lonely as the African veld.

I took Haraldsen and Peter John from Fosse by road, while Mary with maid and baggage and Jack Godstow travelled by rail by way of

London. I had always made a practice of taking my keeper Jack to
Laverlaw on our annual visits, partly that he might act as my loader
at grouse-drives, and partly to give him a holiday in a different sort
of world. Also he made a wonderful gillie and companion for Peter
John. Jack was a living disproof of the legend that the English coun-
tryman is not adaptable. He was in bone and fibre a Cotswold man,
and yet wherever he went he met friends, and he had a knack of getting right inside whatever new life he was introduced to. There was
something about him that attracted good will – his square face with
little greying side whiskers, and his steadfast, merry, brown eyes.

So in the first days of July there was a very pleasant party at Laverlaw – Barbara Clanroyden and her daughter, Mary, Haraldsen, Peter
John, and myself. But there was no Sandy. I gave him a lift to the
aerodrome that night we met at Lombard's house, and since then I
had seen nothing of him. I had an address in London, not a club but
a bank, to which I wrote to report our arrival, but for days I had no
word from him. He was publicly supposed to be at Laverlaw, for the
press had announced his arrival there and his intention of staying for
the rest of the summer. The *Scotsman* and the local papers chroni-
cled his presence at local functions, like the Highland Show, the
wedding of a neighbour's daughter, and a political fête at a house on
the other side of the shire. But I was certain that he had never left
London, and when I met his factor by chance and asked for information, I found that gentleman as sceptical as myself. 'If his lordship
had come north I would have seen him,' he said, 'for there's some
important bits of business to put through. These newspapers are
oftener wrong than right.'

In a week the place had laid such a spell on us that Fosse was
almost forgotten, and the quiet of the glen seemed to have been
about us since the beginning of time. The post came late in the
afternoons, bringing the papers, but my day-late *Times* was rarely
opened, and I did my scanty correspondence by post cards and
telegrams. It was still, bright weather with a light wind from the east,
and all day we were out in the strong sunshine.

If we saw no strangers there was a perpetual interest in our little
colony itself. There were the two keepers, Sim and Oliver, both
long-legged Borderers whose forbears had been in the same glen
since the days of Kinmont Willie, and who now and then in their
speech would use phrases so vivid and memorable that I understood
how the great ballads came to be written. There was the head shepherd Stoddart – Sandy kept one of the farms in his own hands – a
man tough and gnarled as an oak-root, who belonged to an older

dispensation. He had the long stride and the clear eye of his kind, and his talk was a perpetual joy to us, for in his soft, lilting voice he revealed a lost world of pastoral. Under his tuition I became quite learned about sheep, and I would accompany him when he 'looked the hill,' and thereby got the hang of a wide countryside. Also to my delight I found Geordie Hamilton, the Scots Fusilier who had been my batman in the War. He had been mixed up with Sandy in his South American adventure, and had been installed at Laverlaw as a sort of 'Laird's Jock,' a factotum who could put his hand to anything, and whose special business it was to attend his master out-of-doors, much what Tom Purdey was to Sir Walter Scott. Geordie had changed little; his stocky figure and his mahogany face and sullen blue eyes were the same as I remembered; but above the ears there was a slight grizzling of the shaggy dark hair.

The days passed in a delightful ease. We walked and rode over the hills, and picnicked by distant waters. The streams were low and the fishing was poor, though Peter John did fairly well in the lochs, and got a three-pounder one evening in the park lake with the dry fly. It was only a month to the Twelfth, so Morag the falcon was not permitted on the moors, but he amused himself with flying her at pigeons and using her to scare the hoodies. The months at Laverlaw had made Barbara well again, and she and Mary, with their clan about them, were happy; even Sandy's absence was not much of a drawback, for his way was the wind's way, and any hour he might appear out of the void. It was lotus-eating weather in a land which might have been Tir-nan-Og, so remote it seemed from mundane troubles. When I gave a thought to my special problem it was only to remind myself that for the moment we were utterly secure. The pedlar who took the Laverlaw round from Hangingshaw had his coming advertised hours in advance; the baker's and butcher's carts had their fixed seasons and their familiar drivers; and any stranger would be noted and talked over by the whole glen; while, as for the boundary hills, the shepherds were intelligence-officers who missed nothing. All the same I thought it wise to warn the keepers and Stoddart and Geordie Hamilton that I had a private reason for wanting to be told in good time of the coming of any stranger, and I knew that the word would go round like a fiery cross.

We were all lapped in peace, but the most remarkable case was Haraldsen. It may have been the stronger air, for we were four hundred miles farther north, or the belief that here he was safe, but he lost his hunted look, he no longer started at a sudden sound, and he could talk without his eyes darting restlessly everywhere. He began to find an interest in life, and went fishing with Peter John and Jack, accompanied the keepers and Stoddart on their rounds, and more than once joined me in a long stride among the hills.

It was not only ease that he was gaining. The man's old interests were reviving. His Island of Sheep, which he had been shutting out of his thoughts, had returned to his mind while he was delighting in the possessions of another. Laverlaw was so completely a home, that this homeless man began to think of his own. I could see a longing in his eyes which was not mere craving for safety. As we walked together he would talk to me of the Norlands, and I could see how deep the love of them was in his bones. His mental trouble was being quieted by the renascence of an old affection. Once in the late afternoon we halted on the top of the Lammer Law to drink in the view – the glen of the Laver below us with the house and its demesne like jewels in a perfect setting, the far blue distances to the north, and all around us and behind us a world of grey-green or purple uplands. He drew a long breath. 'It is Paradise,' he said; 'but there is one thing wanting.' And when I asked what that was, he replied, 'The sea.'

Yet at the back of my head there was always a slight anxiety. It was not for the present but for the future. I did not see how our sanctuary could be attacked, but this spell of peace was no solution of the problem. We could not go on living in Laverlaw in a state of mild siege. I had no guess at what Sandy was after, except that he was unravelling the machinations of Haraldsen's enemies; that knowledge was no doubt essential, but it did not mean that we had defeated them. We were only postponing the real struggle. My one solid bit of comfort was that Haraldsen was rapidly getting back to normal. If he went on as he was going, he would soon be a possible combatant in any scrap, instead of an embarrassment.

Then one day that happened which woke all my fears. I had told Peter John that Haraldsen was in danger, and warned him to be very much on the watch for anything or anybody suspicious. This was meat and drink to him, for it gave him a job infinitely more attractive than the two hours which he was supposed to devote to his books every morning. I could see him cock his ears whenever Sim or Geordie had any piece of news. But till this particular day nothing came of his watchfulness.

It was the day of the sheep-clipping at the Mains of Laverlaw, the home farm. The two hill hirsels had been brought down to the valley the night before, and were penned in great folds beside the stream. Beyond was a narrow alley which admitted them in twos and threes to a smaller fold where the stools of the shearers were set up. At dawn the men had assembled – Stoddart and his young shepherd, whose name was Nickson, and the herds from the rest of the Laverlaw estate, many of whom had walked a dozen moorland miles. There were the herds of the Lanely Bield, and Clatteringshaws, and Drygrain, and Upper and Nether Camhope, and the two Lammers, and a man from the remotest corner of Sandy's land, the Back Hill of the Cludden, who got his letters only once a fortnight, and did not see a neighbour for months. And there were dogs of every colour and age, from Stoddart's old patriarch Yarrow, who was the *doyen* of the tribe, to slim, slinking young collies, wild as hawks to a stranger, but exquisitely skilled in their trade and obedient to the slightest nod of their masters. On this occasion there was little for them to do; it was their holiday, and they dozed each in his owner's shadow, after a stormy morning of greetings with their kind.

We all attended the clipping. It was a very hot day, and the air in the fold was thick with the reek of sheep and the strong scent of the keel-pot, from which the shorn beasts were marked with a great L. I have seen a good deal of shearing in my time, but I have never seen it done better than by these Borderers, who wrought in perfect silence and apparently with effortless ease. The Australian sheep-hand may be quicker at the job, but he could not be a greater artist. There was never a gash or a shear-mark, the fleeces dropped plumply beside the stools, and the sheep, no longer dingy and weathered but a dazzling white, were as evenly trimmed as if they had been fine women in the hands of a coiffeur. It was too smelly a place for the women to sit in long, but twenty yards off was crisp turf beginning to be crimsoned with bell-heather, and the shingle-beds and crystal waters of the burn. We ended by camping on a little hillock, where we could look down upon the scene, and around to the hills shimmering in the heat, and up to the deep blue sky on which were etched two mewing buzzards.

We had our luncheon there, when the work stopped for the midday rest, and Haraldsen and I went down afterwards to smoke with the herds. The clipping meal at Laverlaw was established by ancient precedent. There was beer for all, but whisky only for the older men. There were crates of mutton-pies for which the Hangingshaw baker was famous, and baskets of buttered scones and oatcakes and skim-milk cheese. The company were mighty trenchermen, and I observed the herd of the Back Hill of the Cludden, to whom this was a memorable occasion, put away six pies and enough cakes and cheese to last me for a week.

After that we went home, but Peter John stayed behind, for he had decided to become a sheep-farmer and was already deep in the confidence of the herds. In the afternoon I took Haraldsen to visit the keep of Hardriding ten miles off, an ancient tooth of masonry on a crag by a burn. I remember thinking that I had never seen him in better spirits, for his morning at the clipping seemed to have cheered him by its spectacle of decent, kindly folk.

When we got back just before dinner I found Peter John waiting for me with a graver face than usual.

There had been visitors, it appeared, at the clipping that afternoon. One was Little, the auctioneer from Laverkirk. That was to be expected, for 'Leittle,' as the countryside pronounced his name, was a famous figure in the shire, a little red-faced man with a gift of broad humour, whose jokes in the sale-ring were famous through the Lowlands. But he had also a rough side to his tongue, and this, with his profound knowledge of black-faced sheep, made him respected as well as liked. He was a regular guest at the Laverlaw clippings, and was a special friend of Stoddart's. But he had brought a friend with him whom nobody had met before. Peter John described him carefully. An average-sized man, quite young, with a small, well-trimmed moustache like a soldier. He wore riding breeches and cloth gaiters, and a check cap, and carried a shooting-stick. He was Scotch and spoke broadly, but not in the local fashion – Stoddart thought he must come from Dumfries way. His name was Harcus, and Little had introduced him as a rising dealer whom they would soon hear more of, and who was on holiday, taking a look at the Laver Water flocks. He seemed to know a lot about Cheviot sheep.

'Well, he sounds harmless enough,' I said, when I had heard his story. 'A dealer is the kind of fellow you'd expect at a clipping, and if Little brought him he must be all right.'

But I could see from the boy's face that he was not satisfied.

'I didn't much like him,' he said. 'He was too soft-spoken, and he wanted to know too much. Geordie Hamilton said he would ' speir the inside out of a whelk.' He asked all about who was staying here, and if Lord Clanroyden was still here. He said a lot of nice things about Lord Clanroyden which Mr. Stoddart thought cheek. Mr. Stoddart thought he wanted something out of him.'

'There's nothing in that,' I said. 'That's the habit of dealers. He probably wants to buy the Mains hoggs before they're sent to Laverkirk. Was that the only thing that made you suspicious? '

'No-o,' he said slowly. 'There was another thing. He behaved rather queerly about me. I was sitting behind the keel-pot cutting a whistle, and I heard all his talk with Mr. Stoddart and Mr. Nickson. I saw that he had noticed me when he arrived. He pretended not to know we were staying in this house, and when Mr. Stoddart said that you were here he looked surprised, and asked was that the General Hannay that he had heard about in the War? And then he said suddenly, ' Sir Richard's boy's here. I would like to have a crack wi' him,' and Mr. Stoddart had to introduce us. That showed that he must have known all about us before, and that I was your son.'

'That was odd,' I admitted, rather impressed by Peter John's shrewdness. I asked what he had talked to him about, and he told me just ordinary things – what school he was at, what he thought of Scotland, what he was going to do when he grew up – and that he had laughed when he heard of the sheep-farming plan. Stoddart had given the two visitors a drink, and after an hour's stay they had gone down the valley in Little's car.

I said that I didn't think there was any real cause to worry. But Peter John was obstinate, and then he added that which really alarmed me.

'I thought I had better do something about it,' he said, 'so I asked Mr. Sprot – he's the young shepherd at Nether Laver and lives nearest to Hangingshaw – to try to find out when he got home if this Mr. Harcus had been in the village before. Do you know what he told me? That he had been there for three days, and had been staying with Miss Newbigging at the post office. He said he had been to a lot of farms, and had bought the short-horn bull at Windyways that got the second prize at the Highland Show.'

That word 'post office' alarmed me. It was the very place a man would choose for his lodgings if he wanted to make private inquiries. There was no inn in Hangingshaw, and the post office was the natural centre for a big countryside. Also Miss Newbigging, the postmistress, was a most notorious old gossip, and lived to gather and retail news.

'So I thought I'd better ask Geordie Hamilton to go down there' (in this case alone Peter John dropped his habit of 'mistering' everybody, for it was impossible to call Geordie otherwise than by his Christian name). 'He went off on his bicycle after tea. I thought he was the best man for the job, for he's a great friend of Miss Newbigging.'

'That was right,' I said. 'So far I give you good marks. I'll have a talk to Geordie in the morning.'

I dressed for dinner with a faint uneasiness at the back of my head. It was increased when, just as we were drinking our coffee, I was told that Geordie Hamilton wanted to see me urgently. I found him in the gun-room with a glowing face, as if he had made some speed on his bicycle from Hangingshaw in the warm evening.

'Yon man Haircus, sirr,' he began at once. 'Actin' under instructions from Maister Peter John I proceeded to Hangingshaw and had a word wi' Miss Newbiggin'. Sprot was speakin' the truth. Haircus is no there noo, for he gaed off in the car wi' Leittle the auctioneer, him and his pockmanty. But he's been bidin' there the last three days and – weel, sirr, I dinna like the look o' things. I didna like the look o' the man, for he was neither gentry nor plain folk. And gude kens what he's been up to.'

Geordie proceeded with his report, delivered in the staccato fashion of the old Scots Fusilier days. He had found Miss Newbigging alone and had had a friendly cup of tea with her. 'Yon's an awfu' ane to speak,' he said. 'She has a tongue on her like a pen-gun.' The post mistress had been full of her late lodger, and had described him as a 'fine, couthy, cracky body.' He was Galloway bred, but had been a lot in the north of England, and his big market was Carlisle. He told her that he wanted to get in touch with the farmers in these parts, which he said were the pick of the Borders. 'He was aye rimin',' said Miss Newbigging, 'about this bonny countryside and the dacent folk that bode in it.' She had been glad to answer his questions, for he was bringing trade into the parish. When asked if he had been curious about Laverlaw, she had replied that he had, just as every one would be curious about the Big House. He seemed to know all about Lord Clanroyden and to have a great opinion of him. 'I told him that his lordship was supposed to be in residence, but that I hadna clapped eyes on him for months. But says I, that's naethin new, for his lordship comes and gangs like a bog-blitter, though I whiles think that he should pay mair attention to his leddy wife, and her no that strong.' But Miss Newbigging had been positive that she had never given him the names of the party now at Laverlaw. 'Though he might have read them on the letters,' she had added.

On further examination Geordie discovered that Harcus had been what the postmistress called 'a usefu' man about the house.' He had helped her every day to sort out the mail, both the incoming and the outgoing. He had often been jocose about the former. 'Here's ane to Sundhope frae the Bank,' he would say. 'That'll be about the overdraft for the beasts he bocht at Kelso. And here is a bundle for her leddyship. It's bigger than I get mysel' after the back-end sales. But I see there's twa leddyships, Leddy Clanroyden and Leddy Hannay. There's walth o' rank the noo up the Laver Water.'

This had roused Geordie's interest. He asked if Harcus had made a point of looking at the outgoing letters. Miss Newbigging had replied: 'He did, now I come to think o't. I was aye tellin' him there was nae need, for the hale lot gangs to Laverkirk to be sorted. But he was a carefu' man, and he had time on his hands, and he would set them out in wee packs as if he was playin' at the cards. "That's for Embro", he would say, "an that's for the West country, and that heap's for England." He was aye awfu' interested in the English letters, comin' as he did frae Carlisle.'

Geordie, having learned all he wanted, had taken his departure after compliments. Now he sat before me with his shaggy brows drawn down. 'Ye telled me, sirr, to let naething gang by me, however sma', and there's just a chance that there's mischief here. Haircus doesna ken wha's writin' to the folk in this house, but he kens a wheen o' the names that the folk here write to.'

That was precisely the point, and at first I thought that it did not matter. And then, when Geordie had gone, I suddenly remembered that though we were in a sanctuary our party was not complete. There was one absentee, one sheep outside the fold. Not Sandy – he could very well look after himself. It was Haraldsen's child, his daughter Anna.

I started out to look for Haraldsen, but he had gone off with Peter John to dap for trout in the park lake. It was nearly eleven o'clock before they returned, and, as they entered the lit hall from the purple gloom which is all the night that Laverlaw knows in early July, I thought what a miracle recent weeks had wrought in Haraldsen's appearance. He held his head up, and looked you straight in the face, and walked like a free man. When I called to him he was laughing like a care-free boy at the figure Peter John cut in Sandy's short waders. It struck me that it was just in this recovered confidence that our danger lay.

He had often told me about his daughter Anna. She was at a well-known boarding-school for girls in Northamptonshire, called Brewton Ashes, under the name of Smith, the name he had taken when he sought refuge in England. At first he had looked after her in her holidays, and taken her to dismal seaside resorts which he had heard well spoken of. But as his dread of pursuit grew he had dropped all this, and had not seen her for nearly a year. It had been arranged that one of the mistresses, to whom she was attached, should look after her in the holidays, and Haraldsen must have paid for pretty expensive trips for the two, since it was the only way he could make up to the child for his absence. He had always been very careful about letters, writing to her not direct, but through his bank, and he had never dared to show himself within twenty miles of Brewton Ashes.

I turned the conversation on to the girl, being careful not to alarm him, for I didn't want to spoil his convalescence. I pretended that Peter John wanted to write and tell her about Laverlaw, and asked how it was done. He told me that there was a choice of three banks, who all had their instructions.

'It seems a roundabout way,' I said; 'but I dare say you are wise. Do you stick to it rigidly?'

'Yes. It is better so. You never know. . . . Well, to be quite honest, I have broken the rule once, and I do not intend to break it again. That was last Monday. Anna's thirteenth birthday was yesterday, and I made a mistake about the dates, for I have been so busy here that I have grown careless. I could not bear to think that she would have no message from me on that day, so I wrote direct to her at Brewton Ashes.' His smile was a little embarrassed, and he looked at me as if he expected reproaches. 'I do not think that any harm is done. This place is so far away from everybody.'

'Oh, that's all right,' I said. 'You needn't worry about that, but I think you're wise all the same to stick to your rule. Now for bed. Lord, it's nearly midnight.'

But I thought it by no means all right. It was infernally bad luck that Haraldsen should have chosen to be indiscreet just at the time when the mysterious Harcus was in the neighbourhood. I told myself that the latter would make nothing of a letter addressed to a Miss Anna Smith at a country address in England. But I have never made the mistake of underrating the intelligence of the people I was up against. Anyhow, I was taking no chances. I routed out Geordie Hamilton from his room above the stables and warned him for duty. Then I wrote a letter to Sandy in London, telling him all that had happened and my doubts about Harcus. I left it to him to decide whether any steps should be taken to safeguard the girl. Geordie was instructed to set off at once to Laverkirk, twenty miles distant, and post it there, so that it might catch the London mail – Laverkirk was on the main line to the south – and reach Sandy the following evening.

But I wasn't content with a letter. I also wrote out a telegram to Sandy in a simple cypher we had often used before – a longish telegram, for I had to explain how it was possible that the enemy might have got the girl's address. Geordie, when he had posted the letter, was to go to bed in the Station Hotel, be up betimes, and send the telegram as soon as the office was open. I had no fear of espionage in Laverkirk, which was a big bustling market-town with half a dozen post offices.

Then I went to bed with anxiety in my mind out of which I could not argue myself. The happy peace of Laverlaw had been flawed. I felt like the man in *Treasure Island* who was tipped the black spot.

CHAPTER IX

Lochinvar

NEXT DAY THE HEAT-WAVE BROKE in a deluge, and by midday the Laver was coloured and by the evening in roaring spate. Peter John and I went out before dinner, and got a heavy basket with the worm in the pools above the park. The following morning it still drizzled, and we did well in the tributary burns with the fly known locally as the black spider. Burn-fishing has always had its charms for me, for no two casts are the same, and I love the changing scenery of each crook in the little glens. But after luncheon Peter John's soul aspired to higher things. There was a tarn six miles off in the hills called the Black Loch, a mossy hole half overgrown with yellow water-lilies and uncommonly difficult to fish. We had tried it before in a quiet gloaming and had had no luck, though we had seen big trout feeding. Sim had always declared that it only fished well after rain, when its sluggish inmates were stirred by the swollen runnels from the hills. So we set off with Oliver and Geordie Hamilton, warning Barbara that we might be late for dinner.

We did not return till half-past nine. The weather cleared, the sun came out, and the warm evening was a kind of carnival for the Black Loch trout. They took whatever we offered them, but for every five fish hooked four broke us or dropped off. We had to cast over an infernal belt of water-lilies and pond-weed, which meant a long line and a loose line. It was impossible to wade far out, for the bottom was treacherous, and once I went down to the waist. To land a fish we had to drag him by brute force through the water-weeds, and, as we were fishing far and fine, that usually meant disaster. There were two spits of gravel in the loch, and the only chance with a big one was to try to manoeuvre him towards one of these, not an easy job, since one had practically no purchase on him. Peter John, who was far the better performer, managed this successfully with two noble fellows, each nearly two pounds in weight, but he too had many failures. Nevertheless, between us we had two dozen and three fish, a total weight of just over twenty-seven pounds, the best basket that had been taken out of the Black Loch in Oliver's memory.

These two days' fishing had put everything else out of my mind, a trick fishing always has with me. As we tramped home over the dusky sweet-scented moors I had no thought except a bath and dinner. But as we approached the house I was suddenly recalled to my senses. Before the front door stood a big and very dirty car, from which a man in a raincoat had descended. He had no hat, he seemed to have a baldish head and a red face mottled with mud, and his whole air was of fatigue and dishevelment. He was in the act of helping another figure to alight, which looked like a girl. And then suddenly there was a noise in the house, and from it Haraldsen emerged, shouting like a lunatic. He plucked the girl from the car, and stood hugging and kissing her.

When we got nearer I saw that the man was Lombard, but very unlike the spruce city magnate with whom I had been lately connected. He looked tired and dirty but content, and somehow younger, more like the Lombard I remembered in Africa. 'Thank God we're here at last,' he said. 'It's been a roughish passage. . . . What do I want most? First a bath, and then food – a lot of it, for we've been living on biscuits. I've brought no kit, so you must lend me some clothes to change into.' As for Haraldsen, he went on behaving like a maniac, patting the girl's shoulder and holding her as if he thought that any moment she might disappear. 'My happiness is complete,' he kept declaring. This went on till Barbara and Mary appeared and swept the child off with them.

I provided Lombard with a suit of flannels, and we ate an enormous late supper – at least four of us did, while the other three, who had already dined, looked on. The girl Anna appeared in a pleated blue skirt and a white blouse, the uniform, I supposed, of her school. She was a tall child for her years, and ridiculously blonde, almost bleached. She had a crop of fair hair which looked white in certain lights, a pale face, and features almost too mature, for the full curve of her chin was that of a woman rather than a girl. There was no colour about her except in her eyes, and I thought that Haraldsen deserved something better than this plain, drab child. I had whispered that to Mary in the hall before supper, and she had laughed at me. 'You're a blind donkey, Dick,' she had said. 'Some day she will be a raging beauty, with that ivory skin and those sea-blue eyes.'

When we had eaten, Haraldsen went off with the women to put Anna to bed and to look after her wardrobe, for she also was kit-less. Lombard had a couple of glasses of Sandy's famous port, and when we adjourned to the smoking-room, where a peat fire was burning, he stacked himself in an armchair with an air of great content. 'First score for our side,' he said. 'But it has been a close thing, I can tell you. Till about ten hours ago I wouldn't have given twopence for our chances. I'll have to do the devil of a lot of telegraphing to-morrow, but to-night, thank God! I can sleep in peace.'

Then he told his story, which I give in his own words.

Clanroyden (he said) had your telegram yesterday morning. There was a letter too, you tell me? Well, he hadn't had that when I left, but you seem to have explained things pretty fully in your wire. He got hold of me at once – luckily I was sleeping in town, having motored up the day before. There were one or two small matters I had to arrange before I took my holiday, and I had finished them and was going home after luncheon.

He said I must get busy – that the other side had probably got the address of Haraldsen's daughter and might be trusted to act at once. Possibly it was even now too late. I must go down to the school in Northamptonshire and fetch her back to town. He would arrange that she should stay with a great-aunt of his in Sussex Square till he made other plans. He would have gone himself, but he dared not, for he thought he was pretty closely marked, but I was still free from suspicion, and I was the only one to take on the job. He wrote me a chit to the headmistress, Miss Barlock, to say that he was Haraldsen's – Smith's, that is to say – greatest friend and managed his affairs, and that he had authority from him to bring his daughter to him in London for a few days in connection with some family business. He thought that would be enough, for the schoolmistress-woman was pretty certain to know his name, and my appearance, too, he said, was a warrant of respectability. I was to bring the girl straight to Sussex Square, where he would be waiting for me. He said he would expect me before four o'clock, but if there was any difficulty I was to wire at once, and he would send down one of the partners in the bank that paid the school fees.

I rather liked the job of saviour of youth, for I felt that I hadn't been quite pulling my weight in this business, so I started off in my car in good spirits. It was the big Bentley, which I always drive myself. I was at Brewton Ashes by eleven o'clock, a great, raw, red-brick building in a fine park, which I believe was one of the seats that old Tomplin, the oil fellow, built for himself before he crashed. Well, I sent up my card to Miss Barlock, but by the mercy of God I didn't send up Clanroyden's chit with it. I was told that Miss Barlock was engaged for the moment, and was shown into a drawing-room full of school groups and prize water-colours and great bowls of fine roses. The room rather made me take to the place, for it showed that the people there knew how to grow flowers, and there's never much wrong with a keen gardener.

I waited for about ten minutes, and then Miss Barlock's door opened and three people came out. One was Anna, who looked flustered. The others were a man and a woman – a young man in a flannel suit with an O.E. tie, a pleasant-looking toothy chap with a high colour, and a middle-aged woman in a brown linen costume and big specs. A maid took the three downstairs, and I was ushered into the presence of Miss Barlock.

She was slim and grey-haired and bright-eyed, with that air of brisk competence which shy women often cultivate in self-defence. There was obviously nothing wrong with her, but I saw at a glance that she was a precisian and would be a stickler about rules. So some instinct warned me to go canny. Luckily I began by saying only that I was an old friend of Anna Smith's father, and that I had dropped in to see her and give her a message.

Miss Barlock smiled. 'It never rains but it pours,' she said. 'Dear Anna does not often have visits from friends. Her poor father, of course, has not been down for months. But this morning who should appear but Anna's cousins? They and Anna must have passed you as you came in. They brought a letter from Mr. Smith, who asked me to allow them to carry off Anna a week before the holidays begin. They propose, I think, a cruise to the Northern capitals. I readily consented, for the child has been rather wilting in the hot weather.'

At this I sat up and thought hard. It looked as if I was too late, and that the other side had got in first. I decided that it wasn't the slightest good my showing Clanroyden's chit. The others would have a water-tight case, a letter from Haraldsen himself in a good imitation of his handwriting, which perhaps Miss Barlock recognized, for she must have seen it in his early days in England. I thought how clever they had been in sending down an inconspicuous young man and a rather dowdy woman, instead of some smart female with scarlet lips and a distempered face whom the schoolmistress would have suspected. Those two were the very model of respectable country cousins. I couldn't discredit them, for if I told Miss Barlock the truth I would only discredit myself. Clanroyden's letter, even if she didn't think it a forgery, couldn't prevail against the *ipsissima verba* of Haraldsen. I realized I was in a cleft stick and must conduct myself discreetly. The first thing was to see Anna herself.

Miss Barlock glanced at the cards which lay on the writing table. 'Lady Bletso and her son – he is the young baronet – propose to give

Anna luncheon in the Brewton Arms at one o'clock, and then to leave for London. The morning will be occupied in packing Anna's things.' I noted a baronetage on the table which had been moved from the stand of reference books. Miss Barlock was a cautious woman and had looked up her visitors before receiving them. I wondered who the true Bletsos were. I had heard of the name in Yorkshire.

I said cordially that I was glad that Anna's relations were carrying her off for a cruise. Excellent thing, I observed fatuously, to expand the mind of the young. But, having come so far, I would like to have a talk with the child, being her father's friend, and also I had a message to her from him which I had promised to deliver. I would have liked to give her lunch, but since she was engaged for that to her cousins, might we have a short walk in the park together?

Miss Barlock saw no objection. She rang a bell and bade a maid fetch Miss Margesson. Miss Margesson, she informed me, was the girl's chief friend among the mistresses, had been given special charge of her by her father, and had on more than one occasion accompanied her abroad on holidays. Presently Miss Margesson appeared, and the sight of her gave me my first glimmer of hope. For here was one who had none of the repressions and pedantries of the ordinary schoolmistress. She was a tall girl, with a kind mouth, and clever, merry blue eyes. At all costs I must make her an ally.

'Anna Smith's packing is being attended to, Miss Margesson?' her superior asked. 'It will be completed in an hour? Very good. A car will come for her at a quarter to one to take her down to the Brewton Arms, where she will meet her cousins. Meantime, this is a friend of Anna's father who has called to see her. Will you arrange that he has a short walk with Anna in the garden? Yes, now. It cannot be long, I fear, Mr. Lombard,' she added, turning to me, 'for Anna will no doubt desire to say good-bye to her mistresses and her friends.'

Miss Margesson took me downstairs and out into a very pretty terraced garden at the back of the house. She went indoors and presently returned with Anna. For the first time I had a proper look at the child, and what I saw rather impressed me. She's not much of a beauty, as you saw, but I thought that she had an uncommon sensible little face. I don't know much about children, having none of my own, but the girl's composure struck me as remarkable. She didn't look as if she had inherited her father's nerves. The sight of her was my second gleam of hope.

There was no time to waste, so I plunged at once into my story.

'Anna, my dear,' I said, 'we've never met before, but when I was young I knew your grandfather in South Africa and he made me and another man, whose name is General Hannay, promise to stand by your father if trouble came. Your father is in great danger – has been for a long time – and now it's worse than ever. That's why he hasn't been to see you for so long. That's why you're called Smith here, when your real name is Haraldsen. That's why his letters to you always come through a bank. Now *you* are also in danger. These people Bletso, who came this morning and say they're your cousins, are humbugs. Their letter from your father is a fake. They come from your father's enemies, and they want to get you into their power. Your friends discovered the danger and sent me down to bring you away. I'm only just in time. Will you trust me and do what I ask you?'

That extraordinary child's face did not change. She heard me with the same uncanny composure, her eyes never leaving mine. Then she turned to Miss Margesson and smiled. 'What a lark, Margie!' was all she said.

But Miss Margesson didn't take it that way. She looked scared and flustered.

'What a ridiculous story!' she said. 'Say it's nonsense, Anna. Your name's Smith, all right.'

'No, it isn't,' was the placid answer. 'It's Haraldsen. Sorry, Margie dear, but I couldn't tell that even to you.'

'But – but –' Miss Margesson stammered in her uneasiness. 'You know nothing about this man – you never saw him before. How do you know he's speaking the truth? Your cousins had a letter from your father, and Miss Barlock, who is very shrewd, saw nothing wrong with it. They looked most respectable people.'

'I didn't like them much,' said Anna, and again I had a gleam of hope. 'The woman had ugly eyes behind her specs. And I never heard of any English cousins.'

'But, darling, listen to me,' Miss Margesson cried. 'You never heard of this man either. How do you know he comes from your father? How do you know he is speaking the truth? If you have any doubt, let us go together to Miss Barlock and tell her that you don't want to go on any cruise, and want to stay here till the end of the term. In the meantime you can get in touch with your father.'

'That sounds good sense,' I said; 'but it won't do. Your father's enemies now know where you are. They are very clever people and quite unscrupulous. If you don't go away with the Bletsos, they'll find ways and means of carrying you off long before your father can interfere.'

'Rubbish,' said Miss Margesson rudely. 'Do you expect me to believe this melodrama? You look honest, but you may be half-witted. What's your profession? '

'Not one for the half-witted,' I said. 'I'm what they call a merchant-banker,' and I told her the name of my firm. That was a lucky shot, for Miss Margesson had a cousin in our employ, and I was able to tell her all about him. I think that convinced her of my *bona fides*.

'But what do you propose to do with Anna?' she demanded.

'Take her straight to her father.' That I had decided was the only plan. The girl would be in perpetual danger in London, now that our enemies had got on her trail.

'Do you know where he is?' she asked.

'Yes,' I said, 'and if we start at once I can get her there before midnight.'

Then it suddenly occurred to me that I had one convincing piece of evidence at my disposal.

'Anna,' I said, 'I can tell you something that must persuade you. You had a letter from your father on your birthday three days ago?'

She nodded.

'And it didn't come from London enclosed in a bank envelope. It came from Scotland.'

'Yes,' she said, 'it came from Scotland. He didn't put any address on it, but I noticed that it had a Scotch postmark. That excited me, for I have always wanted to go to Scotland.'

'Well, it was that letter of your father's that gave his enemies the clue. One of them spotted the address in a Scotch post office. Your father's friend, Lord Clanroyden, was worried, and he sent me here at once. Doesn't that prove that I'm telling the truth?' I looked towards Miss Margesson.

Her scepticism was already shaken. 'I don't know what to think,' she cried. 'I can't take any responsibility –'

Then that astonishing child simply took charge.

'You needn't, Margie dear,' she said. 'Hop back into the house and carry on. I'm going with Mr. Lombard. I believe in him. I'm going to Scotland to my father.'

'But her things are not packed,' put in Miss Margesson. 'She can't leave like this –'

'I'm afraid we can't stand on the order of our going,' I said. 'It's now just twelve o'clock, and any moment the Bletsos may turn up and make trouble. We can send for Anna's things, and in two days everything will be explained to Miss Barlock. *You* must keep out of the business altogether. The last you saw of Anna and me was in the garden, and you know nothing of our further movements. But you might do me a great kindness and send this wire in the afternoon. It's to Lord Clanroyden – you've heard of him? – he's Anna's father's chief stand-by. He told me to bring Anna to London, but that's too dangerous now. I want him to know that we have gone to Scotland.' I scribbled a telegram on a leaf from my pocket-book.

Miss Margesson was a good girl, and she seemed to share Anna's conviction. She hugged and kissed the child. 'Write to me soon,' she said, ' for I shall be very anxious,' and ran into the house.

'Now for the road,' I said. 'My car is at the front door. I'll pick you up in the main avenue out of sight of the house. Can you get there without being seen? And bring some sort of coat. Pinch another girl's if you can't find your own. The thicker the better, for it will be chilly before we get to Laverlaw.'

I picked up Anna in the avenue all right, and we swung out of the lodge gates at precisely a quarter-past twelve. Then I saw something which I didn't much like. Just outside the gates a car was drawn up, a very powerful car of foreign make, coloured yellow and black. It looked to me like a Stutz. The only occupant was a chauffeur in uniform, who was reading a newspaper. He glanced sharply at me, and for a moment seemed about to challenge us. When we had passed I looked back and saw that he had started the car and was moving in the direction of the village. I guessed that this was the Bletsos' car, and that the man had gone to seek his master. He did not look quite like an ordinary chauffeur.

That was the start of our journey. My plan was to get into the Great North Road as soon as possible – Stamford seemed the best point to join it at – and then to let the Bentley rip on the best highway in England. I didn't see how we could be seriously pursued even if that confounded chauffeur had spotted our departure. But I was all in a dither to reach Laverlaw that night. This young Lochinvar business was rather out of my usual line, and I wanted to get it over.

Well, we got to Stamford without mishap, and after that we did a spell of over sixty to the hour. The morning had been hot and bright, but the wind had shifted, and I thought we might soon run into dirty weather. At first I had kept looking back to see if we were followed, but there was no sign of a black and yellow car, and after a little I forgot about it. Lunch was our next problem, and, as there was a lot of traffic on the road, I feared that if we looked for it in a good hotel we should be hung up. I consulted Anna, and she said that she didn't care what she ate as long as there was enough of it, for she was very hungry. So we drew up at a little place, half pub and

half tea-house, at the foot of a long hill just short of Newark. While
my petrol tank was being filled we had a scratch meal, beer and sandwiches for me, while Anna's fancy was coffee and buns, of which she
accounted for a surprising quantity. I also bought two pounds of
chocolates and a box of biscuits, which turned out to be a lucky step.

We were just starting when I happened to cast my eyes back up
the hill. I have a good long-distance eyesight, and there at the top,
about half a mile away, I saw a car which was unpleasantly like the
Stutz I had seen at Brewton. A minute later I lost it, for some traffic
got in the way, but I saw it again, not a quarter of a mile off. There
could be no mistake about the wasp-like thing, and I didn't think it
likely that another car of the same make and colour would be on the
road that day.

If its occupants had glasses – and they were pretty certain to have
– they must have spotted us. I drove the Bentley as hard as I dared,
and tried to think out our position. They knew of course what our
destination was. They certainly had the pace of us, for I had heard
wonderful stories of what a Stutz could do in that line – and this was
probably super-charged – so it wasn't likely that we could shake
them off. If we stopped for the night in any town we should be at the
mercy of people whose cleverness Clanroyden had put very high,
and somehow or other they would get the better of me. A halt of
that kind I simply dared not risk. The road before us for the next
hundred miles or so was through a populous country, and I didn't
believe that they would try a hold-up on it. That would be too risky
with so many cars on the road, and they would not want trouble with
the police or awkward inquiries. But I had driven a good deal back
and forward to Scotland, and I knew that to get to Laverlaw I must
pass through some lonely country. Then would be their chance. I
couldn't stand up against the toothy young man and the formidable-
looking chauffeur. I would be left in a ditch with a broken head and
Anna would be spirited away.

My chief feeling was a firm determination to go all out to get to
Laverlaw. I couldn't outwit or outpace them, so I must trust to luck.
Every mile was bringing us nearer safety, and if it was bringing us
nearer the northern moorlands, I must shut down on the thought. At
first I was afraid of scaring Anna, but, when I saw her face whipped
into colour by the wind and her bright enjoying eyes, I considered
that there was no danger of that.

'You remember the car we saw at the school gates?' I said. 'The
black and yellow thing? I've a notion that it's behind us. You might
keep an eye on it, for I want both of mine for this bus.'

'Oh, are we being chased?' she cried. 'What fun!' And after that she sat with her head half screwed round and issued regular bulletins.

Beyond Bawtry we got into the rain, a good steady north-country downpour. We also got into a tangle of road repairs, where we had to wait our turn at several single-track patches. At the last of these the Stutz was in the same queue and I managed to get a fairly good view of it. There was no mistake about it. I saw the chauffeur in his light-grey livery coat, the same fellow who had stared at us at Brewton. The others in the back of the car were of course invisible.

Beyond Pontefract the rain became a deluge, and it was clear from the swimming roads that a considerable weight of water had already fallen. It was now between four and five, and from constant hang-ups we were making poor speed. The Stutz had made no attempt to close on us, though it obviously had the greater pace, and I thought I knew the reason. Its occupants had argued as I had done. They didn't want any row in this populous countryside, but they knew I was making for Laverlaw, and they knew that to get there I must pass through some desolate places. Then their opportunity would come.

In a big village beyond Boroughbridge they changed their tactics. 'The Wasp is nearly up on us,' Anna informed me, and I suddenly heard a horn behind me, the kind of terrifying thing that they fix on French racing cars. The street was fairly broad, and it could easily pass. I saw their plan. They meant to get ahead of me, and wait for me. Soon several routes across the Border would branch off and they wanted to make certain that I did not escape them. I groaned, for the scheme I had been trying to frame was now knocked on the head.

And then we had a bit of unexpected luck. Down a side street came a tradesman's van, driven by one of those hatless youths whom every motorist wants to see hanged as an example, for they are the most dangerous things on the road. Without warning it clipped over the bows of the Stutz. I heard shouting and a grinding of brakes, but I had no time to look back and it was Anna who reported what happened. The Stutz swung to the left, mounted the pavement, and came to rest with its nose almost inside the door of a shop. The van-driver lost his head, skidded, hit a lamp-post, slewed round and crashed into the Stutz's off front wing. There was a very pretty mix-up.

'Glory be,' Anna cried, 'that has crippled the brute. Well done the butcher's boy!'

But she reported that so far as she could see the Stutz had not been damaged seriously. Only the van, which had lost a wheel. But there was a crowd, and a policeman with a note-book, and I thought that the whole business might mean a hold-up of a quarter of an hour. I had a start again, and I worked the Bentley up to a steady eighty on a beautiful stretch of road. My chief trouble was the weather, for the rain was driving so hard that the visibility was rotten, and I could see little in front of me and Anna little behind.

I had to make up my mind on the route, for Scotch Corner was getting near. If I followed the main North Road by Darlington and Durham I would be for the next hundred miles in a thickly settled country. But that would take me far from Laverlaw, and I would have the long Tweed valley before I got to it. If I turned left by Brough to Appleby, I should have to cross desolate moorlands, which would give the Stutz just the kind of country it wanted. I remembered a third road, which ran through mining villages where there would be plenty of people about. It was a perfectly good road, though the map marked most of it second-class. Besides, it was possible that the Stutz didn't know about it, and, if I had a sufficient start, might assume that I had gone by either Darlington or Brough. Anyhow, unless it caught me up soon, it would be at fault. Clearly it was my best chance.

But Fate, in the shape of the butcher's boy, had not done its work thoroughly. The rain stopped, the weather cleared, there was a magnificent red sunset over Teesdale, and just as I was swinging into my chosen road with an easier mind, Anna reported that the Wasp was coming into view.

That, as they say, fairly tore it. I had not diverted the hounds and the next half-hour was a wild race, for I wanted to get out of empty country into the colliery part. I broke every rule of decent driving, but I managed to keep a mile or so ahead. The Stutz was handicapped by the softness of the surface after the rain, and by not knowing the road as I knew it. It was beginning to grow dark, and to the best of my knowledge what there was of a moon would not rise till the small hours. My only hope was that it might be possible somewhere in the Tyne valley to give the pursuers the slip. I had tramped a good deal there, in the days when I was keen about Hadrian's Wall, and knew the deviousness of the hill-roads.

I reached the mining country without mishap, and the lights of the villages and the distant glow of ironworks gave me a comforting sense of people about and therefore of protection. Beyond Consett the dark fell, and I reflected uneasily that we were now getting into a wild moorland patch which would last till we dropped down on the Tyne. Somehow I felt that the latter event would not happen unless

I managed to create a diversion. I could see the great headlights of the Stutz a mile behind, but I was pretty certain that when it saw its chance it would accelerate and overhaul us. I realized desperately that in the next ten minutes I must find some refuge or be done in.

Just then we came to a big hill which shut off any view of us from behind. I saw a bright light in front, and a big car turned in from a side-road and took our road a little ahead of us. That seemed to give me a chance. On the left there was a little road, which looked as if it led to a farm-house, and which turned a corner of a fir-wood. If I turned up that, the Stutz, topping the hill behind us, would see the other car far down the hill and believe it to be ours. . . . There was no time to waste, so I switched off our lights and moved into the farm road, till we were in the lee of the firs. We had scarcely got there when, out of the corner of my eye, I saw the glow of the Stutz's lights over the crest, and I had scarcely shut off my engine when it went roaring down the hill fifty yards away.

'Golly,' said Anna, 'this is an adventure! Where is the chocolate, Mr. Lombard? We've had no tea, and I'm very hungry.'

While she munched chocolate I started the engine, and after passing two broken-hinged gates we came to a little farm. There was nobody about except an old woman, who explained to me that we were off the road, which was obvious enough, and gave us big glasses of milk warm from the cow. I had out the map (luckily I had a case of them in the car with me) and I saw that a thin red line, which meant some sort of road, continued beyond the farm and seemed to lead ultimately to the Tyne valley. I must chance its condition, for it offered some sort of a plan. I reasoned that the Stutz would continue down the hill and might go on for miles before it spotted that the other car was not ours. It would come back and fossick about to see which side-road we had taken, but there were several in the area, and it would take a little time to discover our tracks on the farm road. If it got thus far, the woman at the farm would report our coming, and say that we had gone back to the main road. I made a great pretence to her of being in a hurry to return to that road. But, when she had shut the door behind us, we crossed a tiny stack yard, found the continuation of the track trickling through a steep meadow, and, very carefully shutting every gate behind us, slipped down into a hollow where cattle started away from our lights and we had to avoid somnolent sheep.

The first part was vile, but in the end it was joined by another farm-track, and the combination of the two made a fair road, stony, but with a sound bottom. My great fear was of ditching in one of the moorland runnels. After a little it was possible to increase the speed, and, though I had often to stop and examine the map, in half an hour we had covered a dozen miles. We were in a lonely bit of country, with no sign of habitation except an occasional roadside cottage and the lights from a hillside farm, and we passed through many planta-tions of young firs. Here, I thought, was a place to get a little sleep, for Anna was nodding with drowsiness and I was feeling pretty well done up. So we halted at the back of a fir clump and I made a bed for Anna with the car rugs – not much of a bed, for, the weather in the south having been hot, I had only brought summer wraps. We both had some biscuits and chocolate, but the child went to sleep with her mouth full, snuggled against my side, and I wasn't long in following. I was so tired that I didn't want to smoke.

I woke about four. Every little pool left by the rain was flushed rose-pink with the reflection of the sky, and I knew that that meant dirty weather. I roused Anna, and we laved our faces in the burn, and had another go at the biscuits. The air was cold and raw, and we would have given pounds for hot coffee. The whole place was as quiet as a churchyard, not even a bird whistled or a sheep bleated, and both of us felt a bit eerie. But the sleep had done us good, and I was feeling pretty confident that we had puzzled the Stutz. It must have spent a restless night if it had been prospecting the farm roads in north Durham. My plan now was to make straight for Laverlaw and trust to luck.

We weren't long in getting to the Tyne valley near Hexham. The fine morning still held, but the mist was low on the hills, and I counted on a drizzle in an hour or two. Anna looked chilly, and I decided that we must have a better breakfast. We were on a good road now and I kept my eye lifting for an inconspicuous pub. Presently I found one a little off the road, and its smoking chimney showed us that the folk were out of bed. I turned into its yard, which was on the side away from the road, and Anna and I stumbled into the kitchen, for we were both as stiff as pokers. The landlord was a big, slow-spoken Northumbrian, and his wife was a motherly crea-ture who gave us hot water to wash in and a comb for Anna's hair. She promised, too, bacon and eggs in a quarter of an hour, and in the meantime I bought some cans of petrol to fill up my tank. It was while the landlord was on this job that, to stretch my legs, I took a stroll around the inn to where I had a view of the highroad.

I got a nasty jar, for there was the sound of a big car, and the Stutz came racing past. I guessed what had happened. It had lost us right enough in the Durham moorlands, but its occupants had

argued that we must be making for Laverlaw, and that, if we had
tangled ourselves up in by-roads, we must have made poor speed
during the night. They would therefore get ahead of us, and watch
the road junctions for the North. There was one especially that I
remembered well, where the road up the North Tyne forked from
the main highway over the Cheviots by the Carter Bar. Both were
possible, and there was no third by which a heavy car could make
fair going. Their strategy was sound enough. If we hadn't turned
into that pub for breakfast we should have been fairly caught, and if
I hadn't seen them pass, in another hour we should have been at
their mercy.

Yet after the first scare I didn't feel downhearted. I felt somehow
that we had the game in our hands, and had got over the worst snags.
I said nothing about the Stutz to Anna, and we peacefully ate an
enormous breakfast. Then I had a word with the landlord about the
countryside, and he told me a lot about the side-ways into the upper
glens of Tyne. At eight o'clock we started again in a drizzle, and
soon I turned off the main highway to the left by what I had learned
was one of the old drove-roads.

All morning we threaded our way in a maze of what must be about
the worst roads in Britain. I had my map and my directions from the
inn, but often I had to stop and ask the route at the little moorland
farms. Anna must have opened fifty gates, and there were times
when I thought we were bogged for good. I can tell you it was a
tricky business, but I was beginning to enjoy myself, for I felt that we
had won, and Anna was in wild spirits. The sight of bent and heather
intoxicated her, and she took to singing and reciting poems. The
curlews especially she hailed as old friends, and shouted a Danish
poem about them. . . .

Well, that's about the end of my story. We never met the Stutz
again, and for all I know it is still patrolling the Carter Bar. But I was
taking no risks, and when we got into the main road up the Tyne to
Liddesdale, I didn't take the shortest way to Laverlaw, which would
have been by Rule Water, or by Hermitage and the Slitrig. You see,
I had a fear that the Stutz, if it found no sign of us on the Carter or
Bellingham roads, might have the notion of keeping watch on the
approaches nearer Laverlaw. So I decided to come in on you from
the side where it wouldn't expect us. The sun came out after midday,
and it was a glorious afternoon. Lord, I think we must have covered
half the Border. We went down Liddel to Langholm, and up the Esk
to Eskdalemuir, and so into Ettrick. For most of the way we saw
nothing but sheep and an odd baker's van.

Lombard finished with a cavernous yawn. He grinned content-edly. 'Bed for me,' he said, 'and for Heaven's sake let that child have her sleep out. A queer business for a sedentary man getting on in years! I'm glad I did it, but I don't fancy doing it often.'

I asked one question. 'What was the chauffeur in the Stutz like?'

'I only got a glimpse of him,' he replied; 'but I think I should know him if I saw him again. An odd-looking chap. Tall and very thin. A long, brown face, a pointed chin, and eyes like a cat's. A foreigner, I should say, and a bit of a swine.'

I remembered the man who had come to Fosse with the youth Varrinder, and whom Sandy had recognized as Jacques D'Ingraville. We had not been quite certain if he was in the Haraldsen affair, and it had been Sandy's business to find that out. Now I knew, and the knowledge disquieted me, for of this man Sandy had spoken with a seriousness which was almost fear.

CHAPTER X

The Dog Samr

ANNA HARALDSEN'S ARRIVAL made us tighten the precautions at Laverlaw. We were now all assembled there, except the laird, and he might be trusted to look after himself. Lombard showed no desire to leave. He had wound up his business affairs in anticipation of a holiday, and thought that he might as well take the first few days of it in Scotland. He wrote a long account to his wife of his journey, which he read to me with pride – certainly it was a vigorous bit of narrative; and at the end he put in something about staying on to watch events. 'That will please Beryl,' he said. 'She's very keen about this business, and will like to know that I'm doing my bit.' I asked him what events he expected, and he replied that he had a feel in his bones that things would begin to move. That was not my own view, for, short of bombs from an aeroplane, I didn't see what the other lot could do to harm us. Laverlaw was as well guarded as a royal palace.

I have mentioned that Haraldsen was becoming a cured man. Under Peter John's care he had lost nearly all his jumpiness, he ate and slept well, laughed now and then, and generally behaved like an ordinary mortal. You could see that he was homesick, for the sight of Sandy's possessions reminded him of his own. But he had altogether lost the hunted look. The coming of his daughter put the top stone on his recovery. It was as if a nomad had got together a home again. I expected him to be in a great state about the very real risk she had run; I knew that with Peter John it would have come between me and my sleep; but he never gave it a thought. Indeed, he scarcely listened when Lombard told him about it. He wrote to Miss Barlock and sent for Anna's kit, and then shut the lid on that chapter.

But it did one good to see him and the girl together. For a couple of years the two had not met each other. He talked a good deal to her of the Norlands, which she was beginning to forget, and he was always reminding her of things that had happened in the Island of Sheep. I noticed that he tried to appear interested in her stories about school, but on that subject she had better listeners in Mary and Barbara and me, and an infinitely better one in Lombard. He seemed to wish to forget all that had happened in England, as if it had been a bad dream. He reminded me one day with satisfaction that at Laverlaw we were half-way to the Norlands.

One thing was clear – for him that English chapter was closed. Haraldsen was not only a cured man, but a new man, or perhaps he had returned to what he had been before I met him. There was confidence in his voice, more vigour in his eyes, and he held himself and walked like a free man. That was all to the good, for he would be a combatant now, I hoped, instead of a piece of compromising baggage. He was beginning to assert himself, too, and I came to think that, if Lombard was right, and things started to move, Haraldsen himself might be the propelling force. He was becoming restless again, not from shaky nerves, but from some growing purpose. He and Anna had long serious palavers in Norland, and I guessed that he was trying to hammer out some line of action. He might soon take a hand in shaping his own destiny.

Peter John, his former comrade, was now wholly neglected, and Haraldsen and Anna made most of their expeditions together. I had asked myself how my son would get on with the girl, and I soon found an answer. They didn't get on at all. Peter John had never had much to do with women, except his mother, and to some small degree with Barbara Clanroyden and Janet Roylance, because they were the belongings of his friends. I did not believe that he would make friends with any kind of girl, and it soon became clear that, anyhow, Anna was not his kind. Never were there such obvious incompatibles. He talked little, and when you asked him a question it was like dropping a stone into a deep well – you had to wait for the answer. She babbled like a brook. He had a ridiculously formal style of speech – Johnsonian English, his house-master had called it – whereas she revelled in every kind of slang – school slang out of novels, slang from film captions. I found her mannerisms often delightful, for she had not a complete command of English. For example, she would make unfamiliar positives from negative words, 'couth' (as the opposite of uncouth) was a favourite term of praise with her, and, contrary-wise, 'unbeautiful' a condemnation. Peter John thought them merely silly. Then she was always chaffing him, and it was about as much use chaffing Cleopatra's Needle for all the response she got. He treated her with elaborate politeness, and retired into his kennel, as an old house-dog will sometimes do when visitors bring a strange hound.

This went on for the better part of a week. Then suddenly Lombard's prophecy came true, and events quickened their pace to a run.

One afternoon all of us, except Barbara's infant, made an expedition to the shieling of Clatteringshaws, where the shepherd's only daughter – his name was Tarras – was being married to Nickson, the young herd on the home farm. It was a slack time in the pastoral year, before the autumn fairs began, and the whole Laverlaw estate turned out to the ceremony, for Nickson was popular and Tarras was one of the oldest hands on the place. The minister of Hangingshaw was to marry the couple at half-past two; after that there was to be high tea on the green beside the burn; then dancing was to follow till all hours in the big shed. Few of us had seen a Scots wedding, and, besides, Jean Tarras had been one of the Laverlaw maids, so we all set out on ponies to make an afternoon of it – except Peter John who, according to his custom, preferred to walk.

It was divine weather – just as well for the tea beside the burn – and we made a cheerful party. Anna especially was in wild spirits, and I realized for the first time those good looks about which Mary had been so certain. Now that she was in prettier clothes than her school uniform, and had been out a good deal in the sun, she had become an altogether more vivid and coloured being. Her hair had gold glints in it. Her skin had flushed to a sort of golden ivory, and her lovely eyes had become deeper by contrast. She held herself well in the saddle, and her voice rang out over the heather as sweet and true as a bell. She was riding with Mary and Lombard, and I was behind with Barbara and Haraldsen, and I couldn't help telling her father that she was an uncommonly pretty child. The fact was so patent that he didn't trouble even to look pleased.

'Where does she get her name?' I asked. 'Her mother? '

'No, my mother. Anna is a common name in the Norlands. But it is not right for her. She is no Jewish prophetess. If I had the christening of her again, it should be Nanna, who was Balder's wife.'

I remembered vaguely that Balder was some sort of Norse god, and certainly the girl looked a goddess that afternoon. Haraldsen was getting very full of Northern lore these days, for he went on in his queer staccato way to explain that a goddess's name would not do for her either – that she was more like the maidens in the Edda, who had to live in the underworld in a house ringed with fire till a hero rescued them. He ran over a string of those ladies, of whom Brynhild was the only one I recognized.

'Poor Anna,' he said. 'Perhaps she will be like the women in the Sagas, ill-fated because her men are doomed. She may be as proud and sad as Bergthora, but she will never be treacherous like Halgerda.'

I wasn't quite sure what he was talking about. I had read one or two of the Sagas on Sandy's advice, and I observed that they were gloomy anecdotes.

'They are the Scriptures of my race,' said Haraldsen. 'And they have truths from which we cannot escape, though they are sad truths. They are true for me – and for you too, Hannay, and for Lord Clanroyden, and for our kind ladies, and for your son, who is striding yonder as if he were Thor on his travels. You Scots know it too, for you have it in your sayings. There is a weird which none can escape. Fenris-Wolf is waiting in Hell for Odin himself.'

'I should let Fenris-Wolf sleep in this weather,' I told him, and he laughed.

'True,' he said. 'It is not well to think of ultimate things. There is a Norland proverb which says that few can see farther forth than when Odin meets the wolf.'

He stopped and sniffed the scents, a wonderful mingling of thyme and peat and heather blown by a light west wind over miles of moorland. 'This place is like the Norlands,' he said with abstracted eyes. 'I have smelled this smell at midsummer there, when there was a wind from the hills.'

'It's my own calf-country,' I said, 'and I'm glad to think it reminds you of yours.'

'The reminder is not all pleasure. It makes me sad also. There is another of our proverbs – I seem to be quoting many to-day – that strongest is every man in his own house. I am in the house of a stranger – the kindest of strangers.'

'So am I,' I said; 'but I'm not complaining.'

'But you have your home – you can reach it in a day. Anna and I have a home, but it is shut to us. She is like the poor Princess in the tale – there is a ring of flame round her dwelling.'

'Oh, we're going to put those fires out,' I said cheerfully. 'It won't be long till you're as snug in your island as Sandy in Laverlaw and me at Fosse – a dashed sight more snug, for you haven't to pay income-tax. If the worst comes to the worst, I'll come up and join you.'

A sudden queer look came into his face. He had been talking dolefully in a brisk voice, and he had been half laughing. But now his eyes grew grave, just as his father's used to.

'I wonder if I shall ever find peace,' he said slowly. 'We Norlanders get tied up in a skein of fate from which there is no escape. Read in the Sagas, and you will see how relentless is the wheel. Hrut slays Hrap, and Atli slays Hrut, and Gisli slays Atli, and Kari slays Gisli.

THE ISLAND OF SHEEP

My father, God rest him, punishes the old Troth, and the younger Troth would punish me, and if he succeeds perhaps Anna or some child of Anna's will punish him.'

It was in a whirl of outlandish names and with Haraldsen looking as mysterious as a spae-wife that we plashed through the burn and off-saddled on the green of Clatteringshaws.

You could not imagine a pleasanter spectacle. A dozen shepherds had brought their womenfolk, and there was a big contingent of the Laverlaw servants, and an ancient horse-bus had conveyed a party from Hangingshaw village. The minister, an active young man who had got a Military Cross in the War, had come on a bicycle. Stoddart, the head-shepherd on the Mains, was the master of ceremonies, and he was busy with the preparations for tea, with Sim and Oliver as his lieutenants. Tarras welcomed us with that kindly composure which makes a Border shepherd the best gentleman on earth, for he is as sure of himself as any king. There must have been fully fifty guests. The older men were in their Sunday blacks, their regular garb for church, weddings, and funerals, but the younger wore the glen homespun, and the keepers were, of course, in knickerbockers. I noticed that every man had a black-and-white checked necktie, a thing which Sandy always wore at home and which was the Laverlaw equivalent to a tartan. The women were in bright colours, except the bride, who wore white, and I thought how female clothes had been evened up since the War. Most of the girls were fully as well-dressed as Barbara or Janet.

The ceremony in Tarras's little parlour was a suffocating business, but happily it did not last long. Then the blushing Nickson and the very demure bride disappeared up a wooden ladder to shed some of their finery, and we examined the presents laid out in the kitchen. Tarras and his wife did hosts at the tea on the green, and I have never seen a company tuck in more resolutely to more substantial viands. There were hot mutton pies, and cold mutton hams, and all that marvellous variety of cakes and breads in which Scotland has no rival, and oceans of strong tea and rich cream, and beer for those who liked it, and whisky for the elderly. Old Tarras made a speech of welcome, and Barbara replied almost in his own accent, for the American South, when it likes, has the same broad vowels as the Border. And then, after a deal of eating and drinking, all hands set to work to remove the tables, and the company split up into groups, while youth wandered off by itself. Presently dancing would begin in the wool-shed – the fiddlers were already tuning up – and there would be supper some time in the small hours.

The ladies started for home early, and, since I wanted exercise, I sent my pony back with Geordie Hamilton. Lombard professed the same wish, and Haraldsen, who had been a silent figure at the feast, followed suit, so that Geordie departed like a horse-thief who had made a good haul. We were in no hurry, for it was less than an hour's walk home over hill turf, so we went round to the back of the cottage, where some of the older men were sitting on a rock above a small linn, smoking their pipes and talking their slow talk. I remember thinking that I had rarely had so profound an impression of peace. The light wind had dropped, and the honey-coloured bent and the blue of the sky were melting into the amethyst of twilight. In that cool, mellow, scented dusk, where the only sounds were the drift of distant human speech, and the tinkle of the burn, and the calling of wild birds, and the drowsy bleat of an old ewe, I seemed to have struck something as changeless as the hills.

The dogs were mostly congregated round Tarras's back-door, on the look-out for broken meats, and I had just taken a seat on a bank beside Stoddart when a most infernal racket started in their direction. It sounded like the father and mother of dog-fights. All of us got to our feet, but we were on the wrong side of the burn, and it took us some minutes to circumvent the linn, pass through the gates of the sheep-fold, and get to the back-door where bicycles and the Hangingshaw horse-bus were parked. For the last dozen yards we had the place in sight, where a considerable drama was going on.

The centre of it was Stoddart's dog, the patriarch Yarrow. He was about twelve years old, and in his day had been the pride of the countryside, for he had won twice at the big sheep-trials. I dare say he was an arrogant old fellow, and said nasty things to the young collies, for it isn't in dog nature to be a swell without showing it. But as Stoddart's dog he had a position of acknowledged pre-eminence, and at clippings and speanings and lamb sales he took precedence, and was given, so to speak, the first lick from the plate. But now he must have gone a bit too far. Every dog in the place had it in for him, and with bared teeth was intent on his massacre.

The old beast was something of a strategist. He had got into the corner where the peat-shed projected beyond the cottage wall, so that he couldn't be taken in flank or in rear, and there he was putting up a sturdy fight. He had a dozen enemies, but they had not much notion of a mass assault, for if they had come on in a wave they would have smothered him. What they did was to attack singly. A little black-and-tan dog would dart forward and leap for his neck, only to be hurled back by Yarrow's weight, for though his teeth were old and blunt, he was a heavy beast, and could have given pounds to anything else there. But some of his assailants must have got home, for he had an ear in tatters, and his neck and throat were blotched with blood.

His opponents' game was the old one of the pack, learned when their ancestors hunted on the plains of Asia. They meant to wear the old fellow down, and then rush in and finish him. Stoddart saw what they were after, and flung his stick at them, roaring abuse. I would have bet any sum that, but for us, in ten minutes the poor old beast would have been dead.

But I would have been wildly wrong, for suddenly Yarrow changed his plan, and the fight was transformed. Instead of standing on the defence he attacked. With lips snarling back over his gums, and every hair on his thick collar a-bristle, and with something between a bark, a bay, and a howl, he charged his enemies. He didn't snap – his teeth weren't good enough – he simply hurled his weight on them, using jaw and paws and every part of him as weapons of offence. Far more important, he let them see that he was out for blood. He didn't want to save his hide now, but to rend theirs. I have never seen such determination in any animal, except in African wild game. Yarrow's twelve years by Stoddart's fireside were forgotten. He was no more the household pet, the shepherd's working partner, the prize-winner at shows to be patted and stroked; he was a lightning-bolt, a tornado, a devouring fiend. . . . There was a cloud of dust and fur, and then the whole mob streaked into flight. One went between my legs, one tripped up Lombard, several felt the weight of their masters' crooks. As for old Yarrow, he had fixed his stumps in the hind-leg of a laggard, and it took Stoddart all his time to loose them.

I stopped to laugh, for it was one of the best finishes I had ever seen. Each shepherd was busy rounding up and correcting his own special miscreant, and Lombard, Haraldsen, and Peter John and I were left to ourselves. I got a glimpse of Haraldsen's face and gripped his arm, for I thought he was going to faint. He was white as paper, and shaking like a leaf. He looked just as he had done that morning on Hanham sands when the whitefront had escaped from Peter John's falcon.

Words came slowly from his pale lips. He was drawing a moral, but it was the opposite of the Hanham one. But the first words were the same.

'It is a message to me,' he croaked. 'That dog is like Samr, who died with Gunnar of Lithend. He reminds me of what I had forgotten.'

By now Stoddart had dragged Yarrow indoors to be washed and

bandaged, and the other shepherds were busy with their own dogs. The gathering twilight showed that it was time for us to set out for home. Haraldsen followed us mechanically as we crossed the paddock where Tarras grew his potatoes, and the meadow where he cut his bog-hay, and breasted the long slopes which the westering sun had made as yellow as corn. He walked with great strides, keeping abreast of us, but a little to the right, as if he wished to be left alone to his gloomy Scandinavian meditations. But there was something new about him that caught my eye. He was wearing a suit of that russet colour called *crotal*, and it somehow enlarged his bulk. He kept his head down and poked forward, with his great shoulders hunched, and he had the look of a big brown bear out for action. There was fight and purpose in his air which before then had only been a lounging, loose-limbed acquiescence. Now there was something of old Yarrow when he had gathered himself up for the final rush.

At the watershed of the glen we stopped by consent, for the view there was worth looking at with its twenty miles of rounded hills huddling into the sunset. There was a little cairn on which Lombard and I seated ourselves, while Peter John as usual circled round us like a restless collie. Then Haraldsen spoke:

'I must leave you soon – Anna and I – at once,' he said. 'I have been too long a trespasser.'

'We're all trespassers on Sandy,' I said.

He didn't listen to me. He was in his proverbial mood, and quoted something from the *Hava-mal* (whatever that may be). It ran like this: 'Stay not in the same house long, but go; for love turns to loathing if a man stays long on another's floor.'

'Oh, nonsense!' I said. 'We're not here cadging hospitality. We're all in the same game, and this is part of it.'

'That is what I mean,' he answered. 'We are not playing it right. I, at any rate, have been a fool.'

We waited, for he was labouring with some thought for which he found it hard to get words. But it was only the words that were lacking, for every line of his face spoke of purpose.

He put his big hand on my shoulder.

'In January, do you remember, on the Norfolk shore? I saw the goose escape the hawk by flying low. I thought that I too might escape by being quiet and humble. . . . I was wrong, for humility drains manhood away, but does not give safety. To-day I have seen the virtue of boldness. I will no longer be passive, and try to elude my enemies. I will seek them out and fight them, like Samr the hound.'

All three of us sat up and took notice, for this was a Haraldsen we had not met before. Except for his shaven chin he might have been his father. He had identified old Yarrow with some Saga dog, and he seemed to have got himself into the skin of an ancestor. His great nose looked like the beak of a Viking galley, and his pale eyes had the ice-blue fanaticism of the North.

'I have been forgetting my race,' he went on. 'Always a weird followed us, and Fate was cruel to us. But we did not run from it or hide from it, but faced it and grappled with it, and sometimes we overthrew it. I have been a coward and I have seen the folly of cowardice. I have been sick too, but I am a whole man again. I will no longer avoid my danger, but go out to meet it, since it is the will of God. . . .'

'*Quisque suos patimur Manes.*' A voice spoke below us, but I did not know what the words meant. Lombard did, and perhaps Peter John, though I doubt it.

We turned to find Sandy. He had come quietly up the hill while we had been talking, and had been eavesdropping at our backs. He was wearing an old grey flannel suit, and looked pale, as if he had been too much indoors lately.

'How on earth did you get here?' I asked.

'Flew. Archie Roylance dropped me at Chryston, and that's only five miles off. I was just in time to kiss Jean Tarras and drink her health. . . . You were saying, when I interrupted?' and he turned to Haraldsen.

On Haraldsen's face there was no sign of surprise at Sandy's sudden appearance, for he was far too full of his own thoughts.

'I was saying,' he replied, 'that I will skulk no longer in a foreign country or in other men's houses. I will go home to my own land and there will fight my enemies.'

'Alone?' Sandy asked.

'If need be, alone. You have been true friends to me, but no friends can take from me the burden of my own duty.'

Sandy looked at him with that quick appraising glance of his which took in so much. I could see in his eyes that, like me, he had found something new in Haraldsen which he had not expected, and which mightily cheered him. His face broke into a smile.

'A very sound conclusion,' he said. 'It's the one I've been coming to myself. I've come up here to talk about it. . . . And now let us push on for dinner. Laverlaw air has given me the first appetite I've had for weeks.'

CHAPTER XI

We Shift our Base

THAT NIGHT AFTER DINNER we held a council of war, at which we all agreed that Peter John should be present. That was a comfort to him, for since Anna's coming he had been rather left out of things. Sandy, as was his habit at Laverlaw, wore the faded green coat of a Border dining club, but it didn't make him look, as it usually did, a Scots laird snug among his ancestral possessions. His face had got that special fining-down which I so well remembered, and his eyes that odd dancing light which meant that he was on the warpath again.

We had heard nothing of him for weeks, so I had a good many questions to ask.

'What have I been doing?' he said. 'Going to and fro on the earth. Trying to get a line on various gentry. My old passion for queer company has stood me in good stead, and by voluptuous curves I've been trying to get in on their flanks. One way and another I've learned most of what I wanted to know. Several of the unknown quantities I can now work out to four places of decimals. We're up against a formidable lot – no mistake about that.'

'More formidable than you thought?' asked Lombard.

'Ye-es,' he said slowly. 'But in a different way. That is my chief discovery.'

'What was your method' I asked. 'Have you been up to your old tricks?' I turned to Lombard. 'Perhaps you don't know that he's one of the best quick-change artists in the world.'

'Partly,' Sandy replied. 'I've had quite a lot of fun in the business. But I met some of them in my own name and person. We had better be clear about one thing – they know all about us. Dick they marked down long ago; and Lombard since he levanted with Miss Anna. They don't know our motive, but they realize that we are backing Haraldsen. If I've got a good deal of their *dossiers*, they've got plenty of ours. You'd be surprised, Dick, to know how zealously they have been searching into your tattered past, and I'm glad to think that what they found has made them fairly uncomfortable. They've been pumping, very cleverly and quietly, all your old pals like Artinswell and Julius Victor and Archie Roylance. They even got something out of Macgillivray, though he wasn't aware of it.'

'What do they make of *you?*'

Sandy laughed. 'Oh, I puzzle them horribly. I've got the jade tablet, so I'm in the thick of it, and they're gunning for me just as much as for Haraldsen. But I'm a troublesome proposition, for they understand quite well that I've taken the offensive, and they've an idea that when I fix my teeth in anything I'm apt to hang on. That's the worst of my confounded melodramatic reputation. It sounds immodest, but I've a notion that they've got the wind up badly about me, and if we had only the first lot to deal with I might make them cry off. . . . Only of course we haven't.'

'What's the new snag?' I asked.

'Patience,' he said. 'We'll go through the list one by one. First, Varrinder, the youth with the rabbit teeth. We can count him out, for he'll worry us no more. He was what I suspected – an *indicateur*, and at heart a funk. I laid myself out to scare Master Varrinder, and I succeeded. He was very useful to me, so far as his twittering nerves allowed him. Yesterday he sailed, under another name, for Canada, and he won't come back for a long, long time. Next, Dick.'

'Albinus,' I said.

'Right. He's the second least important. Well, I've seen a lot of Mr. Erick Albinus. I played bridge with him at Dillon's, which cost me twenty pounds. We went racing together, and I had a boring but illuminating day. I gave a little dinner for him, to which I made a point of asking one or two of his City friends about whom he is most nervous. He's a nasty piece of work, that lad, and it beats me how people tolerate him as they do, for he's the oily *faux bonhomme* if there ever was one. He's in the job for greed, for financially he's on the edge of Queer Street, and also Troth has some kind of family pull on him. But I think I could scare him out of it, like Varrinder, if I wanted to. But I don't. I've decided that he's safer in than out, for he has a big yellow streak in him, and, though he's a clever devil, he'll be a drag on his friends in the long run. So I've remained on good terms with Mr. Albinus, and he flatters himself that he has thrown dust in my eyes, more power to him.

'Now we get to bigger business. Troth – Mr. Lancelot Troth. I've come to a clear decision about Troth. He's a ruffian, but I don't think he's altogether a rogue. A fine distinction, you say. Maybe, but it's important. First, he has his friends who genuinely like him, quite honest fellows, some of them. I got myself invited to the annual dinner of his Fusilier regiment, where he made a dashed good speech. I gathered that in the War he was a really good battalion officer, and very popular with the men. I did my best to follow his business tracks, and pretty tangled they are, but my impression is that he is more of a buccaneer than a swindler. He's a bold fellow who runs his head now and then against the law, because he likes taking risks. Did you ever read *The Wrong Box*? There's a touch of Michael Finsbury in Troth.'

'Did you meet him – I mean as yourself?' I asked.

'Indeed I did. Had quite a heart-to-heart talk with him. I went down to his office, sent in my card, and begged for a few minutes' conversation on private business. There was a fine commotion in that office, a client was cleared like a shot out of his private room, and he told his secretary that on no account must we be disturbed. I suppose he thought that I had come to offer terms. I was the guileless innocent – asked if he had read my letter to the *Times* – said I was very anxious to get all the information I could about old Haraldsen, and that I had heard that he had known him in South Africa. That puzzled him, and in self-defence he became very stiff and punctilious – said he had had nothing to do with Haraldsen, though his father might have met him. You see, he hadn't yet linked me up with you, Dick, and was playing for safety. Then I said that I was trying to get on the track of Haraldsen's family – believed he had a son somewhere, and could he help me to locate him? I had come to him solely as a matter of business, for I had heard good reports of his skill. I said I had got this jade tablet, which I couldn't possibly stick to, and that I proposed to present it to the British Museum unless I could find Haraldsen's heirs, in which case they should have it.

'That fetched him. He suggested luncheon, and took me to one of the few old City places remaining where you feed in a private box. He insisted on champagne, so I remembered a saying of my father's, that if a man gave you champagne at luncheon, you should suspect a catch. He was very civil and forthcoming, and began, quite cleverly, to dig things out of his memory which his father had told him about Haraldsen. He dared say that with a little trouble he could get some information for me about the people who had a claim to the equities in Haraldsen's estate. We parted on excellent terms, after some highly technical talk about spring salmon in Caithness, and he promised to ring me up as soon as he had anything to tell me.'

'Did he?' Lombard asked eagerly. He was the one of us who knew most about Troth.

'No. For in the next day or two his scouts linked me up with Dick

– Laverlaw was enough for that – and he must have realized that I knew everything and had been playing with him. But I rang him up myself and got a very dusty answer. However, he agreed to see me again, and I made him lunch with me at Claridge's – planted him down in the middle of a crowded restaurant, where he couldn't make an exhibition of himself. For I meant to make him lose his temper, and if that had happened in his office the end would only have been a shindy. I managed it all right. I orated about old Haraldsen, that wonderful figure half-saint and half-adventurer, and the sacred trust that had been laid on me, and so forth. He listened with a squared jaw and ugly suspicious eyes while I strummed on the falsetto. Then he broke out. ' See here, Lord Clanroyden,' he said. ' I've had enough of this stuff. You've been trying to fool me and I don't like it. I see what your game is, and I don't like it either. You take my advice and keep out of this business, or you'll get hurt, big swell as you are. Old Haraldsen was a scoundrel, and there's some of us who have a lot to get back from him and his precious son.'

'I opened my eyes and started on another tack. I said that all this shocked me, and I'm hanged if I didn't get him to believe that I meant it. You see, I was the new-comer who might have heard any kind of story from the other side. He actually seemed to want to put himself right in my eyes, and he gave me his own version. What it was doesn't signify, except that he has a full-sized vendetta on his hands inherited from his father, and isn't going to forget it. I must say I respected his truculence. It was rather like the kind of family legacy you have among the Indian frontier tribes. I pretended to be surprised, and not altogether unsympathetic, and we parted on very fair terms. I had got the two things I wanted. I had kept the gang uncertain what part I meant to play, and I had taken the measure of Troth. A bit of a ruffian as I have said, but not altogether a rogue. If he were the only one in the show I think he might be squared. He wants what he considers to be his rights, not loot in the general way. But of course he's not alone, for there's a bigger and subtler mind behind him. Can you put a name to it? '

'Barralty,' said Lombard and I in unison.

'Yes, Barralty. He is the mind all right. I had to get a full view of Barralty, so I approached him from all kinds of angles. I've told you already about the Bloomsbury party, where he was a king among the half-baked. I followed up his trail in the City – Lombard started me on that – and my conclusion is that the Lepcha business hasn't done him much harm. He has still plenty of money in the ordinary way, though not a hundredth part of what he wants, and his reputation is still high. I thought I'd have a peep at his political side, so I got Andrew Amos to arrange that I should attend a private conference between some of the intellectuals and the trade-union leaders – I was a boiler-maker from the Clyde and a fairly shaggy comrade. His performance there rather impressed me, for he managed to make himself a bridge between two utterly different worlds – put the idealistic stuff with a flavour of hard good sense, and the practical view with a touch of idealism. There's a considerable future for him in politics, if he decides that way.

'Then I thought that I'd better make his acquaintance. You know Charles Lamancha's taste for freak parties? Well, I got him to give a dinner at the club – himself, Christopher Stannix, an Under-Secretary, a couple of bankers, and Ned Leithen, and I had myself placed next to Barralty. Of course by this time he knew all about me, for the Laverlaw party had begun, and his friends had discovered the way we have tied up Haraldsen's fortune, so naturally I was considered the villain of the piece. He made no mistakes that night. He was very polite to me, and talked intelligently about my Far East Commission and foreign affairs generally, and even condescended to be enthusiastic about this Border country in which he said he often motored. He did not attempt to pump me, but behaved as if I were an ordinary guest of whom he had heard and whom he was quite glad to meet. There was some pretty good talk, for Stannix always manages to put life into a dinner table, and Barralty kept his end up. He had a wrangle with one of the bankers over some financial point, and I thought he put his case uncommonly well. So did the others, for he was listened to with respect. There's no doubt that he has a pretty solid footing in the world, and there's no mistake about his brains. He's as quick as lightning on a point, and I can see him spinning an immense web and keeping his eye on every thread in it.'

'I told you that weeks ago,' said Lombard. 'Barralty is as clever as the devil. But what about the rest of him – besides his mind?'

'I'm coming to that. That was the thing I most wanted to know about, and it wasn't easy to get cross-bearings. I had to dive into queer worlds and half-worlds and, as I've already said, I found that my unfortunate liking for low society came in useful. I found out most of what I wanted, but it has been a long job and not a particularly pleasant one. One piece of luck I had. There was bound to be a woman somewhere, and I scraped up acquaintance with Barralty's particular friend. She's a lovely creature, a red-haired Jewess, who just missed coming off as a film-star. Heaven knows what her real name is, but she calls herself Lydia Ludlow.'

'She came to tea at Fosse,' Peter John put in. 'I remember her name. My mother said she was an actress.'

'Dick,' said Sandy solemnly, 'I think Peter John should be in bed. But I won't enlarge upon Miss Ludlow, except to say that she was hard to get to know, but that she repaid me for my trouble. I was an American film magnate, very well made up, and I don't think she is likely to recognize me again. I had a wonderful scheme for a super-film about Herod Agrippa, which would star her. So we had a number of confidential talks, in which Barralty's name cropped up as a friend who would take a share in the venture. You see, it was to be a great Anglo-American show, a sort of proof of the unity of art and the friendship of the Anglo-Saxon race. I learned from her a good deal about Barralty. He is her slave, it appears, but the fetters don't gall, for his success is to be her success. The two of them represent a pretty high-powered ambition, and Miss Ludlow won't let the pressure slacken.'

'What's your conclusion?' I asked. 'A first-class brain, but how much stuff behind it?'

'Not a great deal. I have collected all my evidence and carefully weighed it, and that is my verdict. Barralty has three spurs to prick him on – ambition, greed, which is part of his ambition, and his lady. But he has a lot of tethers to keep him still – fear of his reputation, fear of his skin, all sorts of funks. He's not the bold class of lad. Rather a sheep in wolf's clothing. If things were as they were a year ago, I believe we could settle the whole business out of hand.'

'You mean – what?' Haraldsen spoke for the first time.

'Well, we could do a deal with Troth, a reasonable deal, and I believe he would stick to it. I could scare Albinus as I have scared Varrinder. And in spite of Miss Ludlow I think I could scare Barralty. Only you see that is impossible now, for a fifth figure has appeared, who puts a darker complexion on the thing. Before, it was not much more than melodrama, but now the tragic actor is on the boards. For the real wolf has arrived.'

'We knew for certain that D'Ingraville was in it after Lombard's escapade,' I said.

I had to tell Sandy some of the details of Lombard's story, for he had not heard them.

'Yes,' he said reflectively. 'He must have been the man who drove the Stutz.' He referred to a pocket diary. 'There were three days when he slipped away from me, and now I know what he was doing. Otherwise I didn't let him often out of my sight. No, I never was in his sight, but there wasn't much he did in those weeks in London that I didn't know. You see, I was on my own ground and he was a stranger, so I had a pull on him. He tried a little *contre-espionage*, but it was clumsy. I've been sitting tight and watching him, and all I can say is, that if he was formidable in Olifa he's a dashed sight more formidable to-day.'

I whistled, for I had Sandy's Olifa doings clear in my head, and I remembered just how big a part D'Ingraville had played there.

'He's a beast of prey,' Sandy went on. 'But in Olifa he was a sick beast, living an unnatural life on drugs which must have weakened his nerve. Now he's the cured beast, stronger and much more dangerous than if he had never been sick. It's exactly what happens with a man who gets over infantile paralysis – the strength of will and mind and body required to recover from the disease give the patient a vitality and self-confidence that lasts him for the rest of his days. I don't know why God allowed it and by what magic he achieved it, but D'Ingraville to-day is as fit a man as any of us here, and with ten times our dæmonic power. . . . And he isn't alone. You remember, Dick, the collection of toughs that Castor called his Bodyguard. I thought that all of them had been gathered in, but I was mistaken. Two at least survive – the ones called Carreras and Martel, the Spaniard and the Belgian. At this moment they're with D'Ingraville in London, and you may bet they're in with him in this show.'

'But Martel was killed in your last scrap,' I put in. 'What was the name of the place? Veiro? You told me so. I don't remember about Carreras, but I'm positive about Martel.'

'So I thought,' said Sandy; 'but I was wrong. Carreras managed to leak out quite early, but I thought Martel was one of the bag at Veiro. But he's very much alive. I could take you any day into a certain Soho restaurant, and show you Martel in a neat blue suit and yellow boots having his *apéritif*. The same lithe, hard-trained brute, with the scar over his left eye that he got from Geordie Hamilton. We have the genuine beasts of prey on our trail this time, Dick, my lad. . . . And I'll tell you something more. We could have bought off, or scared off, the others, I think, but there's no scaring D'Ingraville's pack, and there's only one price to buy them with and that's every cent of Haraldsen's fortune and my jade tablet. D'Ingraville, I understand, is particularly keen on the jade tablet – naturally, for he's an imaginative blackguard.'

'But how will the old lot mix with the new?' I asked.

'They won't,' said Sandy grimly. 'But if I'm any judge of men, they'll have to do as they're told. None of them can stand up for a moment against D'Ingraville. Troth, the ordinary, not too scrupulous, sedentary attorney – Barralty, the timid intellectual – what can they do against the real desperado? I could almost be sorry for them, for they're young rabbits in the fox's jaw. D'Ingraville is the leader now, and the rest must follow, whether they like it or not. He won't loosen his grip on either his opponents or his allies. He's the real enemy. My old great-great-great-grandfather at Dettingen led his regiment into action after telling them, ' Ye see those lads on yon hill? Well, if ye dinna kill them, they'll kill you.' That's what I say about D'Ingraville.'

'So much for the lay-out,' I said. 'What do you propose to do about it? '

'At first I was for peace,' Sandy answered. 'I thought that the gang could be squared or scared. I knew that D'Ingraville couldn't, but I fancied he might be dealt with in another way – he and his Body-guard. I saw the Olifa Embassy people, but it's no good. There's not enough positive evidence against them to make extradition possible. Besides, even if there were, it wouldn't solve Haraldsen's problem. These hounds will stick to his track, and, unless they could be decently strung up, there's no lasting security for him. So I take it that things have come to a crisis. At any rate they're coming, and we must face it. It's no good our sheltering here any longer. I dare say we could stave them off for a bit, but it would be a rotten life for everybody, and some day they would get under our guard. We must fight them, and choose our own ground for it, and, since they are outside civilization, we must be outside it too.'

'I don't see the sense of that,' I said. 'This is a law-abiding country, and that will cramp D'Ingraville's style. If we go down into the jungle the jungle beasts will have the advantage.'

Sandy shook his head.

'First, you can't bring things to the point in a law-abiding land. Second, a move will cramp the style of Troth and Barralty worse than ever. Third, D'Ingraville is a product of civilization, and I'd be more afraid of him in a Paris street than on a desert island. So I agree with what I overheard Haraldsen say when I overtook you on the hill. We must fight the last round in the Island of Sheep.'

Then Haraldsen spoke.

'That is my resolution,' he said in his slow, quiet voice. He stood up and stretched his great form to its full height, much as I had seen his father do on that moonlit hill long ago. 'I will do as the old dog did this afternoon, and snap back at my tormentors.'

'Right,' said Sandy. We all felt the tension of the moment, and he wanted to keep the temperature down. 'I think that is common sense. I will arrange that the papers announce that you are going back to the Norlands. We had better divide up. I have a friend, a trawler skipper in Aberdeen, who will take you. By the way, what about your daughter? '

'Anna goes with me. I should be a wretched man if she were out of my sight. Also, it is right that she should share in my destiny.'

'I dare say that's wise. If you left her here, they might make a hostage of her. Dick, you can go by the monthly Iceland boat, which sails next week from Leith, and you'd better take Geordie Hamilton. I will come on later. You may be certain that the pack will be hot after us as soon as they learn our plans. Laverlaw and Fosse and Mary and Peter John and Barbara and the infant will be left in peace.'

There was a small groan from Peter John. He had been listening to our talk with eyes like saucers. 'Mayn't I come too?' he pled.

'No, my lad,' I said, though his piteous face went to my heart. 'You're too young, and there's no duty in it for you. We can't afford camp-followers.'

'But I will not permit it,' Haraldsen cried passionately. 'I go to meet my fate, whatever God may send, I and my daughter. But I will not have you endanger yourself for me. You have been most noble and generous; but your task is over, for you have restored me to myself and made me a man again. I go to my home to fight out the battle there with one or two of my own people. You, my friends, will remain in your homes, and thank God that He has given you peace.'

'Not I,' I said. 'I promised your father to stand by you, and I'm jolly well going to stick to that. Besides, I'm getting fat and slack, and I need fining down. I wouldn't be out of this for all your millions. What about you, Lombard? '

'I'm on,' was the answer. 'I swore the same oath as you, and I want some exercise to stir up my liver. I've tidied up my affairs for a month or two, for I meant, anyhow, to take a long holiday. Beryl won't object. She's as keen on this job as I am.'

I had spoken briskly, but my heart was in my boots. I was certain that Mary would raise no objections, as she had raised none in the 'Three Hostages' business, but I knew that she would be desperately anxious. I had no fears for her and Peter John, for the battle-ground would be moved a thousand miles off, but I saw a miserable time ahead for those that I loved best.

Haraldsen stared at us and his eyes filled with tears. He seized on Lombard, who was nearest him, and hugged him like a bear. I managed to avoid an embrace, but he wrung my hand.

'I did not know there was such honour in the world,' he said with his voice breaking. 'Now indeed I may be bold, for I have on either side of me a friend.'

Then he looked at Sandy, of whom he had hitherto been rather in awe.

'But of you, Lord Clanroyden, I can ask nothing. You have sworn no oath, and you are a great man who is valuable to his country. Also, you have a young wife and a little baby. I insist that you stay at home, for this enterprise of ours, I must tell you, will be very difficult. And I think it may be very dangerous.'

'Oh, I know that,' was the answer. 'Barbara knows it too, and she would be the first to tell me to go. I have a bigger interest in this than any of you. Give me some beer, Dick, and I'll tell you a story.'

I filled up his tankard and very deliberately he lit his pipe. His eyes rested on each of us in turn – Lombard a little flushed and excited, me rather solemnized by the line things were taking, Peter John who had suddenly gone pale, and Haraldsen towering above us like a Norse rover. In the end they caught Haraldsen's eyes, and some compelling force in them made him pull up a chair and sit down stiffly, like a schoolboy in the headmaster's room.

'Three days ago,' said Sandy, 'I had a little trip across the Channel. I flew to Geneva, and there got a car and motored deep into the Savoy glens. In the evening I came to a small, ancient chateau high up on the knees of the mountains. In the twilight I could see a white wedge poking up in the eastern sky, which I knew to be Mont Blanc. I spent the night there, and my host was D'Ingraville.'

We all exclaimed, for it sounded the maddest risk to take.

'There was no danger,' Sandy went on. 'I was perfectly certain about my man. He belongs to a family that goes back to the Crusades and has come badly down in the world. That little dwelling is all that is left to a man whose forbears once owned half Haute Savoie. There's a sentimental streak in D'Ingraville, and that hill-top of his is for him the dearest thing on earth. I had discovered that, never mind how, and I wasn't afraid of his putting poison in my coffee. He's a scoundrel, but on a big scale, and he has some rags of gentility left.

'Well, we had an interesting evening. I didn't try to bargain with him, but we exchanged salutes, so to speak, before battle. I wanted to find out the mood he was in, now that he was a cured man, and to discover just how far he meant to go. There's no doubt on that point. He is playing up to the limit. He is going to skin Haraldsen, and perhaps Troth and Barralty into the bargain. But there's more in it than greed. Once it might have been possible to buy him off with an immense sum – but not now, since he knows I'm in it. He has come to regard me as his eternal enemy. The main quarrel now is not between Haraldsen and the Pack, but between D'Ingraville and me. He challenged me, and I accepted the challenge.'

He must have seen disapproval in my face, for he went on.

'There was no other way, Dick. It wasn't vanity. He might go about the world boasting that he had beaten me, and I would never give it a thought. I'm quite content that he should find his own way to Hell. But there's more to it than that. He's what is left over from my Olifa job, and till those remains are swept up, that job isn't finished. I can't leave the thing half done. I can't let that incarnate devil go loose in the world. If I shirked his challenge I should never sleep in my bed again.'

There had come into Sandy's face that look that I had seen once or twice before – on the little hill outside Erzerum, in Medina's library in Hill Street – and I knew that I might just as well argue with a whirlwind. He was smiling, but his eyes were solemn.

'He saw me off next morning in a wonderful mountain dawn. ' It's good to be alive in such a world,' he said. '*Au revoir*. It will not be long, I hope, till we meet again.' Well, I'm going to hurry on that meeting. I'm going to join him on your island, and I think that one or the other of us won't leave it.'

PART III

The Island of Sheep

CHAPTER XII

Hulda's Folk

I HAD NEVER BEFORE SAILED in northern waters, and I had pictured them as eternally queasy and yeasty and wind-scourged. Very different was the reality in that blue August weather. When Lombard, Geordie Hamilton, and I embarked in the Iceland boat at Leith, there was a low mist over the Forth, but we ran into clear air after the May, and next morning, as we skirted the Orkneys, the sea was a level plain, with just enough of a breeze to crisp it delicately, and in the strong sunlight the distant islets stood out sharp and clear like the kopjes in a veld morning.

But the fine weather did nothing to raise my spirits. I had never started out on a job with less keenness or with drearier forebodings. Lombard put me to shame. This man, whom I thought to have grown soft and elderly, was now facing the unknown, not only composedly but cheerfully. He had a holiday air about him, and would have been glad to be in the business, I'm positive, even though he had never sworn that ancient oath. I began to think that the profession of high finance was a better training than the kind of life I had led myself. Part of his cheerfulness was due to the admiration he had acquired for Sandy, which made him follow as docilely as a small boy in the wake of a big brother. I yielded to no one in my belief in Sandy, but we had been through too many things together for me to think him infallible. That rotten Greek sentence that Macgillivray had quoted stuck in my mind. Both Sandy and I had had amazing luck in life, but luck always turned in the end.

My trouble was that I could not see how the affair could finish. We were to get to grips, in some remote island which was clean outside any law, with a gang that knew no law. That could only mean a stand-up fight in the old style. No doubt Haraldsen would have his own people, but the Norlanders were not a warlike folk, and, though we would have numbers on our side, I wasn't prepared to be cocksure about the result. If we beat them off, it might put the wind up Troth and Barralty for good and all, but it would have no effect on D'Ingraville. Not unless we killed him. If, on the other hand, we were beaten, God knows what would happen to Haraldsen and his daughter – and to the rest of us, and especially to Sandy. There could be no end to the business unless either D'Ingraville or Sandy perished. It looked like one of those crazy duels that the old North-men used to fight, and I remembered that they always chose an island for the purpose. The more I considered the business, the more crazy and melodramatic I thought it. Two sober citizens, Lombard and myself, were being dragged at the chariot wheels of two imaginative desperadoes, for Sandy had always a kind of high-strung daftness about him – that was where his genius lay. And it looked as if Haraldsen had reverted to some wild ancestral type.

But most of all I was worried about those we had left behind. Mary I hoped did not realize the full danger, for I had always put the affair to her as a piece of common blackmail. We had gone to settle Haraldsen in his home, and see that he was comfortable, and the worst that could happen would be that we might have to read the Riot Act to some vulgar blackmailers. Sandy must have put it in the same way to Barbara – at least, I fervently hoped so. Neither knew anything about D'Ingraville. But Mary was an acute person who missed very little, and was extraordinarily sensitive to an atmosphere. She was greatly attached to the Haraldsens, and would never have hinted that I should back out of my duty towards them. But I was pretty certain that she understood that that duty was a more solemn thing than the light holiday task I had pretended. She had said noth-ing, and had bidden me good-bye as if we were off to Norway to catch salmon. Yet I had a notion that her calm was an enforced thing, for no woman had ever more self-control, and that her anxiety would never sleep till she saw me again. She would remember that August morning at Machray when I had gone out for an ordinary day's stalking, and had been found by her twenty hours later sense-less on the top of a crag with Medina dead at the bottom.

With these thoughts in my head I got no good of the bright after-noon, as we skirted the northern butt of the Orkneys and approached the Roost through which our course lay. Suddenly I noticed that the ship was slowing down. The captain, a placid old Dane with whom I had made friends, joined me.

'We take another passenger, General,' he said. 'One who was too late for us at Leith. We were advised of him by wireless. He will have to pay the whole fare between Leith and Reykjavik, or there will be trouble with your British port authorities.'

I followed his eyes and saw approaching us from the land a small motor-boat, with a single figure in the stern.

'It is a man,' he said, handing me the glasses. 'Some Icelander who has tarried too long in Scotland, or some Scot who would come in for the last of the Iceland salmon.'

There seemed something familiar about the shape of the passenger, but I went below to fetch my tobacco pouch, and I did not see the motor-boat arrive. What was my amazement, when I came on deck again, to find Peter John! He was wearing one of my ulsters, and had his kit in a hold-all. Also, he had Morag the falcon on his wrist. There he stood, looking timid and sheepish like a very little boy. He said nothing, but held out a letter.

It was from Mary. She said simply that she couldn't bear the sight of her son's tragic face. 'He has been wandering about like a lost dog,' she wrote. 'I think some sea air would be good for him, for he has been rather limp in the heat lately. And if there is any trouble he might be useful, for he is pretty sensible. He has promised me to keep an eye on you, and I shall be happier in my mind if I know he is with you. Cable from Hjalmarshavn, please, to say he has arrived.'

That was all. Peter John stood very stiff, as if he expected a scolding, but I wasn't inclined to scold. It was a joy to have him with me, and that Mary should send him after me convinced me that she was not really anxious – though I doubt if that conclusion did justice to her stoicism. Then a thought struck me. The boy knew how dangerous our mission was, for he had heard Sandy expound it.

'Did you tell your mother that there was some risk in this business?' I asked.

'Yes. I thought that was only fair.'

'What did she say? '

'She said that she knew it already, and that she would feel easier if I were with you to take care of you.'

That was Mary all over. Another woman would have clutched at her boy to keep at least one of her belongings out of danger. Mary, knowing that a job had to be done, was ready to stake everything to have it well done.

Peter John's solemn face relaxed into a smile when he saw the change in mine.

'How did you get here?' I asked.

'I flew,' was the reply. 'I flew to Inverness and then to Kirkwall. The only difficult things were the motor-boat and the wireless message.'

At that I laughed.

'I don't know that you can take care of me. But there's no doubt you can take care of yourself.'

We came to the little port of Hjalmarshavn, the capital of the
Norlands, in the same bright, west-wind weather. The green hills
behind the black sea-cliffs, the blue tides creaming white on the little
skerries, the wall of dimmer peaks to the north, all seemed to sleep
in a peace like that of the Blessed Isles in the story. In Hjalmarshavn
there was a gentle bustle, and about a thousand varieties of stinks,
from rotting seaweed to decaying whale. The houses were painted in
a dozen colours, and the little bay was full of many kinds of small
craft – fishing smacks, whale boats, kayaks, and primitive motor-
launches. The only big craft were the Grimsby trawlers, and a
steamer flying the red and white Danish flag which had just come in
from Iceland. Ours was the first passenger ship for a fortnight that
had arrived from the south, so the other lot had not preceded us. I
made inquiries and heard that the Aberdeen trawler had arrived
three days before, and that Haraldsen had at once gone on to his
island.

We hired a motor-boat, and that afternoon rounded the south end
of the main island, skirted its west side, and threaded our way
through an archipelago of skerries till we were abreast of Halder, the
second biggest of the group. Its shore was marvellously corrugated,
deep-cut glens running down from peaks about 3,000 feet in height
and the said peaks sometimes ending in mighty precipices and sometimes falling away into moorish levels and broad shingly beaches.
Presently on our port appeared a low coast-line, which from the map
I saw was the Island of Sheep. It was separated from Halder by a
channel perhaps two miles wide, but its character was wholly different from its neighbour. It reminded me of Colonsay, a low, green
place cradled deep in the sea, where one would live as in a ship with
the sound of waves always in one's ear.

Then I saw the House, built on high land above a little voe, half
castle, half lighthouse it seemed, belonging both to land and water.
There are no trees in the Norlands, but even from a distance I could
see that some kind of demesne had been laid out, with stone terraces
ending in little thatched pavilions. Below it, close to the shore, nes-
tled a colony of small dwellings. What caught the eye was the amazing greenness. After the greys and browns of the Shetlands the place
seemed to be as vividly green as an English meadow in May. The
lower part of the House was rough stone, the upper part of a dark
timber, but the roof was bright green turf, growing as lustily as in a
field. When in the early twilight we put in to the little jetty, I seemed
to be looking at a port outside the habitable world in some forgotten
domain of peace.

As long as I live I shall remember my first step on land – the whiff of drying stockfish from the shore, the black basalt rocks, the clumps of broad-leaved arch-angelica, and the oyster-catchers piping along the shingle.

Haraldsen and Anna were awaiting us. Haraldsen was wearing the native Norland dress, coat and breeches of russet home-spun, with silver buttons at collar and knees, homespun stockings and silver-buckled shoes, and a queer conical cap of dark blue and red. He looked half squire and half pirate, but wholly in keeping with his surroundings. Anna had a navy-blue skirt and a red jumper, bare legs, and buckled raw-hide mocassins.

'You have brought the boy,' Haraldsen said after his first words of greeting. His eyes looked troubled.

'His mother sent him after us,' I said. 'He is supposed to take care of me.'

'He is very welcome,' was the answer, but his brow was furrowed. I could see that a second child in the party seemed to him to add heavily to his responsibilities. . . . Little did either of us guess that these two children were to be our salvation.

Very different was Anna's greeting. She seemed to have shed the English schoolgirl, and with that all her tricks of speech and manner which had annoyed my son. Hitherto, as I have said, she had treated him cavalierly, and driven him to a moody silence. Now she was a hostess in her own house, and she had the manner of a princess welcoming a friend to her kingdom. Amazingly handsome she looked, with her brilliant hair and eyes, and her ivory skin coloured by the sea-winds and lit by the sun. She took the boy's hand in both of hers.

'I am very glad to see you, Mr. Peter John,' she said. 'We shall have great fun together.'

I was not prepared for such a palace as the old Haraldsen had built. I had accepted the family fortune as a fact, but had seen no evidence in a hunted man and a rather shabby schoolgirl. Now I realized that there must be great wealth in the background. Above the low cliffs the land had been levelled, and there were wide lawns as fine as England could show, for in that moist climate the turf was perfect. There was some attempt at flowers too, roses and larkspur and simple annuals, but only in sunken hollows to avoid the winds, which in the Norlands can blow like the wrath of God. The House itself was of three storeys, sheltered on three sides by a half moon of hills, while the bulk of Halder across the channel was there to break the force of the eastern blasts. Following the old Norland fashion, the ground floor was mainly storerooms, as in a Border keep, with the living-rooms above them, and the bedrooms in the top storey. It was all new except at one end, where stood a queer little stone cell or chapel, with walls about five feet thick. This, according to the tale, had been the home of an Irish hermit, who in the dark ages had found a refuge here till the heathen Northmen were the death of him.

The entrance was by a flight of steps which seemed to be hewn out of the living rock. First came a vast hall, at least a hundred feet long and the full height of the house. This had been constructed, I suppose, on the model of a Viking hall, and in it one seemed to cheat the ages. Where the old Haraldsen had got the timbers I do not know, but they were hoar-ancient, and the black-oak panelling was carved in wild grotesques. The furniture was ancient and immense; there was a long dining-table which would have accommodated fifty Vikings, and gigantic chairs which only Falstaff could have decently filled. For decorations there were some wonderful old pieces of tapestry, and a multitude of ship models of every age in silver and ivory and horn and teak, which must have been worth a ransom.

That was the state apartment, and a pretty comfortless one. But on either side of it were other rooms – a big drawing-room, expensively furnished, but as barren of human interest as a museum, and like a museum full of collector's pieces; a smoking-room, on the walls of which hung every kind of Norland implement from the Stone Age downward; a billiard room, with a collection of sporting trophies, including many of the old man's African heads; and above all a library. That library was the pleasantest room in the house, and it was clearly Haraldsen's favourite, for it had the air of a place cherished and lived in. Its builder had chosen to give it a fine plaster ceiling, with heraldic panels between mouldings of Norland symbols. It was lined everywhere with books, books which had the look of being used, and which consequently made that soft tapestry which no collection of august bindings can ever provide. Upstairs the bedrooms were large and airy, with bare oak floors, and not too much furniture, but with all modern comforts.

What struck me especially was that everything was of the best and probably of high value. It seemed queer to be contemplating a siege in a treasure house.

'The treasures were my father's,' said Haraldsen. 'Myself I do not want possessions. Only my books.'

The entertainment was as good as the lodging. There was an old steward called Arn Arnason, who wore the same clothes as his master and looked like Rumpelstiltzkin in the fairy-tale, and he had under him four elderly serving maids. I gathered from Haraldsen that it was his habit to send his motor-boat once a week to Hjalmarshavn for letters and such things as he imported. But the island itself produced most of his supplies. He had his own cows for milk, the mutton was about the best in the world, and he cured his own hams and bacon; he grew all the simpler vegetables, including superb potatoes: the sea yielded the fish he wanted, not to speak of lobsters, and there were sea-trout and brown trout to be had from the lochs. Indeed, I never ate better food in my life – simple food, but perfect basic material perfectly cooked. In two things only it deviated into luxury. There was a wonderful cellar in which the sherry and the madeira in particular were things to dream of, and following the Northern fashion, our meals began with a preposterous variety of *hors d'oeuvre*. Peter John, till he learned better, used to eat of so many small outlandish dishes that he had no room for solid food.

We went early to bed, but before turning in I had one word with Haraldsen about serious business.

'We are well in front,' I said. 'Any news of our friends? '

'None. We have a telephone to Hjalmarshavn, and I have arranged to get word of all strangers who arrive there. But I do not think they will come by Hjalmarshavn.'

'Any news of Lord Clanroyden?'

He shook his head. 'No doubt he will soon telegraph, and we will get the message by telephone. He said he would follow at once.'

I asked one other question, and got an answer which sent me to bed with an uneasy mind. 'What men have you on the island?'

He looked perturbed.

'There is Arn Arnason in the house,' he said. 'There are the three gardeners, Dahl and Holm and Evansen. Down at the harbour there is Jacob Gregarsen, who is in charge of the motor-boat. And there is also Absalon the fowler, who is bed-ridden. All these are old men, I fear.'

'Good God!' I cried. 'I thought you had a lot of hefty youths.'

'It is my blunder,' he said penitently. 'I had forgotten. There were a score of young men on the Island of Sheep, but now they are all abroad. Some have gone to Greenland and Iceland after cod, and some are at the halibut fishing. One, on whom I counted most, sailed last month for America.'

The clear blue weather ended that night. Next morning we were back in the typical Norlands, a south-west wind which brought scuds of rain, and mist over all the hills. Halder, as seen across the Channel, was only a grey wraith. The fashion of the household was for a skimpy *petit déjeuner* and then an elaborate midday meal. Haraldsen had some business of his own, so Lombard, Peter John, and I got into oilskins, and, escorted by Anna, started out to prospect the island.

Its main features were simple, and, since they are important to my story, I must make them clear. The place was about six miles long, and at the greatest two miles wide, and it lay roughly north and south. The House stood about two-thirds of the way up, and the highest ground, only five or six hundred feet in altitude, was just behind it. Towards the north end the land was broken moorland, with two or three small lochs full of trout, and the butt itself was a sheer cliff of at least four hundred feet, over which one of the lochs emptied in a fine waterfall. All that part of the coast was rugged and broken, little gullies descending from the uplands to a boulder-strewn shore.

Below the House, as I have said, was a small voe, with to the south a village close to the water. South of this again were stretches of sand, and, since the coast there ran out to a point, there was good shelter for boats in almost any wind. The southern part of the island was quite different in character. The ground fell to only a few feet above sea-level, and the shore was either sand or sprawling reefs. Inland there was a waste of bent and marsh, with several swampy lochs which looked as if they might furnish difficult fishing. Peter John's eyes brightened as we circumnavigated the place, for it was plainly a paradise for birds. A shout from him called my attention to a pair of purple sandpipers. In the Norlands no shooting is permitted on land, and only for a short season on the sea, so the islands are pretty well a sanctuary. It was absurd to see curlews almost running between our legs like tame pheasants, and so shy a bird as the golden plover coolly regarding us from a rock two yards off. That great bog must have been at least four square miles in extent, and it was alive with every kind of bird. It wasn't easy to get my son away from it.

Towards the south end the land rose slightly to hummocky downs, and the sea began to poke its fingers into it. There must have been a dozen little inlets, and a big voe a quarter of a mile wide into which one of the lochs discharged a stream. Seatrout were jumping merrily at the stream mouth. I wished to Heaven that I had come here for a holiday and not on a grim job, for I never saw a more promising fishing-ground. We walked to the mouth of the voe, where a swell was breaking under the wind, and looked out on low mists and a restless sea.

We had two days of dripping weather, and, since there was nothing I could do, I put in some hard thinking. Our total strength when

Sandy arrived would be four reasonably active men, two children, three or four ancient servitors, and a batch of women. My picture had vanished of a lot of stalwart young Norlanders prepared to fight for their master. That was bad enough, but my real perplexity was what we should be called on to fight about. Sandy had been clear that we must come here to bring things to a head, but I hadn't a notion what that head would be.

I could see perfectly well the old game of Troth and Barralty. It would be easy enough to descend on a lonely island and terrify a nervous recluse into doing their will. It might not have been so difficult to lay their hands on him in England, a stranger in a strange land, and frighten him into compliance. But now he had formidable friends about him, and they knew it. Lombard was a figure in the City, Sandy was a famous man, and I had a reputation of sorts. Haraldsen's enemies were men of a certain position, and one at least was a man of devouring ambition; they couldn't afford to go brazenly outside the law when there were people like Sandy to advertise their trespasses. A raid even on the Island of Sheep would be too clumsy a piece of folly. Besides, it would be futile. Even if they had the bigger man-power, we could summon help. I understood that there were only half a dozen policemen in the Norlands and these not of much account, but a telephone message to Hjalmarshavn would certainly fetch volunteer support, and there was a Danish Government boat cruising somewhere about the fishing-grounds. A wireless message from Hjalmarshavn would bring it to the succour of law and order.

Gradually I argued myself into the conviction that the enemy would not come at all, that, like the wicked, we had fled with no man pursuing, and that the best thing Lombard and I could do was to make a fishing holiday of it. That of course couldn't last for ever. We couldn't roost indefinitely in these outlandish parts, for we had all a good deal to do at home. I decided that I would give the place a fortnight's trial, and then, if nothing happened, we would consider Haraldsen safe and go back to England.

But my decision did not greatly comfort me, for I could not get Sandy's words out of my head. He had been positive that a big climax was impending; and, besides knowing more of our enemies than the rest of us, his instinct wasn't often at fault. And then I remembered the words Macgillivray had spoken in the spring. I remembered the mysterious D'Ingraville, whom I had never seen. He was a different proposition from the others; he had no reputation to lose, no prestige to endanger; he was the outlaw at war with society who would stick at nothing to get his desire. Troth and Barralty were only the jackals that the lion forced to go hunting with him to find him game. Also he had a definite rendezvous with Sandy, and would not fail to keep it. With D'Ingraville in the affair there were no limits. He would bring things to a brute struggle, with death and treasure as the stakes. And we were not only feeble; with two children on our hands we were hopelessly vulnerable. By cunning or by force he would find out our weak points and play ruthlessly to win.

The upshot was that by the second afternoon I was as nervous as a hen; I longed for Sandy to cheer me, but there was no sign or word of him. The thick weather and the leaden prospect, only a rain-drummed sea and the ghost of Halder, and wet bogs and sweating black crags, did not raise my spirits. We could see the Channel fairly plain, and in those two days nothing passed up it except a drifter out of its course, and a little steamer flying the Danish flag which Arnason said was a Government ship sent out for the purpose of marine biology. It hustled north at a great pace, with a bone in its teeth, as seamen say. The fishing fleets were miles to the west, and the Iceland boats took the other side of Halder. I felt that the mist shut us into a dark world far away from the kindly race of men, a world into which at any moment terrible things might irrupt. Though I had Peter John at my side, an impression of deep loneliness settled on me. Also a horrid premonition of coming disaster, which I could not get rid of. A ridiculous sailor's rhyme haunted my memory:

> 'Take care, beware
> The Bight of Benin –
> One comes out
> Though forty go in.'

But the third morning the wind shifted to the east, and we woke to steel-blue skies, Halder clear in every cranny, and calm sunlit seas. The tonic weather reminded me of South Africa, where in the Boer War I used often to go to bed supperless on the wet ground and wake whistling from pure light-heartedness. I simply could not keep up my reasoned gloom, and all the rest of us fell into the same cheerful mood. It was difficult to believe that this fresh shining place could ever harbour evil folk and dark deeds. Also there came a message from Sandy, telephoned on from Hjalmarshavn. It didn't say much – only, 'Delayed, but coming on. Expect me when you see me,' but it seemed to lighten my responsibility. The Hjalmarshavn office didn't give the date and the place from which it was sent, and it was too much to expect from it a written confirmation.

That day, and for the next day, we put care behind us. Haraldsen came out of his silent spell, and played the host manfully. He took us down to the village and showed us the life of the place – the dry-houses for the fish, the queer old women spinning and weaving and making their native dyes of lichen and seaweed, wild geranium and clover. After the whale and the codfish the important animal was the sheep, which gave the island its name, funny little shaggy fellows with wonderful fleeces. 'Sheep's wool is Norland gold,' was a local proverb. It was a strange clachan, full of uncanny stinks, for the winter fodder for the cows was dried whale's flesh, and you could smell it a mile away. I had a great talk with old bed-ridden Absalon, the fowler, who was a 'king's bonder,' a yeoman whose family for generations had had a croft direct from the king. Haraldsen farmed his land for him, since his two sons had both perished at sea. He sat up in a bed made of ship's timbers, and told yarns, which Haraldsen translated, of seal hunts when there were still seals in the Norlands, and great walruses that had drifted down from the Arctic, and whale hunts when the waters of the voes were red with blood. His crooked old hands clawed at the blankets, and his voice was as wild as a solan's, but he had the benign face of an apostle.

I came out of his house a happier man, and my cheerfulness was increased by the sight of the Danish marine biology boat putting into the bay in Halder across the Channel. Gregarsen, the man in charge of our motor-boat, told me that her name was the *Tjaldar*, and that she had been trawling off the northern capes. 'This wind will last,' he said, 'for her men are cunning, and only choose that anchorage when it blows steady from the east.' Somehow I felt that the trim little ship kept us in touch with civilized things.

Haraldsen, as I have said, was a good host these days, but he was a queer one. At Laverlaw, when he had got over his nervous trouble, he was very like an ordinary Englishman, apart from a slight foreign trace in his speech. But on his native heath he was a Norlander, steeped in island lore, rejoicing in his home with the passion of a returned exile. He, who had been sparing of words, was now almost garrulous, as if he wanted to explain himself to us and let us into the secrets of his life. He used to recount the folk-tales as if he believed in them – how the seals were the souls of Pharaoh's soldiers who had been drowned in the Red Sea, and the wren who picked at the seams of the houses was the mouse's brother changed into a bird by the Trolls' enchantment. The Trolls by his way of it were the chief plague of the Norlands – with pixies and mermaids as runners-up. They were Hulda's Folk – Hulda being a sort of she-devil – and they were always on the watch to do mankind a mischief. They ship-wrecked boats, and hag-rode the cattle, and sucked the blood of young lambs, and even kidnapped little girls – and here his eye would turn anxiously to Anna.

Then he was full of the islands' history, from the famous old saga of Trond of Gate, which is the Norland epic, to the later days when Algerian pirates raided the coast and sent the people into the hills and the sea-caves. By and by I saw the meaning of his talk. He was reminding himself – and us – that in the Norlands life had always been on a razor's edge, and that what he had to expect in the near future was what all his kin had had to face in the past. Clearly it was a comfort to him that he was following a long tradition. He had none of my scepticism; he believed that Fate was waiting for us as certainly as that the sun would rise to-morrow.

He was unlike what be had been at Laverlaw in another sense, for his nerves were all tuned up again, but in a different way. He had become high-coloured in his talk, exalted, rhetorical, speaking often like somebody in a book, as if the words were not his own. There were times when he seemed almost 'fey,' his eye wild, his voice harsh and shrill, and his language like an Israelitish prophet. That was gen-erally when he was telling us some legend, into which he flung him-self as if it had been his own experience. One strange thing I noticed – he was always talking about fire, as if fire were the Norland weird. In that damp, salty place fire scarcely seemed the perilous element; one would have thought wind and wave the real enemies. But it was always through fire that his house marched to triumph, and by fire that the luckless ones perished. It was fire that Hulda's Folk employed to work their most evil deeds. It was fire that somehow at the back of his head he dreaded for himself and his belongings. 'Then fire came,' he would say, as if it was the natural conclusion to all things.

The happy people were Anna and Peter John. The old stiffness between the two had gone, and they had become like brother and sister. She was the mistress of the island, and she had a guest who was worthy of its treasures, for the boy had a whole new world to explore and was wildly excited. A good deal of the place was like Scotland, except that the heather was poor. There were pastures beside the burns, as bright with flowers as any English meadow. I never saw a better bloom of mint and meadow-sweet, ragged robin and cranesbill; flag-irises and a kind of marsh-marigold were every-where, and the drier slopes were gay with ragwort. The hay was mostly tall clover. On the hills the tormentil grew as I have never seen it grow elsewhere, and the old women used to pound its roots in querns as a substitute for hops. The birds were mostly familiar, but the quantity of them was unbelievable – guillemots and razor-bills, puffins as tame as sparrows, and gannets from a colony on the western cliffs. That was on the water, and on the land there was every moor bird known to Peter John except the grouse. There were no hawks, except one Iceland falcon which we got a fleeting glimpse of in the Channel. Peter flew Morag a good deal, and she brought in snipe and curlews for the pot; and she was nearly the end of one of the funny little blue Iceland cats at a cottage door.

I think that I have mentioned that my son was no horseman, but under Anna's coercion he got himself on one of the Norland ponies, and they quartered the island together. But the real passion of both was the sea, a novelty to Peter, who was inland bred. In the soft, bright weather they were hours in or on the water. Peter was a fair swimmer, but Anna was magnificent – old Arnason had a joke that she was web-footed, being descended from seals, which she refuted by displaying her shapely feet.

There was no great variety of craft to play about in – only the motor-boat which Jacob Gregarsen looked after, and which was never used except for an emergency trip to Hjalmarshavn for supplies and once a week to fetch the mail; and one or two ancient Norland boats, double-ended things with high sterns and stern posts, about twenty feet long and very broad in the beam. But there were a couple of kayaks in the houses, the Eskimo kind like a Rob Roy canoe, and these were taken down to the water and launched, and provided the children with their chief amusement. Anna could handle hers brilliantly, and make it turn over like a turtle and right itself, and Peter John was an apt pupil. The two of them racing about in the voe and adventuring out into the Channel were like nothing so much as a pair of diving ducks. The trouble was to get them home for meals, for those long-lighted days were deceptive, and, since neither had a watch, they would wander in about mid-night, thinking they were in time for dinner. Anna's great hope was for a shoal of whales to come in and the whole Norlands to assemble for a whale hunt. She had only seen one in her life, but the memory of it was vivid. The whale was the small pilot-whale – what they call the 'ca'in whale' in Scotland – and I heard her discoursing to Peter John of the wild excitement of the chase, and its manifold perils. She spoke like a bloodthirsty young Viking, and was deter-mined that they should join the hunt in their kayaks and be in at the death. I was determined in my own mind that there should be no such escapade.

Anna was wholly care-free, for Haraldsen had not told her the reason of his return to his island, and Peter John was under bond not to enlighten her. He, of course, knew the whole story, and since he was always on the move, I warned him to keep his eyes open for anything that seemed suspicious. He always carried his field glasses, and I was confident that nothing was likely to come to the island without his spotting it. It was well to have such a scout, for the place, except for the House and the village, was at the moment wholly unpeopled. He saw that I was anxious, and he did his best to live up to my instructions. The first day of the fine weather he had nothing to report. The second day he announced that in a voe on the other side of the island he had discovered signs of a visit from some petrol-driven craft. When I told Haraldsen this he paid no attention. 'Some trawler put in for water,' he said; 'many of them carry boats with out-board motors.'

But on the third day the boy came to me with a grave face.

'Gregarsen says that the motor-boat is out of order. Something has gone wrong with the engine – something bad – and he'll have to get a man from Hjalmarshavn to repair it.'

'How on earth did that happen?' I asked crossly, for the motor-boat was our only transport to the outer world. 'He has not had it out.'

'It happened in the night, he thinks. He says some fools have been monkeying with it.'

I went down to the harbour and had a look at it. Sure enough there was bad mischief. The sparking-plug had gone, and the main feed pipe had been cut through. Gregarsen was a stupid elderly fellow, with a game leg which he had got at the Greenland fishing, and he had only an elementary knowledge of mechanics.

'How did this happen?' I demanded, for he could speak a kind of American-English, having once been a hand on a Boston tramp. 'Have you been walking in your sleep?'

He shook his head. 'Hulda's Folk,' he said darkly.

The thing made me very uneasy, for the damage had been done by some one who had had tools for the purpose. There was nothing for it but to telephone to the little shipyard at Hjalmarshavn and get them to send up a man. I did not do this at once, for I was trysted with Haraldsen to walk to the north end of the island, and put it off till we returned to luncheon.

I did not enjoy that walk, for I kept puzzling over the motor-boat, and I could not shake off the feeling that something was beginning to flaw the peace of the island. The accident was utterly incomprehensible to me, except on the supposition that Gregarsen had been drunk, or had gone temporarily insane and had forgotten what he had done. It was a nuisance, for next day we should have been sending to Hjalmarshavn for letters, and I longed for some word from Sandy. I felt myself set down on a possible battlefield with no sign of the commander-in-chief. Haraldsen's conversation did not cheer me. He was as mysterious as a spae-wife, and his only answer to my complaint was, 'What must be, will be.' Also the weather suddenly began to change. By midday the blue of the sky had dulled, and the heavens seemed suddenly to drop lower. The clear outlines of the Halder hills had gone, and the Channel, instead of a shining crystal, became an opaque pebble. 'Ran is stoking his ovens,' was all Haraldsen said on the subject, and it did not comfort me to know that Ran was a sea-god.

Immediately after luncheon I rang up Hjalmarshavn, but could not get through. There was nothing wrong with the apparatus in the House, and the trouble was probably at the other end, but the motor-boat business had filled me with suspicions, and I set out alone in the afternoon to trace the telephone line. It ran on low posts by the back of the garden and then down a shallow cleft to the beach not a quarter of a mile south of the village. It was clearly all right as far as the water's edge. But then I had a shock. It entered the sea in a copper casing from a little concrete platform. There seemed something odd about the look of that take-off, and I ran my hand down the cable. I lifted up an end which had been neatly cut through.

That put the lid on my discomfort. The fog was thickening. While walking with Haraldsen I had been able to see the other side of the Channel and witness the *Tjaldar*, returning from one of her dredging expeditions, settling snugly into her little harbour. But now Halder was blotted out, and I could only see a few hundred yards of sea. I felt as if we were being shut into a *macabre* world where anything might happen. We and our enemies, for that our enemies were near I had no manner of doubt. They had cut our communications and had us at their mercy – three men, two children, and a batch of ancients. Where they were, how they had got here, I never troubled to think. I felt them in the fog around me – Hulda's Folk, who had their own ways of moving by land and sea.

I ran back to the House in what was pretty near a panic. Lombard and Haraldsen had gone for a walk, and to give myself something to do I overhauled our armoury. We had half a dozen rifles, four shot-guns, and plenty of ammunition. There was a revolver for each of us, and a spare one which I had destined for Peter John.

At the thought of him all my anxiety was switched on to the chil-dren. If there were evil things afoot in the island they might be at their mercy. Haraldsen and Lombard returned for tea, but not Anna and Peter John. When he heard my story Haraldsen came out of his Nordic dreams and became the distracted parent. The fog had drawn closer, and our search could only be blind, but we got together the garden staff and Gregarsen, and set out in different directions.

The dinner-hour came and there was no sign of them. In the dim, misty brume which was all the northern night, we stumbled about the island. Midnight came and we were still searching. In the small hours of the morning they had not returned.

CHAPTER XIII

Marine Biology

THAT MORNING ANNA AND PETER JOHN had gone off for the day, with sandwiches in their pockets, to explore in kayaks the voes at the south end of the island. They ate their luncheon on a skerry which the tide had just uncovered, and which was their idiotic notion of comfort. The sea was like a pond, and the mist was slowly coming down, but Anna, after sniffing the air, said that it was only a summer darkening and would clear before evening. Then she proposed an adventure. The *Tjaldar* had returned to its home at Halder, and over the Channel came the sound of its dropping anchor.

'Let's pay a call on it,' said Anna. 'Perhaps they'll ask us to tea. Marine biologists are nice people. I've been to tea with them before, when the old *Moe* was here.'

Peter John demurred. No embargo had been laid on their crossing the Channel, but he dimly felt that the trip would be considered out of bounds.

'That doesn't matter,' Anna retorted. 'We haven't been forbidden to go. Besides, in this weather they won't see us from the shore. We'll be back long before dinner. There's not a capful of wind, and it's as safe as crossing a voe. We're not likely to get such a chance again.'

Peter John said something about currents, but Anna laughed him to scorn. 'There's a rip two miles north, but here there's nothing to trouble about. I've been across in the kayak often. You're a land-lubber, you know, and I'm a seadog, and you ought to believe me. I believe you when it's about birds.'

Peter John felt this to be true. Children have a great respect for each other's *expertise*, and Anna had shown an uncanny knowledge of the ways of boats and tides and the whole salt-water world. She bore down his scruples with another argument. 'My father would send us across any time we wanted, but it would be with Gregarsen and the motor-boat, which wouldn't be any fun, or in the long-boat, which is as slow as a cow. In these wieldy little kayaks we'll slip over in no time. If you like, I'll give you five minutes' start and race you.'

No boy can resist a 'dare,' so Peter John acquiesced, and they got into their kayaks and headed for Halder, Morag the falcon sitting dejectedly on her master's knee.

The mist came down closer, but it was only a curtain of silk, through which Halder rose like a wraith. They did not race, but presently fell into an exciting conversation, so that the kayaks often rubbed shoulders. For Anna was telling of the whale-hunts, which she had held forth to Peter John as the chief glory of the Norlands. Only once in her memory had the *Grind* come to the Island of Sheep, for generally they took the wider channels beyond Halder. But that once was stamped for ever on her mind, though she had only been a little girl at the time. She told how the fiery cross was sent through the islands, by means of beacons on every headland; how every man at the signal tumbled into his boat and steered for the rendezvous; how the rendezvous could not be missed, for all the sea-ways were full of people, and the *Grind* only came in clear weather. She described how the boats guided the school of whales, as dogs headed sheep, trimming their edges and slowly forcing the leader into one of the voes. Once the leader entered the rest followed, and the voe would be churned white with blind and maddened monsters. Then came the killing, which Anna could only imagine, for her nurse had hurried her away from the scene; but all the same she described it as she had heard of it from others, and she made a barbaric tale of it. Peter John listened with interest, and at the end with disapproval.

'It sounds pretty beastly,' he said.

'Perhaps it is,' said the girl; 'but a lot of good things are beastly, like killing pigs and using live bait. Anyhow, it puts money in the pockets of our poor people, and gives them food and lighting for the long winter.'

'All the same, I'm sorry for the whales.'

'That's silly,' she replied. 'You're not sorry for haddocks and halibut and sea-trout. Fish are cold-blooded things and don't feel.'

'Whales aren't fish,' said the student of natural history, but he was overborne.

Their discussion had brought them across the still water into the shadow of Halder, and they looked up to see the *Tjaldar* above them. The kayak is a noiseless thing, and the fog had helped them to approach it unperceived. It sat at anchor very trim and comfortable, with a thin spire of smoke rising from the galley funnel, and a pleasant odour of food drifting from it. Some one was emptying ashes from the stokehold.

'Couth little craft,' said Anna appreciatively. 'I smell tea. Let's hail her. *Tjaldar* ahoy!'

The voice brought a face to the bulwark. It was the face of an elderly man, dark and aquiline and rather puffy. He wore a yachting-cap and a flannel suit, but he did not look any kind of sailor. He seemed puzzled and a little startled.

'That will be one of the Danish scientists,' Anna whispered. Then she raised her voice.

'You're the marine biologists, aren't you? We've come to call on you from the Island of Sheep across the Channel.'

She spoke in Danish, but the face showed no intelligence. Then she repeated her words in English, and the man seemed to understand.

'Wait. I will ask,' he said, and disappeared.

He was back in a minute accompanied by another man, a tall fellow with a sunburnt face, wearing an old Harris tweed jacket, and with a pipe in his teeth.

'Where did you youngsters spring from?' the second man asked.

'I'm Miss Haraldsen from the Island of Sheep – and this is my friend, Peter John. We're visitors. May we come aboard? '

'You certainly may,' said the man with the pipe, and he seemed to wink at his companion. The port ladder was lowered and the children tied up the kayaks to its bottom rung, and carefully transhipped themselves. It takes some skill to get out of a kayak.

When they reached the much-encumbered deck they found that three sailors had joined the party.

'Just wait here a second, my dears,' said the man with the pipe, and he and the others went forward, leaving Anna and Peter John with the three sailors. The boy saw nothing but a rather untidy deck, very different from the shipshape vessels of his fancy. There seemed to be uncommonly little free space, and what looked like a gigantic net was clumsily heaped abaft of a stumpy mast. The deck-hands were busy at the vessel's side. But the girl's experienced eyes darted about, and saw more.

'This is a funny place,' she whispered. 'I don't much like it, Peter John. These men aren't a trawler's crew – they've no sores on their hands. Trawlers' men are always getting stung and poisoned. They aren't Danes either – at least, they don't look like it. What are they doing with our kayaks? '

'They're getting them aboard.'

'Whatever for?' The girl's voice had suddenly a startled note in it. 'Look here, I don't like this. . . . Just look at the trawl. It's absurd. It has no otter-boards. . . . There's something wrong with this ship. Let's make them launch the kayaks again and get off.'

'We can't quite do that,' said Peter John. 'I think we must see it through now – wait, anyhow, till these men come back.' But Anna's suspicions had infected him, and he looked uneasily at the little kayaks as they were swung up on deck.

He turned in obedience to a smothered squawk from Anna. A woman was coming towards them – a woman in a white serge frock with a fur cape thrown over her shoulders. She was bare-headed and had wonderful red hair. It was now Peter John's turn to long for the kayaks, for he recognized some one he had seen before, the beautiful Miss Ludlow who, two months ago, had come to tea at Fosse.

The pretty lady advanced smiling. At the sight of her Morag the falcon showed the most lively displeasure. Had Peter John not tightened the lead she would have sought a perch with malevolent purpose on an exquisite red coiffure.

'What a wicked bird!' said the lady. 'You're sure you've got it safe. . . . How nice of you to come to see us! You must be ravenous for tea. Come along, my dears, but I think you'd better leave the bird here.'

So Morag's lead was fastened to a stanchion, and she was left in a very ill temper ruffling her wings on a spare yard. The children followed the lady to a deck-house, which was half chart-room and half cabin. It was a snug little place, and on an oilskin-covered table tea was set out, an ample meal for which their souls hungered. There were three men sitting there, the dark, sallow one to whom they had first spoken, the sunburnt one with the pipe, and another, a tall, slim man with a thin face, high cheek-bones and a moustache which was going grey at the tips. All three rose politely at their entrance and bowed to Anna.

'Here are our visitors,' said the lady; 'and I'm sure they are hungry. They have come over from the Island. The fog is getting thicker, and I don't think we can let them go till it clears. What do you think, Joe?'

'It wouldn't be safe,' said the tall man. 'We must wait anyhow till the Skipper returns. The dory should be back in an hour or so.'

A steward brought in hot water and a big plate of toasted scones. The lady made tea, and much conversation. The sallow man she called Erick, and the sunburnt man Lancie, but most of her remarks were addressed to the tall man called Joe. She prattled of the weather and the Norlands, of London, of Cowes, of ships, and the sea. It was very clear that this company was English, and had nothing to do with marine biology, and Anna's eyes showed her bewilderment.

When the tall man spoke it was to ask questions about the Island of Sheep. His manners were good, and he showed no intrusive curiosity, but it was plain from the others' faces that this was a topic that interested them. They talked much as a yacht's party might have talked who had come into strange latitudes and had suddenly got news of other fellow-countrymen.

'Your father is at home?' the man called Lancie asked. 'He has a wonderful place over there, hasn't he? We heard about it at Hjalmarshavn. Are you two brother and sister? '

'We're no relations. This is my friend, Peter John Hannay. He is English. He is staying with us.'

Four pairs of eyes seemed to open wider.

'Are you by any chance Sir Richard Hannay's son?' the man called Joe asked, with a sudden eagerness in his voice.

Peter John nodded. 'Yes, and Sir Richard is staying with us,' added Anna.

'We must return your call,' said the lady. 'I've always longed to meet Sir Richard – and your father too, my dear.'

Peter John's mind had been working furiously, ever since the sight of Miss Ludlow had opened for him the door on a dark world. Anna was bewildered, but only because the *Tjaldar* was so different from the old *Moe*, and she had had to revise her marine biology notions, but the boy knew enough to realize that they had blundered into the enemy's camp. He had heard Sandy's talk, and I had told him the whole story, and ever since his coming to the Island of Sheep his business had been to be on the watch. Behind all his escapades with Anna had been this serious preoccupation. The sight of Lydia Ludlow had awakened him, and now in this little cabin he was face to face with Haraldsen's enemies, the sallow Albinus, the stalwart Troth, the lean, restless Barralty. Only one was missing, the most formidable of them all. At any cost he and Anna must get off and carry the fateful news.

'We should be going,' he said as he got up, 'or our people will be anxious.'

'You can't go in this weather,' said Barralty. He too rose and opened the door, and sure enough a solid wall of vapour had built itself beyond the vessel's side.

'I've got a compass,' said Peter John, 'and we can't miss the way.'

'We daren't risk it,' said the man. 'We should never be able to face your father if anything went wrong.'

'They must wait till the Skipper comes back,' said Troth, and the others agreed.

Peter John was getting desperate. 'We're rather grubby,' he said. 'Could we wash our hands?'

'Certainly,' said the lady. 'Come down to my cabin, both of you.' She seemed to Peter John to look meaningly at the others and slightly nod her head. She took Anna's hand and led her out, and the boy followed. He lingered a little beyond the door, and he heard, or thought he heard, some one of the three exclaim: 'My God, we have got the trump card now. This will keep the Skipper in order.'

Miss Ludlow took them down a steep companion into a narrow alley lined with cabins. The big one at the end was hers, and she ushered the children into it with the utmost friendliness. 'You'll find everything you want there, my dears,' she said. 'Towels and hot water. The bathroom is next door. I'll come down presently to fetch you.'

But as she left them she drew behind her a sliding door at the end of the passage. Peter John darted after her and tried its handle. It was locked from the outside.

Anna proceeded to scrub her hands and use a pocket comb to tidy up her hair. 'This is a queer ship,' she said, 'and queer people. But they're kind, I think. They're ordinary yachting folk, but the *Tjaldar* isn't much of a yacht. Too much of a grubby trawler for their nice clothes.'

Peter John was looking out of the port-hole into the wall of fog.

'They aren't kind,' he said. 'They're our enemies – your father's and my father's. They're the people who tried to catch you at school. They're the people we were always on the look-out for at Laverlaw. I must tell you all I know, for we're in an awful hole.'

There and then in that dim cabin he told her the story as he knew it, told her many things which Haraldsen had jealously kept hidden from her, and gave point and shape to suspicions which had long lain at the back of her head. He may have told the story crudely, with a boy's instinct for drama, but Peter John was also a realist who made no mistake about the fundamentals. She sat quiet as a mouse, but at the end she gave a low cry.

'They're going to attack our island? And we've let ourselves be made prisoners? Oh, Peter John, it is all my fault! I dragged you on this silly expedition.'

'It is my fault, for I should have remembered. You see, I knew and you didn't.'

Two miserable children clung to each other, while the fog thickened without and the cabin darkened.

Meantime, in the deck-house they had left, there was a feverish council. From what I learned later I can reconstruct the scene as if I had been listening outside the door. In an hour's time the man called the Skipper would arrive, and three men and one woman had much to talk of before then. I can picture their rapid, confused speech, their alternations of eagerness and diffidence, their sudden confidence dashed by sudden fears. Always in the background there must have been this shadow of fear. For the absent Skipper had become to them no longer a colleague but a master. They were people whose plans lay well inside the pale of what we call civilization. They had reputations to lose, ambitions which demanded some respect for the conventions, comfortable lives which they were not inclined to sacrifice. But they had become yoked to one who cared for none of these things, a man from the outlands who had long ago discarded their world. They were like schoolboys playing at pirates who had suddenly found themselves enrolled under the authentic Blackbeard. Barralty, I fancy, was the worst scared. Albinus was the common rogue who had already known the shady side of the law. Troth was a robust fellow, a sportsman accustomed to risks who would not be greatly rattled till he knew the full extent of the trouble. But Barralty was the brittle intellectual, who found himself in a world where his old skill went for nothing, and with him was the woman who had worked with him, and who now saw all their careful schemes on the edge of a fulfilment more disastrous than failure.

Troth must have spoken first, for he had the coolest head.

'Things are brightening,' he said. 'This is a piece of luck for us, for we've got our hostages. Now we can deal.'

'You think so?' said Barralty, in a voice which he tried to keep calm.

'Well, we've got the girl, and she's what Haraldsen cares most for in the world. And we've got the boy, who's the apple of Hannay's eye. There's only Lombard left, and he doesn't count for much. There's no word of Clanroyden.'

'What has happened to Clanroyden? '

'God knows! Run out, perhaps. . . . No, he's not that kind of fellow. The Skipper must have put a spoke in his wheel, for he's devil enough for anything.'

' Have you got a line on the Skipper's plan? '

'Plain enough. Old-fashioned piracy. He'll descend on the Island like a marauding Viking and hold 'em up. If they show fight, as they're likely to, he'll kill. He'll get what he wants and he don't care a damn for bloodshed. When he has got it he'll disappear, he and his gang, into the outer darkness, as he has done before. I daresay he'll play fair with us – I don't know – but we'll have to disappear with him. Do any of you fancy spending the rest of your lives being hunted up and down the globe, even if your pockets are full? D'Ingraville won't mind it, for it's his profession, but what about you, Barralty? What about you, with your big ideas about public life? What about you, Lydia? You like your little comforts. What about you, Erick? No more race-meetings for you, my lad, and flutters at Monte? '

'My God!' Barralty groaned. 'Can't we bring the man to reason?'

'We can't, for all the reason, as he sees it, is on his side. He knows what he wants a little more clearly than we ever have, and he has the power behind him. We're only passengers – he's the fighting force. What can we do to stop him? He has his two infernal trusties from South America, Carreras and Martel – the very sight of them gives me the creeps. He has his crew of gunmen. He's going to implicate us all in his gangster business, so that we'll all hang together.'

'But he can't compel us if we object,' Albinus groaned.

'Can't he? I haven't got him fully taped, but he's the biggest size in desperado I've ever struck. I know what's in your mind, Erick. You think that we might make terms on our own account with the people on the Island. I've had the same idea myself, but I tell you it won't do. The Skipper knows that game too well. If we try to double-cross him he'll shoot.'

I can picture those four scared conspirators sitting for a moment dismally silent, till Troth's vigour woke them.

'But now things look better,' he said. 'We have got the materials for a civilized deal. Thank heaven for these blessed children! I don't much like using kids in this business – if you remember, I always stuck out against it before – but needs must when the devil drives. The Skipper can't be fool enough to neglect such a chance. It gives us a sitter, when the other way is an ugly gamble.'

'But do we want the same things?' Barralty asked. 'We want a good deal, but the Skipper may want everything. And remember that Haraldsen isn't alone. He has Hannay with him, and Hannay by all accounts is a tough customer.'

'That will be the moment for the double-crossing if the Skipper plays the fool,' said Troth grimly. 'Once we get to bargaining we put the lid on his bloody piracy, and that's what we most want.'

Then the Skipper arrived.

I picture his coming into the stuffy cabin, his face shining with fog crystals, and his pale eyes dazed by the sudden light.

'An hour till dinner,' he said, with a glance at the chronometer. 'There's time for a hot rum-and-milk, for it has been perishingly cold in the dory. But I've done my job. The reconnaissance is complete, gentlemen. To-morrow is The Day.'

Troth told him about Anna and Peter John. He listened with head lifted, rather like a stag at gaze, a smile wrinkling his lean cheeks.

'Fortune is kind to us,' he said. 'Now we can add point to our first cartel. For one kind of possession we can offer another – and a dearer.'

But there was that in his voice which made Barralty look up anxiously.

'Surely that alters our whole plan,' he said. 'Now we can treat, where before we could only coerce.'

'I do not think so, my friend.' D'Ingraville spoke lightly, as if the matter were not of great importance. 'They will not treat – not on our terms. You want much, no doubt, but I want all, you see, and men will fight for their all.'

'But – but –' Barralty stammered. 'Haraldsen cares for his daughter above everything, and Hannay for his son.'

'Maybe,' was the answer. 'But Haraldsen and Hannay are not all.'

'Lombard does not count.'

'I do not think of Lombard. I think of Lord Clanroyden.'

'But Clanroyden isn't there.'

'Not yet. But he will be there to-morrow.'

'How do you know? Have you any news?'

'I have no news. I have heard nothing of Clanroyden since we left London. But I know that he will be there, for I have an assignation with him, and he will not fail me. And Clanroyden will never yield.'

'But what do you mean to do, man?' Troth asked.

'I mean to follow the old way, the way of my Norman kinsfolk. Fate has been marvellously good to us. There is no man on the Island except those three – to-morrow they will be four – only dotards and old women. The telephone is cut and they have no boat. The fog will lift, I think, by the morning, but the Island will be in a deeper fog which cuts it off from the world. We shall have peace and leisure to do our will. If they listen to us, so much the pleasanter for everybody. If they fight we shall fight too, and beyond doubt we shall win.'

'Win!' Barralty muttered. 'What do you mean by win?'

'Everything,' was the answer. 'I shall get my will, though I leave a house in ashes and an island of dead men.'

'And then?' It was Lydia's strained voice that spoke.

'Then we disappear, leaving a riddle in the Norlands which no man will ever expound. Trust me, I have made my plans – for you, my friends, and for you, my fair lady. You may have to face some little adjustments in your lives, but what of that? *Le mouvement c'est la vie.*'

He lifted his glass and looked towards Lydia, drinking the last mouthful as if it were a toast.

'And now,' he said, 'let me have a look at our hostages. Martel,' he cried to some one outside the door, 'fetch the babes.'

Peter John takes up the tale again. . . . The children had sat in a stupor of misery and fright, unable to think, deaf to all sounds except the thumping of their hearts. 'We must get away,' the boy had repeated at intervals, and the girl had replied, 'We must,'; but the words were only a kind of groan, so destitute were they of any hope. What Anna thought I do not know, but Peter John's mind was fuller of mortification than of fear. He had failed in his trust, and by his folly had given the enemy a crushing vantage.

They lost count of time, and it may have been an hour or two hours before the sliding panel in the alley opened and a face showed in the cabin door. A hand switched on the light. They saw a man slightly over the middle height, wearing sea-boots and a seaman's jersey – a man who did not look like a sailor, for he had a thin, shaven, pallid face, a scar on his forehead, and eyebrows that made a curious arch over weak, blinking eyes. When he spoke it was with a foreign accent in a hoarse, soft voice. 'You will come with me, please,' he said. 'M. le Capitaine would speak with you.'

The sight of the man sent a spasm of sharp fear through Peter John's dull misery. For he knew him – knew him at least by hearsay. Sandy at Laverlaw had taken some pains to describe to us the two members of the old Bodyguard of Olifa whom D'Ingraville had with him. This was the Belgian Martel – there could be no mistake about the scar and the horseshoe brows. At the door of the deck-house stood another man, a tall stooping fellow whose hatchet face and black beady eyes were plain in the glow from the cabin. This was beyond doubt the Spaniard Carreras. The wolf pack was complete.

'Don't answer anything,' the boy whispered to Anna. A stubborn silence was the one course left to them.

But there was no inquisition. Peter John had the impression of a company mighty ill at ease. The smooth geniality of tea-time had gone, and the four who had then entertained them seemed to have lost interest in their visitors and to be much concerned with their own thoughts. The pretty lady had become haggard and rather old, while Troth had lost his robustness and sucked his pipe nervously. Barralty had become a wisp of a man, and Albinus a furtive shadow. Only the newcomer radiated confidence and vitality. For a moment Peter John forgot his fear, and looked curiously at the tall man whom at Fosse he had assisted to put into the stream. He was so taut and straight that he had the look of an unsheathed sword. His pale eyes glittered like ice, and his smile had as much warmth in it as an Arctic sun. Magnificent, wonderful, terrible, inhuman, like some devastating force of nature. Yet, strangely enough, the boy feared the reality less than the picture he had made in his head. This was a wild thing, like Morag, and wild things could be tamed, curbed, or destroyed.

The Skipper bowed to Anna and nodded pleasantly to Peter John.

'You must be our guests for the night, I fear,' he said. 'We are not a very commodious ship, so you mustn't mind rather rough beds. You will want to turn in soon. What about supper?'

It was Anna who replied. 'We don't want any supper, thank you. But we'd like to turn in, for we're both very sleepy.'

'Right. Show the young lady and gentleman to their quarters, Martel. Mr. Hannay will berth forward, and Miss Haraldsen can have Miss Ludlow's couch. Good-night and pleasant dreams.'

That was all. The two followed Martel the way they had come, and Anna was left in the big cabin, where a bed had been made up for her on the couch. Martel did the expected thing, for he took the key from the inside of the cabin-door and pocketed it; then he pulled the sliding panel which automatically locked itself. The sight of Anna's desolate face was the last straw to Peter John's burden. He followed Martel on deck, feeling as if the end of all things had come.

Suddenly an angry squawk woke him to life. Morag, hungry and drenched with fog, sat on her perch in a bitter ill-temper.

'May I take my falcon with me?' he begged.

Martel laughed. ' I guess you may if you want company. Your ugly bird will be better below deck.'

Peter John found himself in a little cubby-hole of a cabin under the fore-deck. It was empty except for a hammock slung from the ceiling, and a heap of blankets which some one had tossed on the floor. There was a big port-hole which Martel examined carefully, trying the bolts and hinges. 'Don't go walking in your sleep and drowning yourself, sonny,' was his parting admonition. He did not clamp it down, but left it ajar.

Peter John's first act, when he found himself alone, was to open the port-hole wide. It was on the port side, looking west, and close to where they had embarked on the *Tjaldar* in the afternoon. The fog was thinning, and a full moon made of what remained a half-luminous, golden haze. The boy had a notion of getting out of the port-hole and trying to swim to the Island, but a moment's reflection drove it out of his head. He was not a strong swimmer, and he could never manage two miles in those cold Norland waters.

Then a squeak from Morag gave him another idea. There was no light in the cabin except what came from the moon, but he tore a leaf from a little writing-book which he kept for bird notes and printed on it a message. '*In Tjaldar, which is enemy ship,*' he wrote. '*Expect immediate attack. Don't worry about us for we are all right.*' He wrapped the paper in a bit of silk torn from his necktie, and tied it round Morag's leg. Then he slipped the leash, and cast the bird off through the port-hole. Like a stone from a catapult she shot up into the moonlit fog.

'An off-chance,' he told himself, 'but worth taking. She's savagely hungry, and if she doesn't kill soon she'll go back to the House. If she's seen there Mr. Haraldsen has a spare lure and knows how to use it. If he gets the message he'll at least be warned.'

The action he had taken had put sleep out of his head and had cheered him up for the moment. He could make nothing of the hammock, so he sat himself on the heap of blankets and tried to think. But his thoughts did him no good, for he could make no plans. His cabin door was locked and the key in Martel's pocket. Anna was similarly immured at the other end of the ship. They were prisoners, mere helpless baggage to be towed in the wake of the enemy. Oddly enough, the Skipper did not seem to him the most formidable thing. The boy thought of D'Ingraville as a dreadful impersonal force of nature, like a snow blizzard or an earthquake. His horror was reserved for Carreras and Martel, who were evil human beings. As he remembered Martel's horse-shoe brows and soft sneering voice he shivered in genuine horror. The one was the hungry lion, but the other was the implacable, cunning serpent.

How long he sat hunched on the blankets he does not know, but he thinks it must have been hours. Slowly sleep came over him, for body and mind and nerves were alike weary. . . . Then that happened which effectually woke him. The disc of light from the porthole was obscured by something passing over it, slowly and very quietly. He looked out, and saw to his amazement that one of the kayaks was now floating on the water beneath him, attached to a rope from above.

As he stared, a second object dropped past his eyes. It was the other kayak, which lightly shouldered the first and came to rest beside it.

His hand felt for one of the lowering ropes and he found it taut. Grasping it, he stuck his feet through the port-hole, wriggled his body through and slid down the rope. Almost before he knew he was sitting in a kayak, looking up at the dim bulk of the vessel.

Then came another miracle. A human figure was sliding down the rope from the *Tjaldar's* deck, and he saw that it was Anna, coming down hand over hand as lightly as a squirrel. She saw him, dropped into the second kayak, and reached for the paddle. All was done as noiselessly as in a dream. There was a helper on the deck above, for the taut rope was dropped after her and swished gently into the water.

Anna kissed her hand to the some one above, seized her paddle, and with a slow stealthy stroke sent her kayak out into the golden haze. As Peter John clumsily followed suit, she turned on him fiercely, 'Quiet, you donkey,' she whispered. 'Don't splash for your life. Hang on to me and I'll tow you.'

In half a dozen strokes the little craft were out of sight of the *Tjaldar*.

CHAPTER XIV

The Ways of the Pink-Foot

THEY HAD TRAVELLED a quarter of a mile before Peter John spoke. 'How did you manage that?' he asked excitedly.

Anna slackened pace and dropped into line with him.

'I didn't. It was the man – the one with the funny eyebrows – the one the Skipper called Martin or some name like that.'

Peter John emitted a groan of dismay.

'But he's Martel – the worst of them – my father told me. It's a plot, Anna. He didn't mean any good to us.'

'He's let us escape, anyway, and that's the good I want. I had dropped off to sleep on that beastly couch when he woke me up, and said I'd better be off, for this was no place for kids. He made me follow him up on deck, keeping in the shadow so that we shouldn't be seen. There was no one about anyhow, and not a light except the riding-light. He had already got the kayaks in the water, and he said you would notice them, for they were beside your port-hole, and if you didn't we'd go down and rouse you up. When he saw you sitting in a kayak, he said it was what he expected, for you were a bright citizen.'

'It's all a trick,' Peter John groaned. 'Martel's the worst devil of the lot. He wants us to escape so that we can be caught and brought back, and so give them an excuse to bully us.'

'That sounds to me silly,' said Anna. 'I they wanted to treat us rough there was nothing to prevent them anyhow. I think the man is friendly. He's a Norlander.'

'He isn't. He's a Belgian.'

'Well, he speaks Norland as well as my father. And he knows about the Islands. He was out in the dory this afternoon, and he says the *Grind* are coming. He says that they will rendezvous at the Stor Rock – the *Grind* always have a rendezvous. I don't know why he told me that, but he seemed to think it important, for he said it several times. Only a Norlander could know about such things.'

'He may know Norland, but he's a Belgian and the worst of the lot. My father told me. What else did he say? '

'He said that we must hurry like the devil, and we weren't to go straight to the House. If we could shape any kind of course we were to go to the south part of the Island, to the Birdmarsh. That looks as if he thought the Skipper would be after us. I believe he meant well by us, Peter John, and anyway we're free again.'

'We won't be long free,' said the boy. He had his compass out, and halted for a moment to steady it. 'I don't trust him one bit, Anna. A course due west will bring us to the House, and that's where we steer for. If we can't make it, then we'll do the opposite of what Martel said and try for the north.'

'I don't care where we land,' said the girl, 'as long as it's on the Island.'

The boy held up his hand and listened.

'If they find out we're gone – or if Martel tells them – they can overhaul us in ten minutes with their outboard motor. Do you hear anything, Anna?'

The fog was breaking up into alleys and strips of moonlit sea, rayed round them like the points of a star. There was no sound, not even the ripple of water or a gull's cry.

'Come on,' Anna urged. 'We must be a quarter of the way across, and every moment counts. Take longer sweeps, Peter John, like me, and don't behave as if you were making butter-pats.'

Then for half an hour there was no further speech. The boy had not the girl's effortless skill, and put much needless strength into his strokes, so that his shoulders soon began to ache, and his breath to shorten. The fog was oddly intermittent. Now they would be in a circle of clear sea, now back in a haze so thick that Peter John had to keep his compass on his knee, and Anna closed in on him for guidance. On one such occasion she observed that Morag had been left behind, and that she wished well to the first hand that touched her.

'She hasn't,' was his answer. 'I flew her out of the port-hole, and tied a message to her varvel. If she doesn't kill, they may get her at the House.'

'What message?' Anna asked.

'Only that you and I were all right, but that they had better look out for squalls.'

Then, when they were in one of the patches of clear air, there fell on their ears the unmistakable sound of a motor behind them.

'Now we're for it,' said Anna. 'Heaven send the fog thickens. I was right about Martel. He told me not to go straight for the House, and that's what we've done, and they've naturally followed us. . . . Where are you heading for now?'

The compass had dropped to the bottom of the kayak and Peter John had altered course to the north-west.

'Martel said south,' said Anna.

'That's why we are going north,' was the answer.

Mid-channel in the small hours with an enemy close behind you is no place for argument. Anna followed obediently, the more as she saw that the new route was taking them into thicker weather. Presently on their port beam they heard the chug of a motor, but could see nothing when they screwed their heads round. Now they were back in dense fog, and the compass was brought into use again. Fear and the sense of pursuit had given both a fresh vigour, and the little craft slipped gallantly through the water. The moon was setting, and its golden light no longer transfused the sea-mist, which was becoming cold and grey. Soon it would be dawn.

Then suddenly they got a dreadful scare. The sound of a motor broke just ahead of them. They stopped and held their breath, living by their ears, for their eyes were useless in the brume. . . . The noise came nearer – soon it was not twenty yards ahead – but they saw nothing. Then slowly it died away towards the west.

'That was their second motor,' said Peter John. 'It had a different sound from the other. '

'Who was right?' said Anna triumphantly. 'I said we should trust that Martin man, but you wouldn't. We've disobeyed both the things he told us to do, and the result is we've been jolly nearly copped.'

After that there were no more alarms. The fog grew denser as they approached the Island, but it lifted slightly when the lap of the tide told them that they were close to shore. In this part the cliffs rose sheer from a narrow rock-strewn beach, but the children had visited the place before, and knew that a landing could be made in one of the tiny bays cut by descending streams. One such they found, where there was a half-moon of sand at the foot of a steep gully in the crags. They beached the kayaks and hid them in the cover of some big boulders. Then, taking hands, they proceeded to climb the ravine, which was stony and rough, but quite practicable. Near the top they found a recess of heath and bracken and there Anna resolutely sat down.

'Thank God for His mercies,' she said. 'If we had only some food I'd be happy. I'm going to sleep, and you'd better do the same, Peter John, for Heaven knows what sort of a day we have before us.'

They had no watch, and Peter John, who could usually tell the time by the sky, was out of his reckoning in those northern latitudes. They slept sound in the nook of rock, and it was only the sun on Anna's face that woke them. The time cannot have been much short of noon.

The mist had gone, and the day was bright and hot, but the visibility was poor. Halder, of which they had a full view, was a cone of dull blue with no details showing, and the Channel between might have been a bottomless chasm, for it had none of the sheen of water.

'It will be fine till three,' said Anna, who knew the Norland weather. 'Then I think it will blow again from the east, and blow hard.'

She stood up to stretch her arms, but Peter John caught her skirt and pulled her back. 'We mustn't show ourselves,' he enjoined. 'Remember, they're after us. Wait here while I reconnoitre' He crawled out of the cleft, and lay prone on a knuckle of rock from which the view was open eastward. He was back in a few seconds. 'The *Tjaldar* has gone,' he whispered. 'No sign of her, and I could see twenty miles of water. It must be pretty late in the day, for I'm desperately hungry. Aren't you? '

'Perishing, but it's no good thinking about it. We'll get no food till we get home. How is that to be managed? I've been taking our bearings from Halder, and we should be about two miles north of the House. There's a track to it on the top of the cliffs, and it's mostly in sight of the Channel, but if the *Tjaldar* isn't there that won't matter. I expect she is somewhere on the west side of the island.'

'What lies between the House and the west side?' Peter John asked. It was about the only part they had not explored.

'There's the hill Snowfell. A little hill compared to the ones at Laverlaw. Then there's a boggy place which we call the Goose Flat, because the pink-foot breed there. Then there's the sea – a rather nasty bit of coast with only one decent landing. . . . Let's bustle and get home. If the brutes are going to attack to-day there's no reason why they shouldn't start early, for just now there's no darkness to wait for.'

They climbed to the top of the gully where it ran out on to the tussocky cliff-top. Peter John, upon whom unpleasant forebodings had descended, insisted on keeping close in cover and showing no part of themselves on the skyline. Presently they looked down on a small tarn, much overgrown with pond-weed, which they remembered as the only lochan which had no boat. The track to the House passed its eastern edge, and by this their road lay.

It was a terribly exposed track, and Peter John regarded it with disfavour.

'Hadn't we better hug the cliff-edge where there's a certain amount of cover?' he suggested.

'You may if you like, but I won't. The Skipper and his lot can't be near the place yet, and I want to be home soon. They'll all be mad with anxiety. I must loosen my bones, for I'm as stiff as a ramrod. I'll race you, Peter John.'

She shook her yellow locks, and before the boy could prevent her was off at a gallop along the track. There was nothing for it but to follow her. He found it hard to catch her up, and the effort put other things out of his head. When they topped the rise, which overlooked the hollow where the House lay a mile distant, they were abreast and going at their best speed.

Then the boy saw something which made him halt in his tracks, clutch at Anna's arm, and bring her slithering to the ground. . . . Behind a rocky knoll three hundred yards off a man was posted.

He had not heard them, for he continued to smoke and regard the House through binoculars. They had only a back view of him, but he was plainly a sailor from the *Tjaldar* by his blue jersey and baggy blue serge trousers. He had some notion of landscape, for he was so placed that he must command any access to the House from the north.

Peter, his hand on Anna's bowed head, lay for a little with his nose in a patch of lousewort. He was thinking hard and studying the environs of the House. Their only chance now was to reach it from the west or south. But west lay Snowfell, where there was scarcely cover for a tomtit. On the south the approaches were better, but to reach the south it was necessary to get to the back of Snowfell and fetch a wide circuit. One ugly thought struck him. If the *Tjaldar* had gone to the west of the island, might it not have all that side under observation? This watcher came from the *Tjaldar*. If the enemy had posted his vedettes up to the edges of the House, was he not likely to be holding the intermediate ground?

Nevertheless, it was their only chance. The two very cautiously wormed their way back over the ridge they had crossed, left the track, and made good speed across a marshy field which was the source of the stream that fed the lochan. They saw no sign of life except a group of Norland ponies, as tame as puppies, who came up to have their noses rubbed, and fell to grazing quietly as soon as they had passed. But, warned now, they made the final ascent of the spine of the island, a continuation of Snowfell, with immense care, pulling themselves up between two patches of bracken to look over the far side.

There was no sign of the *Tjaldar*. The hill fell steeply in screes and rocks to the water's edge. There seemed to be a bay there, the contours of which were concealed by the hump of the cliffs, with a spire of smoke ascending from it. South, the ground flattened out into a mantelpiece, where pools of water glimmered among rushes and peat. Beyond that a bulge of hill cut off further view. There was no sign of life except the white specks, which were birds down in the Goose Flat, a nimbus of screaming gulls over a dead porpoise on one of the reefs, and the column of smoke.

'That's all right,' said Anna with relief. 'They've been here this morning, and that smoke is the remains of a breakfast fire. They have landed that man to keep an eye on the House, and they have gone off in the *Tjaldar* on some other business. Probably they're back at Halder by now to mislead us. Their time is the evening. We can't go over Snowfell, for the picket would see us, but we can get round by the Goose Flat and reach the House by way of the reservoir. Come on, for I'm weak with starvation.'

Anna would have marched boldly down the hill, but Peter John had sense enough to make her keep cover. This was not so difficult as long as they were on the encumbered slopes, for any road had to be picked among secret tangles of rock and fern. But before they came to the Goose Flat they found themselves on short heather and screes and as conspicuous as rooks on a snow-field. Even Anna was sobered.

'Let's run this bit,' she whispered, 'and get it over.'

It was no doubt the best plan, but it failed. They had not covered ten yards before a whistle cleft the silence. A figure showed itself on the edge of the seaward cliff – and then another. To Peter John's horror, as he cast his eye in the opposite direction, a man appeared on the ridge of Snowfell.

'Three,' he groaned.

'Four,' Anna corrected. 'There's another behind us – we must have passed close to him.'

A rib descended from Snowfell, and Peter John saw that if they could get beyond that they would be for a moment out of sight of the watchers, even of him on the hill. The rib bisected the Goose Flat, making a kind of causeway across it. There was no real cover in the Flat, for to any one on the edge whatever tried to hide itself among the short rushes and shallow lagoons would be easily visible. But to gain even a minute or two was something. The children in full view raced beyond the rib, waded into the Goose Flat, and flung themselves behind exiguous tussocks.

'We're out of their sight,' Anna panted; 'but they'll be down here in a jiffy to nobble us. Let's get on. We might beat them and get first to the Bird Marsh. We could hide there.'

'No good,' said the boy. 'If we go south, we'll be in their view in twenty yards, and the man on the hill has only got to walk down to cut us off. The chap behind, too. We're done, Anna, unless they think we've broken back.'

'They can't. They saw us come here.'

'Then we're for it. We might as well have stayed on the *Tjaldar*.'

'Oh, Peter John, what a mess we've made of everything!' the girl wailed.

Suddenly the boy's eyes opened wide to a strange spectacle. Just in front of them the causeway made by the rib of hill was somewhat broken, and a glimpse could be got of the swamp farther to the north. In this gap appeared the foolish heads and poised necks of a little flock of pink-foot. They were young birds who, having been hatched out in the Goose Flat, had spent their early adolescence on the sea skerries, and had now, according to their ancestral habit, returned for a little to their birthplace. They were chattering among themselves, apparently alive to the presence of something novel in front, about which they desired to be better informed.

By the mercy of God Peter John remembered a piece of lore that he had learned from the wildfowlers at Hanham in January. The pink-foot is not a skeery bird. He has resolved that his duty is not to live but to know, and he is nearly the most inquisitive thing in creation. If you want to get in range of him, Samson Grose had said, show yourself, and the odds are that he will move nearer you to discover what sort of thing you are. With young pink-foot, that is; older birds have learned wisdom.

To Anna's amazement the boy got to his feet, while his right hand held her down. . . . She saw the echelon of geese stop and confide things to each other. Every eye of them was on to Peter John, and after a moment's hesitation they began to move forward. They seemed oddly self-conscious, for they did not keep looking in his direction. Some would stop for a second to feed, and all kept turning their heads every way. But the whole flock was steadily drifting south, as if there was some compulsion in their rear. In five minutes they had moved at least ten yards.

The pink-foot were in sight of the watchers, and Peter John was not. Would the watchers draw the inference desired? They must do it at once, for if the geese came too near, they would lose their heads, stream back, and all would be lost. To one who did not know their habits the conclusion must surely be clear. The children were behind them, and their presence there was making them move south. Therefore it was in the north part of the Goose Flat that they must be sought. They had been seen to disappear behind the rib of hill, but they must have crawled back and got in the rear of the geese.

Peter John's heart was in his mouth, as he stood staring at the bobbing heads and projected necks of these absurd pink-foot, who to him and Anna meant everything. At any moment he himself might come within sight of some watcher who had shifted ground. Two lots of human beings, invisible to each other, were regarding some foolish winged creatures with desperate intentness. It was a new way of taking the auspices.

Then on the boy's ear fell that which was like an answer to his prayers. A whistle was blown up on the hillside, and answered by another from the direction of the sea. The pink-foot had been correctly observed. . . . A second later he had confirmation, for something had come north of the geese to alarm them. They stopped their leisurely advance, and straggled to left and right. The watchers had appeared to hunt for the fugitives in the north end of the swamp.

There was no time to lose, for when they found their search fruitless they would undoubtedly cast south. Peter John dragged Anna out of the foot of mud where she sat like a nesting wild-duck, and the two scrambled out of the bog and raced for their lives along the harder skirts of the hill. They did not stop till they had rounded the flank of the *massif* of the Isle, and were looking down on the Bird Marsh and the rolling barrens beyond it. Only once had Peter John glanced back, and that was to see the pink-foot, shaken out of their comfortable ways, bunching for a seaward flight. Once they were in the deep of the Marsh, where Anna knew the paths, they felt reasonably secure, and dared to draw breath again. As Anna cast herself on a patch of heather she could not resist one word of reproach. 'I was right all along about the Martin man. If we had steered south as he told us we should have missed this heart-disease. We might even be home and having breakfast.'

When she had recovered her breath she spoke again.

'That was very clever of you, Peter John. I'll never laugh at you again for being silly about birds. I thought you had gone mad till I saw your plan. It was a miracle, and I feel happy now. We are going to win, never fear.'

'I wish I knew how,' said the boy dolefully. 'We have slipped through them, but we have still to get into the House. . . . I wonder if they've any notion there what's happening. . . . And after that? The brutes are three or four to our one, and they're desperate.'

'I don't care,' said Anna; 'we're going to win. There'll be another miracle, you'll see.' She raised herself and sniffed the air. From where they sat they had no view of the Channel, but the southern part of Halder was in sight. 'We can't see the *Tjaldar's* anchorage. I wonder if she has come back. Look at the sky over there, Peter John. I said the weather would change in the afternoon, and it's jolly well going to. There's the father and mother of a thunderstorm coming up over Halder, and after that it will blow like fury from the east. . . . Lordie, it's hot, and there's a plague of daddy-longlegs. That should mean that the *Grind* are coming. That was what the Martin man said. He may be a scoundrel, but we would have been better off if we had taken his advice this morning.'

Peter John was almost cross. There was no need to rub in the good intentions of Martel, which he knew to be moonshine, and less to babble about pilot whales, when the world was crashing about them. 'Let's start,' he said. 'We'll have our work cut out getting to the House even from this side.'

Anna let her head sink back on the moss.

'I feel dreadfully sleepy,' she said. 'Perhaps it's the storm coming. All the energy has gone out of me. . . . Martin said the *Grind* would rendezvous at the Stor Rock. That's only about seven miles from the south end of this island – half-way between it and Kalso.'

An exasperated Peter John got to his feet and regarded the girl as she lay with her eyes half-closed. She certainly looked very weary – and different, too, in other ways. She had become like her father – her skin had suddenly acquired his pallor, and her eyes, when she opened them, his light wildness. And her mind was still on her preposterous whales.

'You stay here and rest,' he said, 'and I'll go and prospect. There may be some difficult ground to cover, where one will be safer than two.'

'All right,' she said sleepily. 'Come back before the storm begins, for I hate being alone with thunder. . . . I didn't know there were so many daddy-longlegs in the world.'

Peter John, in a mood between irritation and depression, hopped over the tussocks of the Bird Marsh, struck the shore, and trotted northward on the edge of the shingle. Halder was beginning to veil itself in a gloom as purple as a ripe grape, but the Channel was clear, and there was no sign of the *Tjaldar* by the other shore. The air was oppressive and still, but he had the feeling that some fury of nature was banking up and would soon be released.

The road, which the other day had seemed but a step or two, was now interminable to his anxious mind. He came in view of the harbour and the cluster of cottages to the south of it; all was peaceful there. Then by way of the channel of a stream he climbed from the shore, and looked suddenly upon the shelf where the House stood.

There was peace there, too, but he saw various ominous things. There were pickets posted – one on the near edge of the main lawn, one on the hill behind, and one above the voe on the road up from the harbour. These pickets were armed. Their business was to see that none entered the House and that none left it. Even as he stared, the one nearest him detected some movement in the back parts and sent over a warning shot; he heard the bullet crack on the stone roof of an outhouse. These watchers were the terriers to guard the earth till the hunters arrived.

Peter John's first impulse was to dodge the cordon and get into the House. He believed that he could do it, for he must know the ground better than they did. But if he once got in he would not get out again, and Anna would be left deserted. If the House was to be entered it must be in Anna's company.

There was no time to lose, so he turned and made for the Bird Marsh again, no longer hugging the shore, but taking the short cut across the hill. His last glance back showed the *Tjalda*r rounding the cliffs north of the harbour. He felt miserably depressed and utterly feeble. The people in the House must know their danger now, but what good was that knowledge to them? There were three men there to face a dozen and more – the crew of the *Tjaldar* had seemed to him unduly large, and its members had not looked innocent. If Anna and he joined the defence they would only be two more non-combatants. . . . Where, oh where, was Lord Clanroyden? Peter John had come to regard Sandy as the sheet anchor in this affair, the man who had planned the whole strategy, the regular soldier among amateurs. His absence gave him a dreadful sense of confusion and impotence.

Before he reached the Bird Marsh the weather had changed with a vengeance. The purple cloud had crossed the Channel from Halder, and the afternoon had grown as dark as a winter's gloaming. There was no lightning, but the gloom suddenly burst in a tornado of hail. So violent was the fall that the boy was beaten to the ground, where he lay with his back humped, protecting every inch of exposed skin from that blistering bastinado.

This lasted for perhaps five minutes. But when the hail ceased the sky did not lighten. The ground was white like winter and a wind as icy as the hail blew out of the east. He threaded the Bird Marsh to where he had left Anna, listless in the heat of the summer afternoon. . . . The girl had gone. Peter John lifted up his voice and called her, but there was no answer.

She had not followed him, for in that case he would have met her. It was scarcely possible that the enemy could have arrived from the Goose Flat and captured her. East and west lay impassable lochs. She could only have gone south on to the low dunes which stretched to the butt of the island. The hail had obliterated her tracks in the heather, but a few yards on there was a deep scar in a peat-hagg as if some one had slipped. A little farther and there was another foot-mark in the peat. Peter John followed the trail till he was out of the swampy ground and on the thymy slopes.

Suddenly he became aware that there was another sound in his ears beside the whistle of the wind. It came from in front of him, a strange blend of excited shouting and what seemed like the dash of waves on a skerry. At first he thought it the screeching of gulls over a dead porpoise. And then there came a note in it which was human, which must be human – deep voices in the act of giving orders – a note which no animal can compass. He stumbled over the last ridge, and looked down on the big voe into which one of the lochs of the Bird Marsh discharged its waters, and the network of lesser voes which made up the south end of the Island.

The shores of the voe were dense with people, and its surface and that of the lesser voes black with a multitude of boats. But at the heads of each inlet was a spouting and quivering morass in which uncouth men laboured with bloody spears. It was a scene as *macabre* as any nightmare, but it was orderly too. There were men with papers on the shore pricking off figures. . . . For a second his mind wandered in utter confusion, and then he got the answer. Anna's tales had come true. The *Grind* had arrived.

At first he did not realize that this meant salvation. The strangeness of the spectacle lifted it clean out of his normal world. He only knew that Anna was down there, and that he must find her. But as he raced down the slopes the scene before him began to change. Men left their toil and moved to a post midway up the big voe. The boats from the lesser voes began to draw to the same place. The people with the papers in their hands did likewise – one of them was shouting what sounded like an order. Long before Peter John had reached the point at least three-fourths of the people had moved there. . . .

Then as he came nearer he saw a group make a platform of their arms, and some one was hoisted on to it.

It was Anna, but an Anna whom he had not known before. Around her was bent and shingle grimed with blood – men with conical caps, and beards like trolls and wild eyes and blood-stained whale spears – a few women like mænads – and as a background a channel choked with animals dying or dead. She stood on a human platform, like a Viking girl in the Shield-ring, the wind plucking at her skirts and hair, her figure braced against it, her voice shrill and commanding. Something had been re-born in her out of the ages, some ancient power of domination; and something too had been re-born in her hearers, an ancestral response to her call.

She was speaking Norland, of which he understood not one word. What she said, as he learned afterwards, was that pirates were attacking her house and her father, and she summoned the men of the islands to their defence. She struck a note which reverberated through all their traditions, the note of peril from strangers – Norse and Scots rovers, Algerian pirates, who had driven the folk to the caves of the hills. The Norlander is not a fighting man, but he has fighting strains in him if the right chord be touched. Moreover, these men had their blood hot and their spirit high from the *Grind* hunt. . . .

She saw Peter John, and she seemed to use him to point her appeal. An older man spoke and was answered with a frenzied shouting. Certain men were detailed to keep watch on the *Grind* – they drew themselves off from the rest as the speaker called their names. . . . Then suddenly Anna was no more on her platform. She had Peter John's hand in hers, and behind them, racing northward, was the better part of a hundred islanders babbling like hounds, and in each right hand a reddened whale-spear.

CHAPTER XV

Transformation by Fire

FOR SHEER MISERY I give the night when the children were missing the top place in my experience. By dinner-time I was anxious; by midnight I was pretty well beside myself; but when morning came with no word of them, I had fallen into a kind of dull, aching torpor. Haraldsen, Lombard, and I were on our feet for ten hours, and we dragged the ancient servants after us till their legs gave out. My first thought was naturally for the kayaks, and we ascertained that they were not in the harbour. Gregarsen, the skipper of the now useless motor-boat, was positive that the children had been out in them in the morning, but he had a sort of notion that he had seen them return. The sea was like a mill-pond, so they could not have come to grief through ill weather. My special job was to range the coast, but nowhere on the east side of the island was there any sign of the kayaks, and I had to put the west side off till the next day. Lombard tried the fishing-lochs in case there had been a mishap there. As for Haraldsen I don't know what he did except to prowl about like a lost dog. He seemed almost demented, and hardly spoke a word.

When I returned to the House about 5.30, the riding lights of the *Tjaldar* across the Channel were just going out. I had a momentary idea that the children might have gone there, but I at once rejected it. Neither Peter John nor Anna was the sort of person to condemn their belongings to a night of needless anxiety.

At the corner of the lawn, where a high trellis had been erected to shield a bowling green, I found Haraldsen looking a good deal the worse for wear. But he did not look maniacal, as I must have looked. It was rather as if his mind had withdrawn itself from the outer world altogether. His eyes were almost sightless, like those of an old dog which moons about the doors. He had been in a queer 'fey' mood, ever since we arrived on the Island, but Anna's disappearance seemed to have taken the pin out of his wits altogether.

He was staring owlishly at something which was making a commotion at the top of the trellis – staring helplessly and doing nothing about it. It was a bird which had somehow got tangled in the top wires, and was flapping wildly upside-down on the end of a string, and was obviously in a fair way to perish from apoplexy. I saw that it was Morag, caught by her lead.

It didn't take me long to extricate her, and get savagely bitten in the process. I saw the paper round her leg, and with some difficulty unwound it. My first feeling, as I read it, was a deep thankfulness. At any rate the children were still in the land of the living.

They were on the *Tjaldar*. I saw the little ship across the Channel. She had got up steam, and was moving away from her anchorage with her head to the north. But she would return. The message had said that she was our enemies' base, and that on that day they would attack us.

The news pulled me out of my stupefied misery into a fury of action. I shouted at Haraldsen as if he were deaf. 'They've got the children,' I cried. 'Out there on the *Tjaldar*! God knows how, but they've got 'em. They've cut the telephone and wrecked the motor-boat, and to-day they are coming for us. . . . D'you hear? The children are safe so far. But we must prepare to meet an attack. Don't look like a stuck pig, man. At any rate now we have something to bite on.'

I hustled him into the House, where we found a very gummy-eyed Lombard. I raked up some breakfast from a demoralized household, but I remember that none of us could eat much, though we swallowed a good many cups of tea. And all the time I was discussing our scanty defences, simply to keep my mind and those of the others from ugly speculations. . . . We had a pretty poor lay-out. None of the old servants could be trusted with a gun, for your Norlander knows little of fire-arms. The only man who might have been of any use was old Absalon the fowler down at the clachan, and he was bed-ridden. The fighting-men were Haraldsen, Lombard, myself, and Geordie Hamilton – all of us fair shots, and Haraldsen, as I had discovered, a bit of a marksman. Happily we had plenty of weapons and ammunition. But we had a big area to hold, and the House was ill-adapted for defence – it could be approached on too many sides. We were bound to be outnumbered, and we were badly handicapped by the fact that the enemy had the two children as hostages. From what Sandy had told me of D'Ingraville it was not likely that he would be too scrupulous in the use of them. . . .

Sandy! The memory of him was like a blow in the face. What in God's name had happened to him? Here were we up to our necks in a row of his devising, and no word of him! I pictured him held up by an accident somewhere on the road, and frantically trying to get a message through to an island which was now wholly cut off from the world.

I tried to think calmly and picture what an attack would be like. Our enemies were out for business, and their ways would not be gentle. What did they want? To occupy the House and ransack it at their leisure. Yes, but still more to get hold of Haraldsen. He was what really mattered. They must get their hands on him, and force him to do what they wanted. As for Lombard and me, they must silence us. Kill us, or hide us away somewhere for good. Or bribe us. The horrid thought struck me that they would try to bribe me with Peter John as the price.

I have never contemplated an uglier prospect, and the notion that the children were part of it made me sick at heart. No doubt the enemy would begin with overtures – Haraldsen and the House to be handed over – Lombard and myself to sign some kind of bond of conformity. When that was refused they would attack. We might stall them off for a bit and do them a certain amount of damage, but in the end we must be overpowered. . . . Was there any hope? Only to protract the business as long as possible on the chance that something might turn up. I tried to make a picture of Sandy hurrying to our rescue, but got little comfort out of it. If he was going to do anything, he would have been here long ago.

The sole way of spinning out the affair was to keep Haraldsen away from their hands. So long as he was uncaptured they had not won. Therefore he must be got out of the House into hiding. Was there any place of concealment?

He was more reasonable than I expected. He forced his mind back from its wanderings, and his eyes became more like those of a rational being. He saw my point. I had been afraid that his bellicosity would make him refuse to keep out of the scrap, but Anna's loss seemed to have weakened the spirit in him. He agreed that our only chance was to delay his own capture as long as possible. . . . There was one hiding-place known only to Anna and himself. I have mentioned that to the north of the House, at the end of a kind of covered arcade used for pot-plants, stood the little stone cell of an Irish hermit who had brought Christianity to the Norlands and had been murdered by the sea-rovers. The elder Haraldsen had restored this, and had put a roof on it, not of living turf like the House, but of ordinary thatch. In the floor of the cell the workmen had discovered steps which led downward to the sea, ending in a cave in the cliffs at the north side of the harbour. The discovery had been kept secret – which was the only alternative to blocking the place up – and the entrance was through a trap carefully concealed by a heavy bench which old Haraldsen had had made of driftwood.

This seemed to be what we wanted. I told Haraldsen that he must get to it at once, taking with him a lantern and a packet of food. If the worst happened and we were all scuppered or kidnapped, the attack would still have failed if he remained at large. I told him not to try to get out at the sea end, for then he would be certainly taken, but to stay tight in the passage till the enemy had gone, and then to try what he could do in the way of getting help. The one thing that mattered was that he himself should keep out of their hands. Addled as his wits were, I think that he understood this. He looked at me with eyes like a willing, but stupid, dog's. Arn fitted him out with food and light, but the last thing he did was to go up to his bedroom and fetch a light sporting rifle and some clips of cartridges. 'I shall feel safer with this,' he said, and I saw no harm in his being armed. The enemy might find the passage, and the show conclude with a scrap in the bowels of the earth. I saw him into the cell, watched his lantern flickering down a stone staircase like a precipice, and pulled the bench back over the trap. There can have been no lack of ventilation in that passage, for a current of air drew up it like a tornado.

Then Lombard and I set ourselves to barricade the House. It wasn't a great deal that we could do, for the place was big and rambling, and had not been built for defence. We shuttered the windows, and stacked furniture at the doors, and at the back parts, where the entrance was simplest, made a kind of *abattis* of derelict machines like chaff-cutters and mangles and even an old weaver's loom. The ancient servants were no use except to watch certain entrances and give timely warning. To Geordie Hamilton, who was something of a shot, I gave the front of the House, his post being a little pavilion at the south end. He was to let nobody approach the main door, and challenge anybody who showed his face on the Terrace. Lombard I placed in command of the rear. He distrusted his prowess with a rifle, and preferred to trust to four double-barrelled shot-guns. There was not much of a field of fire in the back parts, owing to the rise of the hill, and any assault there was likely to be close-quarters fighting. For myself I chose the roof, which gave me a prospect of the whole terrain. I could see little of the Island, for the lift of the hill blocked the view to north and south and west, but I had the Channel clear before me, and that would give me early news of the *Tjaldar*.

So I sat down among the lush greenery of the roof, with a chimney-stack as cover, a revolver in my pocket, a couple of .240 magazine rifles beside me, and my spirits as low as I ever remembered them. The thought of Peter John made me sick at heart. The message on Morag's leg said they were both safe, but that was nothing; they were on the *Tjaldar*, and that meant in the enemy's power. D'Ingraville wasn't likely to fling away such a trump card. He would use these helpless children to the limit as bargaining counters, and if I refused to deal, he would not be scrupulous about the counters. . . . I remember wondering just how far his colleagues would approve of his methods – Troth and Barralty and the rest, who were probably more particular about the kind of crime in which they dabbled. But D'Ingraville would not pay much attention to the whimsies of sedentary folk who by this time must be putty in his hands. . . . I longed to see the *Tjaldar* appear, for, though that would mean the beginning of the end, it would also mean that I was within a mile or so of my son. I tried to concentrate my mind on a plan, but I simply could not think. I must wait and see how D'Ingraville opened the action.

It was a mild morning, growing closer as it neared midday. The visibility was only moderate, but the Channel was clear, and there was no *Tjaldar* in it. . . . Five minutes after twelve, just when I was thinking of taking a look round our defences, I saw the first sign of the enemy. Some one keeping well in cover came over the skirts of Snowfell, and took up position to the north of the House, about half a mile off. My glass showed me that he had a seaman's boots and jersey, and that he was armed. The timing must have been good, because five minutes later the sudden clamour of a flock of black-backed gulls to the south made me turn that way, and I saw a second man of the same type ensconce himself just behind the reservoir and rake the House and the gardens with his glasses. I knew now what was happening. D'Ingraville was getting his vedettes placed, so as to prevent any movement out of the House. The earths were being stopped before the pack came up. . . . I turned my glass on Snowfell. There were two men squatting on its upper screes.

A thought struck me which gave me a moment of comfort. Why did he take these precautions? He must have thought, not only that we were helpless, but that we were unsuspecting. The breakdown of the telephone and the motor-boat might have alarmed us, but we had no cause to assume the near presence of the enemy. Or the *Tjaldar* as his base. But Anna and Peter John knew! Could they have escaped? Could D'Ingraville imagine that they were now in the House? . . . I rejected the vain hope. How could the children get out of the clutches of men who left nothing to chance? Or why should these men imagine that we could escape when we had nowhere to fly to? . . .

Nothing happened for an hour or two. I descended from my perch and made a tour of the House. Geordie Hamilton had seen nothing – he was too low down for any long views. Lombard too had not much of a prospect, and the watchmen on Snowfell were just beyond his radius of vision. I left Geordie lunching solidly off bread-and-cheese and beer, had a pow-wow with Lombard, and returned to my watch-tower. I noticed that the weather was changing. It was getting very dark to the east over Halder, the Channel was being flawed with odd little cat's-paws, and, though it was still close, I had the feeling of being in a hot room next to an ice box – as if something sharp and bitter were just round the corner.

Close on three o'clock there came a diversion. There was a shot behind me, and when I looked over the ridge of the roof I saw some stone splinters clattering off one of the byres. I hastened down to investigate, and found that it was Lombard who had drawn fire. He had remembered that Morag was immured in the cheese-house, and would probably be pretty thirsty. So he had set out to water her, and had been observed by a picket, who had fired a warning shot which sent him back to cover. The earth-stoppers were taking their job seriously.

A few minutes later we got our first news of the hounds. Round the seaward cliff north of the harbour came the bows of a ship. I had not seen the *Tjaldar* at close quarters before, and at first did not recognize her. As seen at her moorings under Halder she had looked a smaller craft. But with my glass I picked out her name. She was showing no colours, for the Danish flag was no longer at her masthead. . . .

I did not see her anchor and lower her boats. For she was no sooner off the mouth of the voe than the gloom which had been brooding over the Channel burst in the father and mother of a storm. I would have been beaten off my perch if I had not found some shelter from the chimney stack. In a minute or two the grass of the roof was white with hailstones the size of a sparrow's eggs. The garden, the terrace, the hillside looked deep in snow. And with the hail came a wind that cut like a knife. It must have been the better part of half an hour before the tornado passed, and I could look seaward at anything but a blinding scurry.

There was the *Tjaldar*, white as a ship marooned in the Arctic ice, rocking in a sea which had suddenly become sullen and yeasty. Her starboard ladder was down, but there was no sign of boats. These must have landed. On her deck I thought I saw the flutter of a woman's dress. . . . And then I looked at the foreground, where a path from the harbour climbed on to the terrace. In the same second of time I saw heads appear above the terrace's edge, and heard Geordie Hamilton's challenge. The heads disappeared. I found a better stance in the corner of my chimney-stack and picked up one of the rifles. I considered that presently I might have to get busy.

The *Tjaldar's* party were no fools. Some of them must have gone south under the cliff to their picket stationed beside the reservoir, and learned from him how we had placed our men. I had hoped that Geordie had kept himself well in cover, but he must have shown himself to the sentry, who told the new-comers of his whereabouts. Anyhow, the next thing I heard was a roar like a bull's from Geordie's little pavilion, and I had a glimpse of a confused struggle there which ended in a sudden silence. The Scots Fusilier had been overpowered, and one of the three defenders put out of action. . . .

The next act followed fast. The terrace became suddenly populous, and the new-comers were unchallenged. D'Ingraville had not underrated his opponents, for to match our miserable trio he had brought at least twenty. I did not count the numbers beneath me, but there were at least a score, and there were also the pickets to be reckoned with. Clearly they knew all about us, for, now that Geordie Hamilton had been dealt with, they seemed at their ease. They were following a prearranged plan, based on exact knowledge of the place, for some made their way to the back parts, and some to the arcade which led to the hermit's cell, but more waited at the foot of the steps which led to the main door. They were grouped in two bodies with an alley between them, and seemed to be waiting for somebody.

Who that was soon appeared. Up the alley came three men. I had no doubt about who they were, for I remembered Sandy's descriptions. D'Ingraville was the tall fellow in the yachting cap and grey flannels – he had grown his beard again and looked like a naval officer, except that his light, springy stride was scarcely the walk of the quarter-deck. The dark, lean man, with the long face made in two planes, was Carreras the Spaniard. And beyond doubt the slim one, in the much-stained blue suit and the cap a little over one eye, was Martel, the Belgian.

Of the others I had only a vague general impression, as of something hard, tough, and ruthless, but well-disciplined. This might be a posse of gangsters, but they would obey orders like a Guards battalion. But the three leaders made the clearest and sharpest impact on my mind. They were perhaps three hundred yards away from me, but their personalities seemed as vivid as if they were in the same room. I had an overpowering impression of a burning vitality which was also evil, a glowing, incandescent evil. It cried out from the taut lines of D'Ingraville, from his poise like that of a waiting leopard. It clamoured from Carreras's white, pitiless face. Above all it seemed to me that it shouted from the Belgian Martel's mean, faun-like presence. It was the last one I hated worst. D'Ingraville was a fallen angel, Carreras a common desperado, but Martel seemed to be *apache*, sewer-rat, and sneak-thief all in one.

They had something to say to us. I moved out from the shelter of the chimney, was instantly seen, and covered by twenty guns. I dropped my own rifle and held up my hand.

'Will you gentlemen kindly tell me your business?' I shouted against the east wind.

It was D'Ingraville who replied. He bowed, and his two queer companions did the same.

'Sir Richard Hannay, isn't it?' he said, and his pleasant voice coming down wind was easily heard. 'We want a talk with Mr. Haraldsen. But it would perhaps save time – and trouble – if I could first have a word with Lord Clanroyden.'

'Sorry,' I shouted. 'Mr. Haraldsen is not at home. He has left the island.'

From where I stood I could see the smile on his face, repeated in those of his two companions. They knew very well that I was lying.

'How unfortunate!' he said. 'Well, what about Lord Clanroyden?'

Did they know that we were without Sandy? Or was this a fishing question? Or did they believe that he was in the House? Anyhow, it was not for me to enlighten them.

'If you have anything to say you can say it to me,' I said. 'Go ahead, for it's devilish cold waiting.'

'A roof-top is scarcely the place for a conference,' said D'Ingraville. 'Won't you come down, Sir Richard, from your eyrie? It's a cold day, as you justly observe, and we might talk indoors.'

'All right,' I said, 'I'll come down.' And then, as I looked at the three men, I had a sudden inspiration. I had meant to ask that D'Ingraville should be their envoy, when I observed the man Martel standing in an odd position, his left arm flung across his chest and clutching the biceps of his right. That was an attitude I had seen before, and it woke in me a wild surmise. It might be meant as a sign. My mind was pretty hopeless, for their desire to talk seemed to me certain proof that they wanted to make terms about the children, but it was just not sodden enough to miss this little thing.

'You can keep yourself for Lord Clanroyden,' I told D'Ingraville. 'I'll do my talking to that other chap – the one on your left. Send him forward, and I'll let him indoors.'

'If there's any dirty work,' said D'Ingraville, his voice suddenly becoming shrill, 'you'll pay for it bloodily. You understand that? '

'I do. I'll leave the door open so that you can keep your eye on me, and plug me if I try to be funny.'

I went downstairs with an ugly void at the bottom of my stomach. Old Arn was on guard at the main door, and had built up a perfect battlement of furniture, which it took some minutes to clear away. When I got the door opened and the east wind in my face, I saw that the three men had moved nearer – close to the foot of the steps. I beckoned to Martel.

'You two stay where you are,' I said. 'This man and I will be inside the hall out of the wind. We'll be well in sight.' I turned and re-entered the House. I heard footsteps on the stone and was conscious that Martel had joined me. My heart was in my mouth, for I was certain that his first word would be about the children and the price we were prepared to pay for them.

I swung round on him. 'Well?' I demanded. 'What do you want?'

But the words died away on my lips.

Said the man called Martel, 'Dick, my lad, we've made rather a hash of this business.'

God knows how he had managed it. There was no ordinary make-up about him, no false moustache or dyed hair or that sort of thing. But in some subtle way he had degraded himself – that is the only word for it. Everything about him – slanting eyebrows, furtive eyes, tricky mouth, slouching shoulders – was mean and sinister, because he chose that it should be so. But when he looked me in the face, with that familiar twinkle in his eyes and that impish pucker of the lips, he was the friend I knew best in the world.

There was just an instant when his eyes had the old insouciance. Then they became very grave.

'We must talk fast, for there isn't much time. I've made a deuce of a mess of things, and I thought I was being rather clever. First – to ease your mind. Peter John and the girl are safe – for the moment, at any rate.'

'Thank God!' I said fervently. Such a load was lifted from my heart that I felt almost confident. But Sandy's next words disillusioned me.

'I've done most of what I set out to do. I've got Barralty and his lot scared into fits. No more high-handed crimes for them! They're sitting in the *Tjaldar* sweating with terror. . . . I've collected enough evidence to keep them good for the rest of their lives, and incidentally to hang D'Ingraville and most of his crowd. Do you realize that up to now we had nothing against him that any court would listen to? . . . So I had to make him commit himself. You see that? He had to attack Haraldsen in his island, and have a show-down once and for all. Well, I thought I had got him taped. I was counting on Haraldsen doing as he promised to do, and having a hefty push of young islanders to defend him. I would know D'Ingraville's plans, being his chief staff-officer, and so could play into their hands. And lo and behold! when I get here, I find there's not a soul in the island but dotards, and the whole place is as unprotected as a stranded whale.' He stopped and sniffed, and then said a strange thing. 'Just the weather for the *Grind*,' he said. 'Gad, that would be a bit of luck.'

Then he demanded, 'Where's Haraldsen?' I told him and he nodded. 'I hope he'll stay in his earth. . . . See here, Dick. The lay-out as I planned it was that D'Ingraville should be encouraged to attack you and so commit himself. But before he had time to do any harm, your supports would arrive and hold him. Well, that's a wash-out, for there are no supports. I have got word to the Danish destroyer that patrols the fishing banks. She's on her way, but she's coming from the Westmanns, and can't be here much before midnight. That gives D'Ingraville time to do the deuce of a lot of damage. I tried to have the attack delayed, and I managed to have it put off till now – it was arranged for this morning – principally because I got them hunting for the children. But now we're for it. It's seven or eight hours till midnight, time enough for D'Ingraville to cut all our throats if he wants to. If he gets hold of Haraldsen there may be some ugly work. If it's only you and Lombard he'll be content perhaps with ransacking the House. How long can you stick it?'

'An hour maybe,' I said. 'We've no manpower to keep them out. They are old hands, and won't give us much of a chance of picking them off piecemeal.'

'They won't,' he said. 'If you can make it three hours we might do the trick. . . . I'll go back and report that you won't treat. I'll say you can agree to nothing without Haraldsen's consent, and that he isn't here, and that you'll do your damnedest to defend his property. I'll try to tangle up things at the other end. I'll have to come over to you some time, but I'll choose my own time for that – the moment when I can be of most use. If D'Ingraville finds that he has been diddled and gets his hands on me, then my number is up, and I won't be any use to you as a corpse.'

As Sandy spoke I had a vivid memory of a bush-crowned hillock in the African moonlight, when, to defend another Haraldsen, Lombard and I had imperilled our lives. I seemed to have done all this before, and to know what was coming next, and that foreknowledge gave me confidence. I must have smiled, for Sandy looked at me sharply.

'You're taking this calmly, Dick. You know it's a devilish tight fix, don't you? The one hope is midnight and the Danish boat. Spin things out till then without a tragedy and we have won. I must be off.' He waved his hand to D'Ingraville at the foot of the steps and turned to go. His last word was, 'Keep Haraldsen off the stage for Heaven's sake. He's our weakest point.' He went down the steps, and the next second I had clanged the great hall-door behind him and dropped the bolts. I left old Arn piling up the barricade again and skipped up to my post behind the chimney-stack, with the intention of doing some fancy shooting. I saw Sandy conferring with D'Ingraville and Carreras, looking once again the murderous scallywag.

Suddenly, in a pause of the wind, a voice rang out, a voice coming from the north, from the hermit's cell at the end of the arcade.

'Off the terrace,' it shouted. 'Back to your sties, you swine, or I shoot.'

It was Haraldsen – there could be no mistaking that voice – but it seemed to be raised to an unearthly pitch and compass, for it filled the place like the rumour of the sea in a voe. D'Ingraville's ruffians were accustomed to the need for cover, and suddenly the whole gang seemed to shrink in size, as it splayed out and crouched with an uneasy eye on the north. All but one – Carreras. I don't know what took the man. Perhaps he was looking for shelter in the lee of the steps and the House – at any rate, he moved forward instead of back. A shot cracked out, he flung up one arm, spun half-left, and dropped on his face.

In an instant every man of them was flat on the ground, worming his way back to the terrace wall which would give refuge from that deadly rifle. Then the voice spoke again, and what it said must have considerably surprised one at least of the crawlers.

'Clanroyden,' it shouted. 'Back to the House with you! Quick, man! Do as I tell you. I can't handle that scum if there's a friend mixed up in it.'

How on earth he saw who Martel was I cannot tell. But it was a foolish move, and it came very near being the end of Sandy. It was the words 'Back to the House' that did the mischief, for they enabled

D'Ingraville to identify the man Martel, when otherwise it might have seemed a mere bluff. At any rate so Sandy thought, for to my horror I saw him scramble to his feet from behind a clump of Arctic willows. He knew his danger, for he twisted and side-slipped like a rabbit. I was choking with fright, for I couldn't get down to the main door in time, and there was Arn's barricade to get out of the way: the front of the House was bare of cover, and till he got round the corner of it he was in the centre of an easy field of fire. But only one shot followed him, and I'm pretty certain it did not come from D'Ingraville; he must have been confident of getting his revenge at leisure. The shot missed its mark – I believe that the reason was that the fugitive at the moment stumbled over the dead Carreras. In a few seconds he was out of my orbit of sight. He would be safe in the back parts for the time being, unless he fell in with a stray picket.

Presently he was out of my mind as well, for all my attention was fixed on D'Ingraville. He had got his main force under cover of the terrace wall – out of Haraldsen's danger, and it was plain enough what he proposed to do. It was child's play to take Haraldsen in flank and rear. The cell's door and window opened to the south, and its inmate could protect himself in that direction, but what could he do against an attack from above by way of the thatched roof? Three sturdy fellows with five minutes' work could uncover the badger's earth.

A figure squeezed in beside me behind the chimney-stack. 'A close call,' said Sandy. 'The bullet went through my pocket. If I hadn't tripped and turned side on, I'd be dead. . . . What's our friend up to? Oh, I see. Fire. They'll burn the thatch and smoke him out. This is our worst bit of luck. If only that damned fool had stuck in his burrow, instead of trying to be heroic. I dare say he's off his head. Did you hear his voice? Only a madman's could ring like that. And he gave me away, the blighter, though God knows how he spotted me! Another proof of lunacy! This show's turning out pretty badly, Dick. In about half an hour D'Ingraville will have got Haraldsen, and very soon he'll have got me, and he won't be nice to either of us.'

A kind of dusk had fallen owing to the cloud-wrack drifting up with the east wind, and the prospect from my roof-top was only of leaden skies and a black, fretful sea. The terrace was empty, but I could see what was happening beyond it, and I watched it with the fascinated eyes of a spectator at a cinema, held by what I saw, but subconsciously aware of the artifice of it all. My mind simply refused to take this mad world into which I had strayed as an actual thing, though my reason told me that it was a grim enough reality. I caught a glimpse of one figure after another among the stunted shrubberies and sunk plots which lay north and east of the hermit's cell. Then an exclamation from Sandy called my attention to the cell itself. There was a man on its roof pouring something out of a bucket. 'Petrol,' Sandy whispered. 'I guessed right. They'll burn him out.'

A tongue of flame shot up which an instant later became a globe of fire. A spasm of wind swept it upwards in a long golden curl. Directly beneath me I saw men appear again on the terrace. It was safe enough now – for Haraldsen could scarcely shoot from a fiery furnace.

D'Ingraville was looking up at us, for he had guessed where Sandy would have taken position.

'You have kept your promise, Lord Clanroyden,' he cried. 'I am glad of that, for this would have been a dull place without you.'

Sandy showed himself fully.

'Thank you,' he said. 'I like to keep my word.'

'You have won the first trick,' the pleasant voice continued. 'At least you have deceived me very prettily, and I am not easily deceived. I make you my compliments. But I don't think you will win the rubber. When we have secured that madman, I will give myself the pleasure of attending to you.'

I have called his voice pleasant, and for certain it was now curiously soft and gentle, though notably clear. But there was something feline in it, like the purring of a cat. There he stood with his wild crew about him, elegant, debonair, confident, and as pitiless as sin. The sight of him struck a chill in my heart. In a very little we should be at his mercy, and it was hours – hours – before there was any hope of succour. I was not alarmed for myself, or even for Haraldsen, who seemed now to have got outside the pale of humanity; but I saw nothing before Sandy except destruction, for two men had wagered against each other their lives. . . . And the children! Where and in what peril were they crouching in this accursed island? . . . .

Suddenly there was a roar which defied the wind and made D'Ingraville's voice a twitter. It was such a thunder of furious exultation as might have carried a Viking chief into his last battle. Out from the cell came Haraldsen. His figure was lit up by the blazing roof and every detail was clear. He was wearing his queer Norland clothes, and his silver buckles and buttons caught the glint of fire. One part of his face was scorched black, the rest was of a ghostly pallor. His shaggy hair was like a coronet of leaves on a tall pine. He had no weapon and he held his hands before him as if he were blind and groping. Yet he moved like a boulder rushing down a mountain, and it seemed scarcely a second before he was below me on the terrace.

There was no mistaking his purpose. The man had gone berserk, and was prepared to face a host and rend them with his naked fingers. Had I been near enough to see his eyes, I knew that they would have been fixed and glassy. . . . Once in Beira I saw a Malay run amok with a great knife. The crowd he was in were almost all armed, but the queer thing was that not a shot was fired at the man, and he had cut a throat and split two skulls before he was tripped up and sat upon by a drunken sailor coming down a side street, who hadn't a notion what was afoot. That was what happened now. There were men behind him with guns, there were twenty men on the terrace with rifles and pistols, yet this tornado with death in its face was permitted to sweep down on them unhindered. A palsy seemed to have taken them, like what happens, I have been told, to mountaineers in the track of a descending avalanche.

What befell next must have taken many minutes, but to me it seemed to be a mere instant of time. I was not conscious till it was all over that Sandy beside me had grabbed my wrist in his excitement and dug his nails into my flesh. . . . D'Ingraville was standing in the front of a little group which seemed to close round him as the whirlwind approached. Haraldsen swept them aside like dead leaves, but whether the compulsion was physical or moral I cannot tell. He plucked D'Ingraville in his arms as I might have lifted a child of three. Then, and not till then, there was a shot. D'Ingraville had used his gun, but I know not what became of the bullet. It certainly did not touch Haraldsen.

Haraldsen held up his captive to the heavens like a priest offering a sacrifice. He had drawn himself to his full height, and in the brume to my scared eyes looked larger than human. D'Ingraville wriggled half out of his clutch, and seemed to be tossed in the air and recaught in a fiercer grip. The next I knew was that Haraldsen had turned north again and was racing back towards the hermit's cell.

Then the shooting began. The men on the terrace aimed at his legs – I saw rifle bullets kick up flurries of dust from the flower beds. But for some unknown reason they missed him. The men near the cell tried to stop him, but he simply trampled them underfoot. Only one of them fired a shot, and we found the mark of it later in a furrow through his hair. . . . He was past them, and at the blazing cell where the last rafter was now dropping into a fiery pit. For a moment I thought he was going to make a burnt-offering of

D'Ingraville, who by this time must have had the life half squeezed out of him in that fierce embrace. But no. He avoided the cell, and swung half-right to the downland above the sea.

By this time he was out of sight of the terrace, but in full view of Sandy and me on the roof-top. We might write off D'Ingraville now, for he was beyond hope. Haraldsen's pace never slackened. He took great leaps among the haggs and boulders, and by some trick of light his figure seemed to increase instead of diminish with distance, so that when he came out on the cliff edge, and was silhouetted against the sky, it was gigantic.

Then I remembered one of his island tales which he had told us on our first arrival – told with a gusto and realism like that of an eye-witness. It was the story of one Hallward Skullsplitter who had descended a thousand years ago upon the Island of Sheep and cruelly ravaged it. But a storm had cut him off with two companions from his ships, and the islanders had risen, bound the Vikings hand and foot, and hurled them into the sea from the top of Foulness. . . . It was Foulness I was now looking at, where the land mouth of the harbour ran up to a sea-cliff of three hundred feet.

I had guessed right. At first I thought that Haraldsen meant to seek his own death also. But he steadied himself on the brink, swung D'Ingraville in his great arms, and sent him hurtling into the void. For a second he balanced himself on the edge and peered down after him into the depths. Then he turned and staggered back. I got my glasses on to him and saw that he had dropped on the turf like a dead man.

A tremendous drama is apt to leave one limp and dulled. D'Ingraville was gone, but his jackals remained, and now they would be more desperate than ever with no leader to think for them. Our lives were still on a razor's edge, and it was high time for a plan of campaign. But Sandy and I clutched each other limply like two men with vertigo.

'Poor devil!' said Sandy at last. 'He can't have known what was coming. Haraldsen must have hugged him senseless.'

'We're quit of a rascal,' I said; 'but we've got a maniac on our hands.'

'I don't think so. The fury is out of him. He returned to type for a little, and is now his sober commonplace self again.' He held out his watch. 'Not yet seven! Five hours to keep these wolves at bay. Hungry and leaderless wolves – a nasty proposition! . . . Great God! What is that?'

He was staring southward, and when I looked there I saw a sight which bankrupted me of breath. The murky gloaming was lit to the north by the last flames of the hermit's cell, but to the south there was a breach in the gloom and a lagoon of clear sky was spreading. Already the rim of the southern downs was outlined sharply against it. In that oasis of light I saw strange things happening. . . . At sea a flotilla of boats was nearing the harbour on a long tack, and one or two, driven by sweeps, were coming up the shore. Across the hill moved an army of men, not less than a hundred strong, sweeping past the reservoir, overflowing the sunk lawn, men shaggy and foul with blood, and each with a reeking spear.

The sight was clean beyond my comprehension, and I could only stare and gasp. It was as if a legion of trolls had suddenly sprung out of the earth, for these men were outside all my notions of humanity. They had the troll-like Norland dress, now stained beyond belief with mud and blood; their hair and eyes were like the wild things of the hills; the cries that came from their throats were not those of articulate-speaking men, and each had his shining, crimsoned lance. . . . Dimly I saw the boats enter the harbour and their occupants swarm into the *Tjaldar* like cannibal islanders attacking a trading ship. Dimly I saw D'Ingraville's men below me cast one look at the murderous invasion and then break wildly for the shore. I didn't blame them. The sight of that maniacal horde had frozen my very marrow.

Dimly I heard Sandy mutter, 'My God, the *Grind* has come.'

I didn't know what he meant, but something had come which I understood. In the forefront of the invaders were Anna and Peter John.

CHAPTER XVI

The Riddle of the Tablet

I HAVE OFTEN WONDERED how we should define the courage of the ordinary rapscallion. A contempt, doubtless, for certain kinds of danger with which he is familiar and which for him have lost the terrors of the unknown. Not a settled habit of mind, for often he will be paralysed by the unexpected, and thrown into a panic by what is outside his experience. The first happened when Haraldsen went berserk and plucked D'Ingraville out of the heart of his gang; the second, when several score of ensanguined Norlanders turned the knees of the gang to water. Certainly it was the wildest spectacle I ever beheld, and he would have been a stout fellow who stood up against that nightmare army of blood-stained trolls. . . . As a matter of fact, two of the gang did put up some kind of resistance with their guns, and perished as if they had been pilot-whales. I doubt if the Norlanders knew what they were doing. Like Haraldsen they had gone back to type – they were their forebears of a thousand years ago making short work of a pirate crew.

The rest, who surrendered like sheep, were not maltreated, but were trussed up like bundles of hay with the home-made ropes that every Norlander carries with him. The detachment in the boats who had swarmed over the *Tjaldar* behaved with extreme circumspection. I fancy that the atmosphere of a modern steamer got them out of their atavistic dreams quicker than their kinsmen on the land. They were civil to Barralty and his friends, though they found it hard to find a common tongue, and, having brought the vessel round to a better anchorage and left everything shipshape about her, they came ashore soberly to take counsel with the rest of us.

For the madness did not take long to ebb. The case of Haraldsen was curious. As soon as I saw that there was no fear of resistance and that the Norlanders were ready to do whatever Anna told them, I started off with Peter John for the top of the cliffs, for Haraldsen seemed to be the one big problem left. I found him sitting up on the turf, with his huge fists stuck in his eyes like a sleepy child. I think it was the sight of Peter John, who had always been his close friend, that gave him a bridge back to the ordinary world.

'Anna's all right, sir,' said the boy. 'She's down there with all the Norland men behind her.'

'Good!' he said. 'They'll do what she tells them. Have the *Grind* come to my island?'

Peter John nodded.

'It is the first time for ten years,' said Haraldsen. 'I must go down and arrange about food and drink. The *Grind* are a hungry and thirsty job, and a dirty one.'

His wits were still wool-gathering, and I tried to steady them.

'You're safe,' I said, 'and the House, and Lord Clanroyden and all of us. You need never give another thought to this trouble.'

'I am glad of that,' he said dully. 'There was a lot of trouble. Where is the tall man with the beard? '

'Dead,' I said, 'in the sea.'

'He would be' was the odd answer. 'He came out of the sea, and he has returned to it.'

Then he yawned, his limbs relaxed, and before I could count five he was fast asleep. I knew better than to waken him. We got together a sort of litter, and had him carried down to the House, where he was put to bed and slept for thirty-two hours. He woke ravenous, had a bath and shaved, and then ate the better part of a ham and emptied three coffee-pots. He remembered not one solitary thing between his discovery that the children were lost and his waking in his own bed, and it wasn't for me to enlighten him. But one thing that berserk fit had done for him: it had drained him for good of timidity. He was now as steady-nerved and confident as his father had been, and a hundred per cent. more restful.

The fishery boat arrived an hour before midnight, by which time we had taken counsel, not only among ourselves, but with the folk on the *Tjaldar* and had settled on our story. It was no good having the true business broadcast to the world. Barralty and his people had gone yachting with D'Ingraville, who had picked his crew and had forced them into an attack on the Island of Sheep for his own purposes. They had refused to come on shore, and had seen nothing of the doings on land. The fortunate advent of the *Grind* had averted tragedy. The children had found the Islanders and had led them to the House, where we had been putting up a forlorn defence. Haraldsen had picked off one of the desperadoes, and had fought with D'Ingraville on the cliff-top to the latter's doom. (Sandy could provide a *dossier* of D'Ingraville which would prevent unavailing regrets about his end.) The coming of the Islanders had led to the general surrender of the invaders, two of the latter being the only casualties.

D'Ingraville's gang was a collection of blackguards of various races which it was left for the Copenhagen courts to sort out and deal with. Most of them were rather urgently wanted by their several countries. The *Tjaldar*, which had been chartered in Troth's name, had the rudiments of a regular crew who had not been mixed up in the piracy, and it was arranged that, under the convoy of the Danish destroyer, she should return to Aberdeen.

With the clearing away of our anxieties came a clearing of the skies. The Norlands seemed to swim into a zone of halcyon weather – sunlit days, calm seas, and wonderful, long-lit, golden evenings. When I came there first I thought I was getting outside the world, and then presently I found that I was indeed outside the world in a nightmarish limbo. Now that the nightmare had gone, the Island seemed a happy place, where life could be worthily lived in the company of sea-tides, and friendly wild things, and roaring mornings, and blissful drowsy afternoons. To me it was Fosse, and to Sandy it was Laverlaw, but both, so to speak, set in a world of new dimensions. To Lombard, the man whom I had once thought of as degenerated into a sleek mediocrity, it was a revelation. It had brought back to him something of his youth and his youth's dreams.

I remember that he and I sat together on the highest point of Snowfell, looking across the empty Channel to Haldar, bright as a jewel in the sunshine. The *Tjaldar* and the fishery boat were at anchor below us; beside us curlew and plover kept up a gentle complaining; around us, except in the east, there was a great circle of glittering sea. The landscape was as delicate and unsubstantial as the country of a dream.

'I shall come back to the Norlands,' said Lombard, shaking out his pipe. 'It was good of you to let me into this show, Hannay; I hope I haven't misconducted myself.'

'You were the steadiest of the lot,' I said warmly. 'You never gave a cheep even when things looked ugliest.'

He laughed.

'I often wanted to. But I'm glad to find I haven't gone quite soft. I never really thought I had. But I've let myself get dull and flat. That's what this business has taught me. I want to get air and space round me, for I live in a dashed stuffy world. . . . So I'm coming back to the Norlands to make my soul.'

I suppose I must have looked at him in surprise, for he laughed again. 'You know well enough what I mean. The Norlands are a spiritual place which you won't find on any map. Every man must discover his own Island of Sheep. You and Clanroyden have found yours, and I'm going to find mine.'

My last recollection is of two meals in the great hall of the House. The first was the night of the coming of the *Grind*, or rather the small hours of the following morning. The Danish fishery boat had arrived; the malefactors were safely stowed away; and, while Haraldsen lay in his bed upstairs, in the hall were gathered the Norlanders who had saved us, both the boat parties and those who had come by land – the officers of the destroyer – Sandy, Lombard, and myself – and Anna and Peter John. The children seemed to have got their second wind, for, having been very tired and drowsy at first, they woke up before midnight to an astonishing vigour. The Danish officers, who knew the Norlands well and also Haraldsen, were the friendliest of souls. As for the Norlanders, to them the Island of Sheep was the home of legend and the Haraldsen family the centre of their mythology. At first they were shy and laggard, for your Norlander is an excellent giver but a poor taker. But they were very hungry, and Arn had provided a feast of fat things, and in twenty minutes they had squared their elbows to the job and were as merry as grigs.

I shall never forget that scene. Arn had supplemented the electric light by several score of candles, and the huge place was as bright as day. The tapestries, the carved grotesques, the many ships' models, the curious panelling – their minutest lines and their subtlest colours were displayed in that fierce radiance. And below sat a company which might have come out of a picture in a child's *Grimm*. Many of the islanders wore their cowls, for they were in doubt as to whether that vast hall should be reckoned a dwelling. And at the head of the long oaken table, in a chair like a galley's beak, sat Anna. I had never seen anything quite like her. She had changed from rough clothes into a white silk gown, and the coronel of lights under which she sat made her seem a creature of gold and ivory. She ruled the feast, too. It was she who gave the toasts; it was she who in musical Norland thanked our preservers. Here was the true fairy-tale princess, the Queen out of the North, and to that wild gathering she lent an air of high ceremonial. But she was a stony-hearted princess, for she insisted on toasting Peter John. I don't know what she said about him, but it got the Norlanders out of their seats and he was hoisted – Morag angrily protesting – on a dozen shoulders. A speech was demanded, and his was of two sentences. 'Thank you all very much. – Anna, you beast, I'll pay you out for this.'

The second meal was the following day, when the *Tjaldar* was about to sail under the convoy of the Danish destroyer, and the islanders had returned to their homes. We had the *Tjaldar* party to dinner, and Haraldsen himself was the host. I have never been present on a more fantastic occasion. Sandy said we had to do it, to mark the close of hostilities, but it was a pretty cruel business for the ex-conspirators. Albinus was a dingy figure, still considerably rattled. Barralty was the frightened intellectual trying to recover his poise, but he was a long way short of getting back his self-esteem. The lady was the most composed. She wore a charming gown, and had the wit not to make any pretences. They had got themselves into an ugly show, and were now quit of it and correspondingly grateful. But they all looked at Sandy in some awe. I gathered that, as Martel, he had been chiefly responsible for scaring the life out of them.

I think I may say that we all behaved well. Lombard talked the City to Barralty and Troth, Sandy had some polite things to say about politics, a great deal of information was vouchsafed about the Norlands, some of Haraldsen's treasures were exhibited, and Miss Ludlow was caressingly sweet to Anna. I should add that old Arn excelled himself, that the food was perfection, and that the best of Haraldsen's cellar was forthcoming. This last point was especially appreciated by Troth, who soon relaxed into bonhomie. I found him a very friendly fellow, with sensible notions about the Essex creeks and tides.

It was he who, before they left, made an attempt at an apology.

'I hope, Mr. Haraldsen,' he said, 'that we're all going to forgive and forget.'

Haraldsen looked down on him from his great height.

'I ask for nothing better,' he said. 'I understand that you feel some grievance against me, Mr. Troth. On my father's account, I think, and for your own father's sake? Well, we are willing that some reparation should be made. Lord Clanroyden will tell you what.'

Sandy took from his pocket something in a chamois-leather wrapping.

'This belonged to the late Mr. Haraldsen,' he said. 'It came into my hands in rather an odd way, about which I wrote to the papers. I do not intend to hand it over to the British Museum. I propose, Mr. Troth, to give it to you in full settlement of any claims you may think you have against the late Mr. Haraldsen's estate.'

He took from a bag the tablet of emerald jade which he had shown us at Fosse.

Troth received it with a face in which surprise, greed, and a kind of shame were mingled. He turned the lovely thing over in his hands, made as if to read the inscription, and then looked at Sandy a little confusedly.

'D'you mean that, Lord Clanroyden?' he asked. 'It's extraordinarily good of you. Of course I give up any claims – I had already given them up. D'you mean me to act on what this tablet may tell me?'

'Certainly.'

'And to keep for myself whatever I may find?'

'Certainly. For yourself, and any friends you want to share with you.'

Troth peered at the inscription.

'One side's in Latin. The other side – the important side – I suppose I can get that translated?'

'It has been already translated,' said Sandy gravely. 'I have seen to that.'

'And you found?' The eternal treasure-hunter was in Troth's voice.

'We found a list of the Twelve Major Virtues and the Ninety-Nine Names of God!'

THE END

WORDSWORTH CLASSICS

General Editors: Marcus Clapham & Clive Reynard

JANE AUSTEN
Emma
Mansfield Park
Northanger Abbey
Persuasion
Pride and Prejudice
Sense and Sensibility

ARNOLD BENNETT
Anna of the Five Towns

R. D. BLACKMORE
Lorna Doone

ANNE BRONTË
Agnes Grey
The Tenant of
Wildfell Hall

CHARLOTTE BRONTË
Jane Eyre
The Professor
Shirley
Villette

EMILY BRONTË
Wuthering Heights

JOHN BUCHAN
Greenmantle
Mr Standfast
The Thirty-Nine Steps

SAMUEL BUTLER
The Way of All Flesh

LEWIS CARROLL
Alice in Wonderland

CERVANTES
Don Quixote

G. K. CHESTERTON
Father Brown:
Selected Stories
The Man who was
Thursday

ERSKINE CHILDERS
The Riddle of the Sands

JOHN CLELAND
Memoirs of a Woman of
Pleasure: Fanny Hill

WILKIE COLLINS
The Moonstone
The Woman in White

JOSEPH CONRAD
Heart of Darkness
Lord Jim
The Secret Agent

J. FENIMORE COOPER
The Last of the
Mohicans

STEPHEN CRANE
The Red Badge of
Courage

THOMAS DE QUINCEY
Confessions of an English
Opium Eater

DANIEL DEFOE
Moll Flanders
Robinson Crusoe

CHARLES DICKENS
Bleak House
David Copperfield
Great Expectations
Hard Times
Little Dorrit
Martin Chuzzlewit
Oliver Twist
Pickwick Papers
A Tale of Two Cities

BENJAMIN DISRAELI
Sybil

THEODOR DOSTOEVSKY
Crime and Punishment

SIR ARTHUR CONAN
DOYLE
The Adventures of
Sherlock Holmes
The Case-Book of
Sherlock Holmes
The Lost World &
Other Stories
The Return of
Sherlock Holmes
Sir Nigel

GEORGE DU MAURIER
Trilby

ALEXANDRE DUMAS
The Three Musketeers

MARIA EDGEWORTH
Castle Rackrent

GEORGE ELIOT
The Mill on the Floss
Middlemarch
Silas Marner

HENRY FIELDING
Tom Jones

F. SCOTT FITZGERALD
A Diamond as Big as the
Ritz & Other Stories
The Great Gatsby
Tender is the Night

GUSTAVE FLAUBERT
Madame Bovary

JOHN GALSWORTHY
In Chancery
The Man of Property
To Let

ELIZABETH GASKELL
Cranford
North and South

KENNETH GRAHAME
The Wind in the
Willows

GEORGE & WEEDON
GROSSMITH
Diary of a Nobody

RIDER HAGGARD
She

THOMAS HARDY
Far from the
Madding Crowd
The Mayor of Casterbridge
The Return of the
Native
Tess of the d'Urbervilles
The Trumpet Major
Under the Greenwood
Tree

DISTRIBUTION

AUSTRALIA & PAPUA NEW GUINEA
Peribo Pty Ltd
58 Beaumont Road, Mount Kuring-Gai
NSW 2080, Australia
Tel: (02) 457 0011 Fax: (02) 457 0022

CZECH REPUBLIC
Bohemian Ventures s r. o.,
Delnicka 13, 170 00 Prague 7
Tel: 042 2 877837 Fax: 042 2 801498

FRANCE
Copernicus Diffusion
23 Rue Saint Dominique, Paris 75007
Tel: 1 44 11 33 20 Fax: 1 44 11 33 21

GERMANY & AUSTRIA
Taschenbuch-Vertrieb
Ingeborg Blank GmbH
Lager und Buro Rohrmooser Str 1
85256 Vierkirchen/Pasenbach
Tel: 08139-8130/8184 Fax: 08139-8140

Tradis Verlag und Vertrieb GmbH (Bookshops)
Postfach 90 03 69, D-51113 Köln
Tel: 022 03 31059 Fax: 022 03 39340

GREAT BRITAIN
Wordsworth Editions Ltd
Cumberland House, Crib Street
Ware, Hertfordshire SG12 9ET
Tel: 01920 465167 Fax: 01920 462267

INDIA
Rupa & Co
Post Box No 7071,
7/16 Makhanlal Street, Ansari Road,
Daryaganj, New Delhi – 110 002
Tel: 3278586 Fax: (011) 3277294

IRELAND
Easons & Son Limited
Furry Park Industrial Estate
Santry 9, Eire
Tel: 003531 8733811 Fax: 003531 8733945

ISRAEL
Sole Agent – **Timmy Marketing Limited**
Israel Ben Zeev 12, Ramont Gimmel, Jerusalem
Tel: 972-2-5865266 Fax: 972-2-5860035
Sole Distributor – Sefer ve Sefel Ltd
Tel & Fax: 972-2-6248237

ITALY
Magis Books s.p.a.
Via Raffaello 31/C, Zona Ind Mancasale
42100 Reggio Emilia
Tel: 0522 920999 Fax: 0522 920666

NEW ZEALAND & FIJI
Allphy Book Distributors Ltd
4-6 Charles Street, Eden Terrace, Auckland,
Tel: (09) 3773096 Fax: (09) 3022770

MALAYSIA & BRUNEI
Vintrade SDN BHD
5 & 7 Lorong Datuk Sulaiman 7
Taman Tun Dr Ismail
60000 Kuala Lumpur, Malaysia
Tel: (603) 717 3333 Fax: (603) 719 2942

MALTA & GOZO
Agius & Agius Ltd
42A South Street, Valletta VLT 11
Tel: 234038 - 220347 Fax: 241175

PHILIPPINES
I J Sagun Enterprises
P O Box 4322 CPO Manila
2 Topaz Road, Greenheights Village,
Taytay, Rizal
Tel: 631 80 61 TO 66

SOUTHERN & CENTRAL AFRICA
Southern Book Publishers (Pty) Ltd
P.O.Box 3103
Halfway House 1685, South Africa
Tel: (011) 315-3633/4/5/6
Fax: (011) 315-3810

EAST AFRICA & KENYA
P.M.C. International Importers & Exporters CC
Unit 6, Ben-Sarah Place, 52-56 Columbine Place, Glen
Anil, Kwa-Zulu Natal 4051,
P.O.Box 201520,
Durban North, Kwa-Zulu Natal 4016
Tel: (031) 844441 Fax: (031) 844466

SINGAPORE
Paul & Elizabeth Book Services Pte Ltd
163 Tanglin Road No 03-15/16
Tanglin Mall, Singapore 1024
Tel: (65) 735 7308 Fax: (65) 735 9747

SLOVAK REPUBLIC
Slovak Ventures s r. o.,
Stefanikova 128, 949 01 Nitra
Tel/Fax: 042 87 525105/6/7

SPAIN
Ribera Libros, S.L.
Poligono Martiartu, Calle 1 - no 6
48480 Arrigorriaga, Vizcaya
Tel: 34 4 6713607 (Almacen)
      34 4 4418787 (Libreria)
Fax: 34 4 6713608 (Almacen)
      34 4 4418029 (Libreria)

UNITED STATES OF AMERICA
NTC/Contemporary Publishing Company
4225 West Touhy Avenue
Lincolnwood (Chicago)
Illinois 60646-4622
USA
Tel: (847) 679 5500 Fax: (847) 679 2494

DIRECT MAIL
Bibliophile Books
5 Thomas Road, London E14 7BN,
Tel: 0171-515 9222 Fax: 0171-538 4115
Order hotline 24 hours Tel: 0171-515 9555
Cash with order + £2.00 p&p (UK)